# I Am Kairu

Gregory McEwan

Copyright © 2015 Gregory McEwan

All rights reserved.

ISBN: 151526064X
ISBN-13: 978-1515260646

FOR RICKY

# I AM KAIRU

BOOKS BY GREGORY MCEWAN

Freedom City
Wash Belly
Ulia
Est'vor: The Golden Flute & The Albino Dragon
Homoria

## CHAPTER ONE
*Kairu*

The golden sun burned brightly against the blue backdrop of an African sky, sending sunbeams downward, inflicting temporary blindness. The parched, cracked earth burned the soles of Kairu's bare feet, and though he had parted from his mother for the first time in all of his eleven years of life, Kairu walked on, elated. It was impossible to contain the joy he felt as he walked away from the quaint village he had always called home. Kairu looked up into the burning disc again and quickly shielded his eyes. It was fascinating, the way the sun seemed to move away from him, though every step forward was an intent to bring him closer to it. Was the sun running away from him? He shut his eyes quickly after another futile attempt to gaze up at the illuminating sphere above.

"You will damage your eyes, Kairu," his father said. "You cannot look into the eyes of fire."

He gazed up at his father's stern frown and wondered why he had not seen his smile for days. Kairu took one last look behind. "Seven suns," he whispered to himself. "...I will see Mama again in seven suns." This, his mother had promised him as Kairu wept earlier that morning. He attempted to glance up at the sun again, quickly remembering what his father had said. He could not look into the eyes of fire. He took comfort in the fact that in seven days, he would journey back home with his back toward the sun. Things would be normal again.

He had never journeyed so far from home, and though his village was barely in view Kairu took another glance behind. The wooden wall surrounding his village and the green canopies above it seemed to fade away into the haze. A strange feeling enveloped him. The sadness he felt elicited the strangest longing for home. He slung his waterskin over his shoulder, looked to his father and mimicked his posture, trying to match his long strides. However, Kairu knew he was still just a boy—a long way from manhood. He was not even half the height of his father. He admired the tribal tattoos on his father's forearm, wondering why he had yet to receive them. Soon, he too would wear the markings of their tribe. "Papa, how long must we go?"

"Do not ask silly questions, boy. I've already told you. Three days," said his father. His dark face was without emotion. Wiping sweat from his face, Kairu's father looked down into his eyes. "Your name is Kairu."

Kairu chuckled. "I know my name, Papa. It means *black one*."

"Yes," his father replied, finally displaying his white teeth behind a guilty smile. "You are Kairu...you are a descendant of the El Molo." He paused and placed a hand on Kairu's shoulder. "Remember this, my son."

Kairu gazed back, puzzled. That sadness enveloped him again. His village was just a tiny speck. He was not far from home; however, Kairu longed for it. He was overcome by the need to play with his friends again and to sit next to his mother inside their dome-shaped hut.

Kairu had his mother's face—everyone in the village had always said this. He was not yet as muscular, but Kairu had his father's lean body. However, he hoped he would become as strong as his father was. He looked at his father's toned arms and legs. *Soon, I will be a man*, thought Kairu. He looked ahead, taking comfort in the fact that his father was with him. There was no need to worry—not with his father there to protect him. "Papa," he asked again, "where are we going?"

It took several moments for his father to reply. His brows converged again. "I think you spent too much time inside that hut with your mother, Kairu. You worry too much, boy." Then he sighed, "Do not worry, my son." His words were laced with uncertainty. "We must find a place for the night…to rest."

He did not wish his father to think him a coward, so Kairu held his tongue. He would ask no more questions. Again, he mimicked his father's strides.

They walked in silence for some time before his father spoke. "You must remember, Kairu," he said. "In life, all things happen for a purpose. We may never know what these purposes are, Kairu. Not all purposes ripen fast, my son." Another sigh. "We must not forget who we are—remember who you are. You are Kairu. You are my son. My father's father is a descendant of the El Molo.

Kairu looked up at his father with tears in his eyes. Why did he feel such sorrow? He could only allay his fears by thinking of home. In seven suns Kairu would be home again. He would rush into his rounded hut and find his mother by the fire. The aroma of roasted fish would rush up his nostrils. His mother would shower his face with gentle kisses, and later, after they had feasted, the family would sit just outside the hut and look up at the night's full moon…

Kairu tugged at the colourful beads around his neck. They were precious to his mother, yet she had given them to him. "Keep them safe, my son," she had told him. Touching the beads calmed him. They were the most beautiful he had ever seen—the large necklace had all the colours in the world, as pretty as a rainbow. As his sorrow ebbed, Kairu thought of his two older brothers. They had not been so fortunate to travel far from home, and, finally, the thought made him smile. His brothers had become brave young warriors. They wore the markings of their people upon their faces. They had had the chance to wear the crown of black feathers upon their heads. Soon he would have a chance too. Kairu considered himself lucky to be going on a long journey with their father.

"Take this, Kairu." His father handed him a shúkà, it was of the brightest shade of red—all the men of his tribe wore red.

As he draped the garment over his shoulders Kairu pondered his parents' efforts to make sure no harm had come to him over the years. Unlike his brothers, he had never been allowed to go out hunting for crocodiles and hippos, or to join his father as he fished the lake. He was never permitted to play for long periods in the sun and received daily oil massages from his mother. He had in his pack enough fish oil to last well beyond seven suns. Kairu was to continue to massage this into his skin twice each day.

They walked until the sun nearly vanished beyond the horizon. Kairu was famished. He had not eaten since early that morning and felt he could not go on. However, if his father could walk on, then he would too. *This must be a test*, thought Kairu. *He wants to see if I'm ready for manhood.* With that thought, Kairu could already envision himself participating in his coming of age dance, shield and long spear held carefully in his hands as he attempted to jump higher than the other boys. He could hear the chanting of the females as he jumped up and down…

The time came for them to rest. "We camp there," said his father, pointing toward the mouth of a cave. He led the way into the pitch-black cave. "Stay behind me, Kairu." As his father approached the entrance of the cave, young Kairu admired his stretched lobes, puzzled by the sudden realization that his body did not possess one mark upon its skin like all the other males of his tribe. In fact, other boys younger than he had had their lobes stretched.

The cave was safe. Kairu assisted with starting a fire and unwrapped dried fish and placed them atop the smooth stones. As they dined his father's rare smile beamed. "Mother taught you well, Kairu."

Kairu did not reply; he would have preferred to discuss the purpose of their journey. The two slept close to the fire within the chilly cave, and as he gazed out the entrance, Kairu studied the glowing moon against the dark canvas of the sky. He was a day's journey away from home, and though he was with his father, Kairu could not escape the haunting feeling of fear that resonated from within. He could not endure the uncertainty surrounding their destination. Finally, Kairu closed his eyes and hoped he would sleep well through the night. "Six suns," he whispered. In just six sunsets, Kairu would be home again and the fear he felt would be no more.

They had travelled for nearly three days and still no sign of a destination. Kairu looked up to the clear skies again, still oblivious to the purpose of his journey. They rested several times during the day but did not linger for long in any one place. The strangest thing was that they met no other travellers along the way.

Finally, after nearly half a day's journey, Kairu saw something in the distance ahead. The haze from the heat of the day blurred the image of what lay before them. "What is that, Papa?" Kairu pointed toward the great stone wall—something he had never seen before. He could see nothing beyond the blurry wall, for it was still very far away. However, for the first time in days Kairu's eyes beheld other people, and he welcomed the change. He was suddenly filled with excitement as other boys as young as he walked next to their fathers, all converging upon the great stone wall that sprouted from the dry, parched ground and stretched upward. He exchanged glances with one boy who had large, sad eyes. Did he see fear in those eyes? The boy's face was round, and like Kairu, he walked to match his father's pace. Like his father, the boy's body was painted, lines of yellow, red and white followed the contours of their faces. There were colourful dots across their foreheads and white lines down the bridges of their noses. This boy could not have been older than Kairu; however, his arms were muscular and his body strong, much in contrast to Kairu's lean frame.

Kairu eventually fell into a long line consisting of men and boys—fathers and sons. A massive gate was opened and one after the other, each pair was met by a scrutinizing gaze. Kairu stood close to the boy with the round face and sad eyes. His father's tribal markings were different than those of Kairu's father. Kairu gave the boy a reluctant nod. The boy nodded back, still looking sad.

As their fathers spoke the boy whispered to Kairu. "I am Prodigal. We journey from the North."

Kairu recalled what his father had told him days before. "I am Kairu," he replied. "…I am a descendant of the El Molo."

"You come from the Maasai?" Prodigal finally smiled.

Kairu looked to his father, for he was unfamiliar with the word "Maasai."

His father nodded. "Yes, Kairu, we are of the Maasai."

Puzzled and somewhat ashamed of his ignorance, Kairu shrugged.

"Your new friend is right, Kairu." His father rested a hand on the shoulder of Prodigal's father and smiled. "We are hunters, Kairu. We are known as the Maasai."

Kairu thought of his family's main diet, fish.

The line moved slowly. Kairu looked through the gate and saw what appeared to be the top of a massive stone building. He quickly closed his eyes as a gush of wind swirled around the crowd, sending clouds of dust upward. He moved closer to his new friend while their father's conversed. "This place, what is it?"

"I do not know," whispered Prodigal. "Papa would not tell me. He keeps secrets."

Kairu glanced up at his father and nodded. "Mine too." He studied Prodigal's dark face and his stare widened in awe. Kairu pointed to the tribal marking on his new friend's face, five bumps forming a circle near the boy's ears. "What is your tribe?"

"I am of the Nuba tribe," replied Prodigal. "We are herders. We are of the mountain people."

Kairu was intrigued. He would have given anything to bear the markings of his people.

They finally stood before the gates. Four warriors stood guard; they allowed them to pass through only after questioning Kairu's father at length. The warrior holding the longest wooden spear asked the questions. Colourful feathers hung from his armbands and massive gold rings dangled from his ears and nostrils. He was lean but he looked strong. The warrior stood boldly and showed no fear whatsoever. The warrior's chest could barely be seen behind the red, yellow, and black beads that adorned his neck, and as his eyes turned to Kairu they instilled fear. The warrior nodded toward the gate and they were allowed to pass. Kairu sighed with relief, though he was still uncertain what awaited him behind those walls of stone.

Amazed that he had walked into a city, Kairu looked around in awe. They were led down a path, then through a marketplace. Finally, the group of fathers and sons were assembled before a set of massive stone steps.

Kairu looked up the steps and suddenly became dizzy. It was way higher than the tallest tree he had attempted to climb.

All eyes looked toward the golden double doors at the top of the steps as they opened. Kairu was uncertain what it was he felt. The views within this city were fascinating; however, as he gazed up at the empty doorway fear enveloped him. It took several moments before the first figure walked through the golden doors. Three men dressed in black robes emerged; however, it was the fourth individual who appeared to possess an aura of importance. His two servants, or aides, after leading the way out seemed to back away from him, their heads slightly bowed. *Is this a shaman?* Kairu could not shift his gaze from this peculiar man. In his right hand, the shaman carried a wooden staff embellished with gold, and his headdress was made of white feathers, large ones extending beyond his shoulders. He wore rings of gold around his forearms. Kairu's first instinct was to question his father about this man and this place, this new, strange world. He had never seen such opulence, such wealth.

The shaman descended with poise and from time to time he fanned his face with his free hand as though he was surrounded by a swarm of flies. He came close so he could see every face before him, but far enough to avoid being touched. He examined the face of every boy; he did not seem to care about the older men. He smiled as his eyes paused on Kairu, and swiftly pointed his staff at him. Two of aides moved in Kairu's direction, and as they placed their hands on his shoulders he looked to his father fearfully. "Papa?" Kairu expected his father's voice to echo throughout the city, but no sound came.

His father stepped aside. Kairu's cloak was tossed to the ground, revealing his bare arms and shaking legs. The robed men lifted him and placed him just several feet away from the shaman. He flinched and gasped as the end of the staff lifted his chin. Kairu's arms trembled, he could not control the rate at which he was breathing. Again, he whispered, looking to his father for help. "Papa..."

The shaman nodded, as if satisfied. With a quick snap of his fingers, the third aide quickly made his way down the steps. In his hand was a leather sack. As the sack was tossed in the air Kairu's eyes moved with it, and when it landed in his father's outstretched hand the sound of the bag of coins made Kairu weep in silence.

"Give him two," said the shaman, with a wider grin, "this one's worth far more than a bag of gold."

And so, Kairu looked on with tear-filled eyes as his father's payment was doubled. He locked eyes with Kairu. "You are Kairu," said his father. "You are a descendant of the El Molo." He stuffed the sacks of gold into his pack. "Remember that, my son of the Maasai." His father turned and walked back toward the gates of the city. He never looked back.

"Papa! Don't leave me, Papa!" But his cries were to no avail. His father would not return for him; Kairu knew this. He watched his father until he was out of sight, and by that time there were several other boys standing by his side, most of them weeping.

Prodigal was chosen last. He was far braver than Kairu could have been. As his father kneeled before him and they pressed their foreheads together, the two exchanged words in a tongue Kairu could not understand. Finally, Prodigal stood, turned from his father and faced the shaman. He bowed bravely, a sure sign he had accepted his fate.

The shaman nodded with a smile, his eyes fixed upon Prodigal. "A willing one." The shaman tilted his head back and laughed aloud.

With his new friend next to him, Kairu ascended the stone steps, and as he neared the golden doors ahead he wondered what awaited them in this vast place built of stone. He glanced behind and decided that he should consider himself lucky to have been chosen. Many fathers and sons were turned away with disappointing looks. Only thirteen boys were selected from the many. But the shaman had given away fourteen bags of gold that day. Kairu looked back at the shaman. What would this man do with thirteen young boys?

They were herded into a chamber like cattle. The smooth walls made it impossible for anyone to climb up toward the high windows. Kairu felt safe with Prodigal by his side. He was no longer afraid. However, he could not avoid the overwhelming torture of sorrow that enveloped him. His father had sold him for nothing more than two sacks of gold—was that all he was worth? As he stood with his back against the wall he could think of nothing else but the truth. His parents had betrayed him, and though he felt confident that they loved him he could not find it within his power to forgive them. *Some day,* Kairu promised, *I will look in their eyes and—*

Kairu quickly remembered what his father had said. Even after betrayal he still held fast to his papa's words; "…all things," Kairu whispered, "happen for a purpose…"

## CHAPTER TWO
## *Prodigal*

His people are warriors. Warriors of the North. Prodigal stood next to Kairu, who clearly struggled to conceal the terror of their unknown future, for none of the boys knew why they had been sold by the ones they loved. *I am of the Nuba tribe,* thought the boy. *I am strong.* This was all Prodigal knew—how to survive. He would keep his promise to his father and stand strong for his tribe. All his life, for as long as he could remember, his father had always prepared him for this day and all along he did not know it. Prodigal met the gaze of every other boy, all like himself. They were of the same age. Like them, Prodigal had travelled far from home but he had come from very far—the Nuba Mountains. Eyeing the other boys, Prodigal was confident that he was the strongest. He had trained, competed with and beaten the best of his tribe as well as others from neighbouring villages. Prodigal was a champion.

They were left within the small chamber with cowled men standing near the door. Now seated next to Kairu, Prodigal admired the boy's beads. They made Kairu appear majestic, and for a split second Prodigal had to look carefully at his new friend, as he could have easily been mistaken for a Maasai girl. He shifted his gaze quickly as Kairu caught him staring.

"They are…were my mama's beads," said Kairu. He caressed the beads, which extended to the ends of his shoulders. The Maasai boy shook his head and bit into his thick lower lip. "She always said I should speak the truth. But she lied to me…they all lied."

Prodigal nodded. "Papa wanted to tell me." He clenched his fist, knowing he should never hate the man who had taught him everything. "I know it now…" The boy paused as memories of his father rushed to the forefront of his mind. *Always, he wanted me to be strong.*

"Why did they leave us here?" At that moment Kairu looked toward the door. Finally, the shaman had come.

Prodigal stared into the eyes of the man all the boys had been referring to as a shaman, for no one knew his name. He would not let the shaman see fear in his eyes. They locked gazes for several seconds until the shaman looked away, smiling wickedly. This man obviously knew what was in store for Prodigal and the others and he seemed to enjoy the fact that most of the other boys, if not all, were terrified.

"Welcome, little ones." The shaman waved his staff toward the boys. His attendants in black stood not far behind. "I am to train you," he said. "It will not be easy, at least not for you." That wicked grin surfaced briefly. "The next few days may very well be the worst you have ever had in your lives but rest assured, they shall prepare you all for an advantaged future." The movement of his arms were prophet-like, but this shaman, as Kairu called him, was the devil. Of this, Prodigal was certain.

The shaman pointed his staff toward the only fat boy. Prodigal's brows converged as he pondered the shaman's words. He could feel the sudden pounding of his heart as the fat boy was stripped naked by the attendants, a fountain of tears gushing from his eyes. "Yes," said the shaman, "I must always have one like you. There should always be one like you." He grinned again, lifting the fat boy's chin with his staff. "Come boy!" The shaman nodded to his attendants. "Take him." The fat boy looked back to the others he left behind, his eyes pleading in vain. No one would help him, not even the brave Prodigal.

The boys left behind with the shaman stood in silence. As for the fat boy, Prodigal had lost sight of him after a white curtain veiled the doorway. Much later a shrill scream echoed. Prodigal's heart pounded, and as much as he would have liked to hold the shaman's gaze, this time he could not. Prodigal felt tears welling up in the corners of his eyes. While the fat boy's screams resonated inside his head.

One by one the boys were taken from the room. Each boy seemed to scream louder than the one who preceded him. Kairu's hands were shaking. The shaman had been brought a stool, upon which he sat and fed upon the fear within the chamber. There were three of them left. Kairu stood between Prodigal and another boy, who stood in a puddle of his own urine. The shaman's attendants had removed his beads and shúkà. Kairu cast his eyes toward the floor. He would not look into the shaman's eyes. The wailing of the tenth boy ceased and the eleventh was led beyond the white curtain. What was it that made these boys cry out so? The thought alone was enough to make Kairu weep. He realized that whatever it was, he would have to face it, for as his father had told him just days past…all things happen for a purpose.

The shaman eyed them both as though they were precious to him. Seated upon his stool, he placed his staff across his knees and rubbed his palms together. "If only the others were like you." The shaman lifted one hand to his lips and kissed the largest of his gold rings on his fingers. "What are you called, boy?" For the first time Kairu focused on the sound of this man's voice. He looked like Kairu and the other boys; however, there was something in the way in which he spoke that made him different.

Kairu lowered his eyes.

"Speak!" The shaman grabbed his staff and stood as though he meant to strike the boy. Prodigal stepped before Kairu, his strong legs spread as if ready to charge. If the shaman was afraid he did not show it or maybe he was not afraid at all; after all, Prodigal was just a boy. The shaman moved swiftly. Gripping Prodigal's neck his cunning smile returned. "Listen, Nuba boy," said the shaman. "Your worthless life belongs to me now." His dark skin glistened, his face quickly became sweaty. "I could break that neck right now and watch you die." His eyes shifted to Kairu. "And the only person who would miss you would be your new friend."

"I am Kairu—"

"I know who you are, boy!" The shaman laughed. "What was it your greedy father said? Let's see...ah, here we go. You are Kairu. You are a descendant of the El Molo...of the Maasai." His laugh sounded more like grunts. "There is so much you have to learn, Kairu. Black one. Yes, I know all about your tribe. I know all the tribes." He turned again to Prodigal, who was rubbing his neck and breathing heavily. The shaman gazed between the two boys knowingly. "Yes. How couldn't I have seen this before? The Gods have sent me gifts." He giggled. "The bonds of friendship..."

The attendants had been waiting behind the shaman, waiting for his instructions. As they went toward Kairu the shaman raised a hand. "No, take them both."

After passing beyond the curtain the walk down a long corridor seemed endless. Kairu found the silence haunting, as he could not even hear the sounds of anyone weeping. What had become of the other boys? Naked, the two boys were led toward cots and handed goblets. "You must drink," said a cowled man. Kairu obeyed and drank the sweet concoction quickly.

After glancing around the room his eyes fell upon a blazing fire across the room. Two cowled men restrained his arm and legs. It was useless to struggle; not even when a third man drew a long glowing rod from the fire could Kairu fight to free himself from their hold on him. Prodigal managed to free himself briefly before the strong men restrained him again. Why did Kairu suddenly feel the need to sleep? He shut his eyes just before hot iron was pressed against his chest, and as he cried out Kairu could smell the burning of his own flesh. He had become drowsy, yet he was aware as he was lifted off the cot. He could feel several hands upon him, and all Kairu could do as weakness enveloped him was to remember what he was. *I am Kairu…I am a descendant of the El Molo. I come from the Maasai…*

He was carried to another place, for through half-closed lids, Kairu saw a wall of white linen. There was a lone figure waiting behind sheer white curtains. Hesitant and still drowsy, Kairu looked up into the faces of the robed escorts. They helped him to stand up on tired, weakened legs and motioned toward the curtains; Kairu obeyed. He staggered back as soon as he laid eyes upon the old man seated next to a massive wooden bath containing steaming fluid with floating rose petals. The bath was inviting indeed, but Kairu could not avoid the milky eyes of the old man, whom he assumed to be blind.

The man's face was wrinkled and his dark skin glistened with sweat. "What are you called?" His white pupils did not move but they were fixed upon Kairu. The El Molo boy's eyes blinked rapidly, as the events seemed to be part of a long, confusing dream.

He gulped back a mouthful of fear. "…I am…Kairu," he replied. "I am a descendant of the El Molo."

"The El Molo, you say?" The old man's grey brows converged. "The forgotten race—the tribe of voices."

Kairu's eyes widened with interest; however, he felt a touch of rage, as this man had called his tribe *forgotten*. "I...I am Kairu," he whispered again with thoughts of his father. "I am a descendant of the El Molo..."

"Kairu." The old man offered a toothless smile. "A fitting name, black one." He caressed his own face as if suddenly thrown back into his own past. "Your skin is the colour of a raven, black Kairu," said the old man. "A beautiful name for a beautiful boy."

"You...can see?" Kairu stepped back, astonished. He held his head as his head ached and another wave of dizziness attacked him.

"I see enough." He smiled again and motioned toward the bath. "Get in." Another toothless grin. "Best you fall there than the cold, hard ground, black one."

The warmth of the water was soothing; however, the scorched skin of his chest burned. Kairu's entire body was immersed and he closed his eyes, enjoying the aroma of the scented water. He was in comfort and had forgotten the old man was there with him. Kairu rested both arms on the edge of the bath, still with his eyes closed. He was comfortable, relaxed and had just begun to drift away into slumber when his arms were restrained. He opened his eyes, terrified to see four dark faces leaning over him. His attempts to struggle were futile, and as his legs were forced apart, Kairu's heart pounded. As he was lifted from the bath and placed upon a cold stone table, his own shrill cry echoed inside his head. His cries were in vain.

"You mustn't struggle, black one," said the old man. "It is for your own good. You cannot go back. Your tribe would be shamed."

With his arms and legs restrained Kairu lifted his head as the old man stood at the end of the stone table. His legs were parted as the milky eyes drew closer. Kairu's head fell backward when the old man's cold hands touched his genitals. The first sting of pain forced him to shut his eyes in agony.

Moments later, he was again immersed into the hot bath. Kairu's body collapsed; his eyes grew dim and the five figures around him became a blur…

## CHAPTER THREE
### *Kingdom of Qev*

It was the middle of the longest season in the kingdom of Qev, summer. For anyone who had made this beautiful kingdom their home, one day in summer seemed just like any other. The skies were always blue and the sun shone bright for most of the day. The days of Qev are long. On this particular day, however, Lucas's life as he had known it would change forever. Bernard, king of all of the realm, was dead. The body had been viewed by thousands—more people had gathered outside the walls of the castle than Lucas, a boy of only twelve, had ever seen in all his life. King Bernard's bier had burned two days past. Though he was loved by all, Bernard Godfrey, known as the old father, was gone forever. It was time for a new ruler of the realm.

Lucas could hear his mother calling for him, but he would not answer. Enjoying the view of a world he did not know was far more appealing. From where he stood Lucas could see vast lands in the distance. Green vales, rushing streams and various birds flying about. He leaned against the stone ledge and cradled his face upon the palms of his hands. If only he could get out for even half the day, Lucas thought, still ignoring his mother's voice. It appeared his siblings had joined their mother in searching for him. Lucas closed his eyes and focused on the feeling of the sun upon his face. Summers were always the best of times. The winters were much shorter, but they were cold and dark. And the season of the rains was simply no fun at all…

"Lucas Godfrey!" His mother sighed as she rushed out onto the balcony. Grabbing his shoulders and turning him around she lightly kissed his lips. "Lucas, what am I going to do with you?" She pulled out a lace hanky and scrubbed his face with it. "Look what you've done to yourself since your warm bath this morning." His mother's grey eyes looked like glass beneath the light of the sun. Today is a very important day for us all, Lucas."

His younger sister, Cylene, ran toward them and pointed an accusing finger at her brother. "Mother, he'll make us late again," she said. "Lucas always ruins everything, doesn't he, Mother?"

"Cylene, I told you to return to your rooms." Their mother lifted her hands. "Why is it that no one ever listens to me?"

Cylene smiled. She was only nine years old, but Lucas could hardly stand her. Noticing her brother's gaze, Cylene stuck out her tongue as she shot him a look of disdain. "You're a disgrace to the Godfrey name," she spat.

After slapping Cylene's face their mother looked down at her hand as though it had done so without her consent. "I asked you to go to your rooms."

"I'm telling father what you did!" Cylene pointed a finger at their mother as if to admonish her. "One day I'll be queen and I'll make you pay."

"Their mother smiled, shaking her head. "Child, I've told you many times to pay attention to your lessons. Protocol dictates—"

"I don't care, Mother. Father is king now and I'm his little princess!"

Lucas smiled mockingly. "Kevan, Orin and I will be kings, not you." He looked to his mother. "Do you think she'll ever understand?"

"But I heard what Father said," Cylene screamed. "I heard you talking. Father said Lucas cares too much about them." She motioned toward the lady-in-waiting as she walked out onto the balcony.

"Take her in and get her dressed for the coronation ceremony." Their mother gave the pretty servant a scathing stare. "And she is not to leave her rooms until I send for her."

The servant curtsied. "Yes, milady."

As they were left alone Lucas's mother tucked the piece of lace into her bosom. "Oh how I hate that girl."

"She can be horrid at times, Mum…," Lucas grinned, "…but she's your own daughter."

Her eyes became blocks of ice. "Don't be silly, dear. You know of whom I speak."

Glancing backward, Lucas studied the city beyond the castle walls. "…Don't mean to bring shame to our family, Mum, but why do we have to live better than they do? Why can't everyone be—"

"It appears Cylene isn't the only one not paying attention to her tutor."

"It's just not fair, Mum."

She wiped his face with her fingertips. "It is just the way life is, Lucas. Do not expect any of this to change. We are just better than the lot of them." She waved toward the city dismissively. "If the Gods felt it was fair to have any of them where we are they would have put them here and us out there…living in that hell."

"But what good is it to have other people live without the things we have, when all the kingdom belongs to us?" This, Lucas could not understand.

"I thank the Gods for not making you my eldest," said his mother.

Lucas did not utter a word, as he knew exactly what she meant. Kevan and Orin can rule all of Qev for as long as they want, thought Lucas. He was more than satisfied with his place in the royal family. With that thought, Lucas smiled wide. "Come on, Mum, I guess we should get ready for Father's coronation.

The library had always been the only place Orin could find peace. There was nothing better than the smell of old parchment mingled with the new—the scent of ink. The bells of the cathedral had tolled all night long—every hour since midnight. Luckily for him, the library was located in the west wing of the castle. Orin had even managed to persuade his father to move his bedchamber just several paces from the things he loved most in all the world: books and scrolls. While his young sister, Cylene, sought after pretty gowns and jewels, and their eldest brother, Kevan, wanted nothing more than to be king, Orin desired the only thing he felt brought true power, knowledge. He and his younger brother, Lucas, were more alike—they were never understood. Lucas's need was to help the poor peasants. At nearly fifteen, Orin knew well enough not to trust the common people. He raised his brows at the thought of his naive brother. They will love you today for throwing them a crust of bread, dear brother, but tomorrow they will deliver your head and your crown to the man who promises bread and water...

Lucas was undoubtedly the family member he loved most, yet Orin saw no need to enlighten his soft-hearted brother. What good would it do me? thought the second in line for the throne of Qev. Orin had read much of his family's history and knew what happens when one fails to look out for his own well-being. The house of Godfrey was not always at the head of things, at least not before the last fifty years.

As he reached for another scroll, the massive doors to the library opened. It was Qev's new queen, his loving mother. "Greetings, Queen of all Qev." Orin sprang from his chair, quill in hand and exalted his mother with a mocking bow. She approached him without uttering a word, staring down at him. Orin was suddenly angered by the fact that even his mother was much taller than he, so he straightened his back and extended his already long neck. "Hello, Mother."

"Your father calls for you." She shot him a scathing look before motioning to the books and scrolls surrounding them. "I've told you before, Orin," she said. "Spend too much time among these dusty scrolls and you'll be forgotten." His mother found her chance to mock him. "You must stand tall, second son. You'll have to if you ever expect your father to notice you."

"I love you too, Mother."

"I love all my children," she scoffed. "I also know the life my children are destined for."

It was pointless to argue with a woman, thought Orin. No, Mother, you've planned the destiny of one child, the lesser ones are mere pawns in your eyes…

She cooed at him. "I see you've nothing to say to that, dear son." She moved toward the door. "Like I said, your father calls for you."

Orin could hardly help himself. "Hmm…I wonder why Father never sent a servant to summon me." He brought the tips of his fingers to his lips. "Oh, he sent the queen…" Orin smiled even as his mother stalked forward and struck him. As he was enveloped by sadness Orin wished that slap to his face had been a warm motherly embrace.

"The Gods were cruel to have given me three sons. One would have sufficed."

As the doors to the library were shut Orin tossed a scroll against the wall. He uttered his next words softly as if to whisper to himself. "You cannot blame the Gods for opening your legs, Mother, nor should you ever regret it." The coronation was several hours away and already Orin had had enough of it. Since his grandfather's sudden death, things within the castle had been turned upside down. All of Qev mourned the king they loved. But there was gossip—such that could cause one to lose his head. Orin packed away his scrolls and prepared to stand before his father, king of all Qev. Why was it his heart pounded whenever his father requested to see him? What had he done now? Orin felt he knew why he was summoned, but as much as he feared to look into his father's eyes he had to withhold what he knew. The truth would not help him, at least not yet…

><<<<<o>>>><

"In the name of the Gods," dear man, "you are advisor to the most powerful man in all of Qev, yet you cannot convince him to rid himself of that vile girl." Bernice endeavoured to wield the power which, within a matter of hours, would become official. Somehow, the look in the advisor's eyes forced her to realize her attempts were to no avail.

As always, Percival bowed politely before his reply. "My dear sister," Percival said. "Do not think for one moment that Earvin wishes to get rid of the poor girl. You, on the other hand—"

"Enough!" Bernice's fists collided with the top of the table with such force that she felt she might have broken a bone. "I am Queen," she blurted. For a moment she felt she were no different than Cylene. Bernice took a long, deep breath. She rose from the writing table and walked toward the window. The castle grounds were swarming with servants, all working hard to add the finishing touches to welcome their new king. If only they knew the swine their precious king really was... Percival cleared his throat and Bernice turned from the window. For a moment she had forgotten he was there within the privacy of her rooms.

"Sister, so much has changed since we were children. This life is real." His smile was forced and did nothing to ease her torment. "Father played those childish games with us far too long." This time his smile was sincere. "But you have to see the irony in it all, Sister. Dreams do come true...by sunset you will be Queen of Qev. You, Bernice. My little sister. Surely you have to be thankful for that. By the Gods you should be."

"Father was a fool." Bernice could hardly stand the thought of the man who had married her off to someone she didn't want or love. "He knew who I wanted, yet he gave me to Earvin."

Her brother finally found an ounce of courage to stand up to her. He always did whenever she spoke of their father. "You let his soul rest in peace. Father did what he thought best...he was a good man."

She swung her body away from her brother. "He was good for you. Good to you—not his daughter." Again she faced Percival. "You came to me and asked me—begged me—to recommend that Earvin place you on his council, yet you fail me." Bernice looked at Percival with tear-filled eyes. "Where do your loyalties lie, Brother?"

"By the Gods, woman!" Percival flung his arms upward and winced as though he were in pain. "Earvin will be king, trust me, he will have hundreds of women looking at him now, regardless of how..." He eyed her nervously as his words faded.

"Go ahead and say it, Brother." Bernice's sorrows had become too much for her to bear. She wept. "Remind me for the thousandth time of his face…tell me again how our father gave me to a monster. Qev's king is an ugly brute. No crown or throne can blot his horrid face out of my mind."

"You mustn't utter such words," Sister. "You, of all people, shouldn't." Her brother looked back toward the doors. "You are bound to serve him, Earvin is your husband—your master and king!"

"Enough of this talk of the laws which bind us in marriage." Bernice laughed cynically. "For you men," she pointed to her brother, "a woman is no more than a thing to warm your beds, and when you get drunk enough you somehow find a way to spill your seed and bring forth wailing brutes."

"You have lost sight of what you have, Bernice. Think of what you've said." Her brother clasped hands pleadingly. "The kingdom is filled with strong young men—even old men if that would please you. Surely," he said with raised brows, "Earvin would not begrudge you—"

"My brother, I thank you for your advice, but now you must go. Leave me!" She had been a fool not to have seen it before. Percival, her brother, adored her husband. The doors shut with a loud bang, reminding her of the prison she had lived in for so many years.

## CHAPTER FOUR
### *Changed*

It was impossible to tell how much time had passed since he and the other boys were sold; however, it had been many suns since his father left him behind for two bags of gold. Yes, his entire tribe had sold him, not just his family. As Kairu lay upon the grass near the stream he could hardly avoid the sorrowful thoughts which had plagued him since the day he had been left with the shaman. He kept his gaze toward the sky, remembering the sound of his father's voice—that morning he walked away from his village so eager to be going on a journey for the first time in his life. *You cannot look into the eyes of fire, Kairu…*

He had not forgotten his father's words. Kairu looked up toward the blazing sun, he had done it so many times and had even promised Prodigal he would not do so again. "Don't be a fool," Prodigal had said. "You will be of no use to anyone if you cannot see?" But what good would it be to have eyes? After all he had suffered—after all they had put him through, what would it matter if he were to go blind or even die? Deciding to keep a promise to his friend, Kairu turned his gaze from the burning disc. His eyes ached. For a moment he saw blackness. Prodigal was right, and so was his father. It was unwise to gaze into the eyes of fire. Becoming bored by the stream, Kairu rose and walked toward the garden. Many years had passed before he and the other boys were permitted to go beyond the walls of the massive building they now called home. The temple was surrounded by yet another wall. Kairu loathed walls. From his rooms he would look out the window in the direction of the city wall—the place his father left him. Had he ever come back? Kairu could not avoid thinking, hoping. Night after night he would have the same recurring dream. His papa pounded the massive gates and though they were never opened he found a way inside the city, threw the bags of gold at the feet of the shaman and took his son home…

He had told Prodigal of his dreams, yet his friend's advice was always what he refused to accept. Kairu could never give up that hope. Kairu could have yielded to the temptation of leaving the temple in the dark of night and running toward the city wall. He was certain he could make it home. But what would his village want of him? Why would they even wish to see him again, especially after what he had become? Kairu caressed his mother's beads. He had become accustomed to wearing a cloak but the days were hot, especially beneath the sun. The nights were cool and the air sweet. The garden was his favourite place to be…so many colours. But the most beautiful sight of all was the bird with gigantic feathers. The shaman called it the peacock. Seeing the beautiful bird, Kairu's smile surfaced. He lay quietly upon the grass and rested his chin upon his arms. For the first time since he had left his rooms his mind was free. The peacock took hesitant steps; however, Kairu was certain the creature had not seen him. He mimicked the way the creature moved its head. Kairu giggled.

"You are hiding again, Kairu." Prodigal playfully kicked his feet.

Kairu growled like a lion as he wrestled Prodigal to the ground. "You scared it away again," said Kairu, frustrated. "I want to tame it."

Prodigal was strong—much stronger than Kairu. He had grown even taller and become more muscular. His skill matched his strength. Flipping Kairu and pinning him to the ground, Prodigal grinned down at him. "I am of the Nuba tribe."

"And I am Kairu." He grinned back. "I am a descendant of the El Molo, I am of the Maasai." As Prodigal released him he rose and brushed blades of grass from his legs. "Did the shaman send you to find me again?"

"You provoke him, Kairu. Do not make things hard for the rest of us." His friend looked toward the temple. "You run away from your lessons and your duties to look at this bird."

"Sorry, friend." Kairu lowered his eyes with guilt. "I do not want to know how to read markings…or even how to make them. They are not the way of the El Molo. I am of the Maasai."

"He is not a shaman, Kairu," Prodigal pleaded. "He made Hani go to sleep two nights with no food for calling him Shaman. His name is Ade, Kairu."

Kairu found Ade within the library, surrounded by many scrolls and the things he called books. He was without his cloak. Wearing nothing but his tribal red shúkà and his beads, Kairu stood by the door and waited while Ade made markings on sheets of parchments. He could not understand why such things were important, even if Prodigal saw the use of parchment, quill and ink as part of their training. Kairu and the other boys were never permitted to act without being told, so after entering the library he was to stand there in silence until Ade commanded him to speak. This, Kairu hated. "You sent for me…teacher?" It was near impossible to abide by such rules.

Ade's voice was not deep. Pushing the scrolls away from him, he rose in anger. "It would be a loss to send you away, boy."

Kairu lifted his chin in victory, as he was seldom punished for his petulance. He refused to speak and allowed Ade to admonish him.

"Kairu"—Ade seldom uttered his or any of the boys' names—"a day shall come when all this will vanish." He spread his arms outward. "You are here now but only for a while. Another life awaits you—not just you. All my creations." Ade picked up his staff.

*I am Kairu. I am a descendant of the El Molo, of the Maasai. I must not fear this shaman.* But what Ade did next shocked Kairu. Kairu's body froze and his heart leapt.

Ade stroked the side of Kairu's face with an empty, sad look in his eyes. "You are beautiful, Kairu. You will weaken the hearts of many—even those of kings. But you lack wisdom, my child. Your survival will depend completely on what I have to teach."

Kairu looked into Ade's eyes, confused by the affection. He began to weep. As Ade embraced him, Kairu's body shook as his sobs escaped. "Papa left me…"

"And now you must be strong." Ade stepped away from him and lifted his chin with the tip of his staff. "I know you hate me, Kairu. It is seen in your eyes, beautiful as they may be…" His teacher moved toward the door with staff in hand. He moved gracefully. "Come, boy, and I shall show you who you are now and what you are destined to become…if you wish it." Teacher Ade led Kairu down the hall toward a wing of the temple he had not ventured to before. They passed no one else as they walked the quiet hallway. Ahead, Kairu saw a door; surely, this was the place Ade intended to take him.

"What is this place?" Kairu entered the room reluctantly while Ade waited by the door. He paused, wide-eyed in astonishment. "It is…like home." The room was small, just like the size of the hut Kairu lived in back in his village. The walls were decorated with tribal emblems and colours. Kairu turned to Ade and opened his mouth to speak.

"Yes, child, all this belongs to me." His eyes sparkled with pride. "I am of the Yoruba tribe, far away from here." Ade looked like a different person now as he smiled. "But I am here now, Kairu. I have seen many other worlds, boy, but this," he motioned toward the contents within the room before placing his palm flat over his heart, "and this, is who I am today. I have not forgotten who I am." Ade paced the room before picking up a small black, wooden statuette. "This is the essence of who I am, Kairu, who I have always been."

The boy looked from the statuette to Ade's eyes, puzzled. He did not utter a word, as Ade continued.

He smiled wide. "I was a boy once, just like you. And just like you, I was sent to a place not much different than this." His smile vanished and his old angry face resurfaced. "I had to leave my tribe, Kairu, just like you did." Ade placed the statuette where he had found it, bowed, then untied the string around his waist. He pulled his robes above his thighs, then carefully loosened his loincloth and allowed it to fall to the floor. Kairu stepped back, frightened by what he saw. "You see, Kairu, we are alike in so many ways."

Kairu winced as memories of the pain inflicted upon him many years past were brought to the forefront of his mind. The day his father left him was one Kairu could never forget; however, he had found ways to forget the pain. He could not contain his rage, though, not after seeing the grotesque sight between Ade's legs. Unlike Kairu, his teacher had been completely emasculated. There were no genitalia. Kairu turned his gaze from Ade. Frightened and disgusted, he had seen enough.

"We are eunuchs, Kairu, that is our purpose." Ade covered himself and picked up the little statuette. He caressed it, his eyes clouded with tears. "I am of the Yoruba people. This is my brother, my twin." He clutched the statue to his chest.

Kairu's brows converged, more confused. "Brother?"

"It is called *Ere Ibeji*." He smiled down at the statuette. "In my tribe, it is believed that twins share the same soul; as my brother and I were twins, this represents him. We are apart now. But his soul is here with me."

"Where is your brother?" Kairu found the answer in Ade's saddened eyes.

"Dead." He hung his head briefly.

Kairu shook his head. "I do not understand, teacher."

"Our word *ere* means sacred image. *Ibi* is to be born. *Eji* is two. This *Ere Ibeji* is a sacred image of my twin brother." Ade took a seat upon an old wooden stool. "I am called *Taiwo*, the first born. My brother, *Kehinde*, the second. But although born first, I am considered the youngest. As *Taiwo*, I was the first to taste the world. The meaning of *Kehinde* is to come after the other."

"But how could you be younger if you came first?"

"These are the ways of the Yoruba, Kairu. I was sent by my older partner to see what the outside world looks like. My cry after I was born was a signal for *Kehinde* to enter the world after me. This was my place. It was my purpose."

Again, Kairu was reminded of his father's words. "Why are you called Ade if you are to be called...*Taiwo*?"

Ade laughed, nodding. "Ade is my other name. It is believed by our people that the first twin is more adventurous and curious, while the twin that comes after is intelligent and cautious." With a sigh, Ade's face was sad again. "The Yoruba believe twins are beyond natural or normal. Many are sacrificed at birth, you see." He looked and answered Kairu's question before it was asked. "No, *Kehinde* was not sacrificed. He died just after following me into the world. My cries were false, you see. I did not fulfill the first purpose of my life. If I had died, my twin would not have followed and would have lived. So, you see," he caressed the *Ere Ibeji*, "by tradition, this was carved as a representation of my twin to settle the imbalance of the souls…"

Kairu understood. "Because you share the same soul?"

"Yes, Kairu." Ade nodded as if satisfied with what Kairu had learned. "I grew up among my people and learned their ways until my father died. My mother took a new mate and was soon with child. As I had failed in my first purpose I was no longer welcome and with my father dead, no longer wanted. Unlike you, Kairu, I was not worth much to be sold. I was given away."

In the privacy of his room Kairu stood near the window, just so he could see the garden below. He had left Ade within his small room holding the *Ere Ibeji*. He would never think of his teacher the way he once did. In a way, after learning of Ade's past, Kairu pitied him. Kairu stripped naked, leaving just the beads around his neck. The beads were made in such a way that they extended halfway up his neck, hung just above his nipples and almost extended to the ends of his shoulders. He hoped the beads would fit much better as his body grew; however, though he would grow taller, Kairu did not expect his body to change much.

He had grown much since his castration. His voice, however, would change little if at all. Ade had worked with all the young eunuchs in order to determine where they excelled. Kairu loved to sing and dance. This, Ade praised; however, he was adamant that all his children learn how to read and write. "This," Ade had told them, "is why my eunuchs are desired more than any other."

Kairu's hands moved over his stomach, down his thighs and then between his legs. It was difficult to still hate his teacher now, so he was thankful that he had not been completely emasculated. Of the thirteen boys, only Kairu and Prodigal received *lesser castrations*, while the other eleven eunuchs received *greater castrations*. For this, Kairu was thankful. He closed his eyes as his fingers moved over the scar where the sack containing his testicles once hung. Ade never explained why this was done. A soft knock at the door brought Kairu away from his thoughts. He dressed and quickly let his friend in.

"You did not join us for supper, Kairu." Prodigal looked to him, concerned.

"I was not hungry." He smiled as best as he could. More than anything, Kairu wanted to share what he had learned from Ade with his friend. He thought carefully before deciding not to utter a word. Ade had taught them all the importance of secrecy and trust. Kairu decided it was time to begin taking these teachings seriously. The eunuchs' teacher seldom explained why certain things were taught or why such time and detail was spent on certain tasks. Ade simply expected them to do all things as best as they could.

Prodigal delivered a playful slap to the side of Kairu's shoulder. "I hope you are not lying to me, black eunuch." He grinned wide. "Black one."

Kairu smiled back as he heard the meaning of his own name. "And what was your mother thinking when she named you? Prodigal."

"My father chose my name." He slapped Kairu's other shoulder. "Come on, Kairu. You must fight back."

"You always win, Prodigal. I am not strong." He aimed a fist toward his friend's chest, which was quickly blocked. Kairu gave in after the pain to his arms became unbearable. He turned his gaze back to the outdoors. It had become dark, and slowly, the night sky was studded with stars. For the first time in many suns, Kairu felt safe. Something had changed within him…something which made him feel as though the temple had become his home. Throwing his arm around his friend's neck, Kairu said, "I am hungry now."

"You are impossible, Kairu," said his friend. "Come with me."

There was much to learn from Ade and his aides, especially the art of reading the skies. Knowing the time of day, Ade had explained once, was very important. As Kairu stood out on the balcony that evening he looked toward the sky as the sun reached its zenith. The evening air was cool and refreshing, just perfect after a long day of singing, dancing and reading. These were just some of the tasks that each eunuch had to carry out each day, not to mention their chores. Before Kairu or the others could enjoy a moment of free time they each had to assist in cleaning the temple. They were expected to make all the beds of the senior aides as well as Ade's. This, Kairu opposed doing, as he had never had to do such things before he was sold to be a eunuch.

In order to have enough time to himself Kairu rose very early in the mornings, took a break in the middle of the day and ensured his chores and lessons were completed before supper. This way he could enjoy quiet moments to himself as he now did out on the balcony. He could hear noise outside the temple walls. The city sounded so alive, so exciting. If only he could see what life outside the temple was like, if just for a few moments. But it was not permitted for any of the eunuchs to go beyond the gates. Ade had forbidden it. Kairu rested his arms atop the ledge and looked over the wall to no avail. He had never been able to see anyone. Again, the thought of being surrounded by walls brought great sorrow. All his life he had lived within the walls of his village. Then one day, when he was finally able to go beyond them with the person he trusted most, he never returned. He was sold—bought by another person that he came to trust with his life, and again caged within the confines of a wall. This time the wall was of stone. He had not uttered a word to Prodigal of his plans—not yet. Kairu had not even decided whether he would tell anyone what he intended to do. *This is the night*, Kairu confirmed.

Later that night, after the aides had checked every room, Kairu waited. He lay in bed with his eyes wide open, determined to see what the world outside the temple walls was like. As he pushed the door open it creaked. Kairu's heart raced. He paused, holding his breath. He had devised a plan. It was quite simple. He left his beads behind, slipped into the black cowl he had taken days earlier, and though it was much too big for him, Kairu girded the waist with a string to avoid tripping. As he passed Prodigal's door he considered waking his friend. *I do this alone*, thought Kairu. *I will tell my friends of my adventure in the morning.*

He made it to the gate fairly quickly. Everything had worked out just as planned. The young black eunuch covered his mouth with his palm to muffle a quick chuckle, for as he looked inside the booth next to the gate he confirmed that the gatekeeper, Sol, was sound asleep. Kairu felt proud of what he had done to Sol. Just before retiring to his room Kairu had brought a cup of ale for his new friend. Sol had no clue that a pinch of sleeping herb had been dissolved inside his cup. The art of healing was another of Kairu's favourite lessons.

Just to make sure, he gently slapped Sol's thin face. The guard's spear had fallen to the floor. Again, Kairu giggled. He moved toward the massive gate and lifted the latch to the small door in the gate, pulling ever so carefully. Kairu slipped through the small opening of the temple gates and looked out into an entirely different world. The night was black, terrifyingly dark. He saw small glows of light in the distance; however, as his eyes adjusted to the darkness and Kairu could see several feet farther, he swiftly darted out into the night.

It took just moments to get away from the gates, and after running so fast and out of breath Kairu paused for a quick respite before walking on. He never looked back. Finally, after walking from one alley to the next and hardly seeing anyone at all, Kairu realized he had lost track of time. He had been wise to avoid crossing paths with strangers; however, he did not realize how far he had gone from the temple. Kairu found himself in a lonely, dark alley, surrounded by small shacks and stalls with no clue how to get back home. The black eunuch was lost.

The city was dark and still—not quite what Kairu had expected. He should have planned more carefully, for what good was it to be within the city when most of its inhabitants were asleep? The night had become cold and the fact that he had nothing else on beneath the black cloak but his loincloth caused him to shiver. His hands were trembling. Kairu was afraid. He walked down alley after alley, feeling as though he were in a maze. The moon was full, and for that Kairu was grateful; however, the moonlight was not enough to show him the way back to the temple. He had lost track of how long it had been since he left; surely Sol would have awoken by now. Panicking, Kairu turned in circles several times before breaking into a run. He had already begun to weep and had just closed his eyes when he collided with another body. His heart slammed against his chest when he looked up into the face of the largest person he had ever seen. The tall tribesman's dark face could barely be seen in the night; Kairu looked into the whites of two eyes and as the stranger spoke he saw strong white teeth.

The stranger's voice rumbled. "Ki ni o." Pushing the cowl from Kairu's face, he smiled in awe. "Lẹwa," he whispered. "Ọmọkùnrin wa ni omobirin." Kairu stepped backward, frightened. His first instinct was to run, but as he did so he tripped. There was no escape. The large warrior stood over him with a toothy grin. He uttered no other words, but as his large palm gripped Kairu's throat the eunuch knew he was in danger and should never have left the safety of the temple. The giant was strong and pushed so hard against Kairu's chest that he suddenly became short of breath. Kairu struggled with all his might, even as the large tribesman pinned him to the ground. Something scratched Kairu's forehead as he moved his head from side to side. The eunuch clawed at the dark face, hoping to find a way to free himself. But he was no match for this warrior's brute strength. He cringed as the stranger raised a hand to strike him. Something made him stop. "Lẹwa." He said that word again, even as he tore Kairu's cloak from his body and dragged him out of the moonlight. Kairu looked up into the whites of those eyes, even as tears streamed from his own. The giant's hand probed his body, all along uttering the word, *lẹwa*. Kairu did not know the meaning of the word and knew he would never forget it. His violator's smile widened as his fingers moved over Kairu's scar. The black eunuch turned his head to the side and looked up toward the moon. He could no longer gaze into those eyes. "Lẹwa," he said again, "lẹwa…lẹw—"

There was a muffled thud before the tribesman stared down at Kairu, wide-eyed in shock. Kairu rolled away as the giant fell forward and landed facedown into the dirt. Above them was Prodigal. Kairu had never been so happy to see his friend.

"Why do you never listen, Kairu?"

## CHAPTER FIVE
### *Diadem*

Thousands had come to court to see the crowning of Qev's new king. Protocol demanded that the royal family sit together, and for Orin, this long spectacle was too much to bear. His sister, Cylene, and their eldest brother, Kevan, relished every moment of the proceedings. Lucas, however, was nowhere to be found. All except King Earvin joined in the search for Lucas to no avail. Lucas would join the grand coronation when he felt the need to do so.

The cathedral, though crowded, was still. Orin watched from behind Kevan's broad shoulders as his father, adorned in the finest robes, walked behind the high priest. The procession was slow and methodical. A choir of boys sang praises to the Gods; nothing sounded sweeter than the sound of song within the walls of the royal cathedral. Having high ceilings and massive stained glass windows, no other place would have been better for a new king to accept his rule and his crown. Orin rolled his eyes in disgust. He had met with his father before the coronation. *What have I done to have* been granted the pleasure of having such loving parents?* He caressed the side of his face where his mother had slapped, before rubbing his neck. Orin watched his uncle Percival across the cathedral, only he had been present to witness his father's palms tighten around his neck. *I am so lucky to have such a protective uncle...*

His father and his mother's brother had questioned him. Orin divulged nothing of the rumours he had heard. He could trust no one—not even his own blood. Of this, Orin was certain.

><<<<o>>>><

Her husband knelt upon a cushion with the royal sceptre in his right hand. His look was solemn; Bernice, his wife, watched him in disgust. Her place was beside her husband, yet protocol dictated that she should sit with the children and look on like any commoner. Bernice felt small and insignificant. How, by the Gods, could a queen feel lesser than a mere maid? The lady-in-waiting—her husband's mistress—stood just steps away from the king. Even as the crown was placed upon her husband's head, Bernice's gaze was fixed upon the wench.

"Oh, Mother," said Cylene, hands clasped with poise and grace, "does father not look magnificent?"

"You must be quiet, darling," replied Bernice. "We mustn't disrupt the proceedings." The last thing she needed to hear was how great Earvin was. *He is only half man,* she thought. *I loved a man far greater—a man who could have loved me back...*

Cylene shed tears as her father repeated the solemn vows, while her mother could only think on the many nights Earvin had spent with a mere servant. "Revolting." She eyed Genesis—this is what she was called. *What a horrid name.*

"All hail the King!" The high priest raised his hands heavenward, his eyes gleaming with love for a man who could have him executed if he stood in his way. Thousands within the cathedral lifted their voices to hail the newly crowned king, and the many thousands outdoors echoed the same praise.

"All hail," mumbled the Queen. She realized then how powerless she was, being a queen only in name. She fixed her gaze upon the father of her children. *He's truly an ugly man…though he had been beautiful once. Rejoice now, King. You may have your consort and your guards. You have your army, even my own brother by your side. But I have my cunning.* Finally, the new queen smiled, for it was time for the family to stand with the King of Qev.

"Oh…Your Majesty!" The scullery maid's body trembled at his touch. With widened eyes, Kevan pressed his body closer against hers. He had forcefully undone the bodice of her dress, exposing firm, full breasts. Pinching her nipple again, Kevan tilted his head to the right, his tongue licking the corners of his mouth. The scullery maid reacted again with a high-pitched squeal. "Oh…my Prince!"

Kevan moved one hand up her chest and gently tightened it around her neck. "It's Your Majesty to you," he commanded. "Say it." As he did this his manhood stiffened. "Yes, tell your king what you want."

The scullery maid paused, and looked up into his eyes, obviously afraid. "But…your father is king—"

Kevan tightened the grip. "And one day I shall be, won't I, cow?"

"Yes…Your Majesty." She had begun to cry.

"Come on now, ruin the fun." He lowered his hand to the maid's breasts; however, her weeping would not cease. Kevan grinned down at her, determined to have what was promised him. The maid covered her face with both hands as the heir to the throne of Qev parted her legs and slipped his fingers inside her. Then came the soft knock at his door. "By all the Gods," he cursed. "What now?" The prince pointed a threatening finger toward the girl's face. "I will find you later. Now go out the way you came…and not a word to anyone about the passages or I'll skin you alive." The scullery maid gathered her things and rushed from the room.

"It smells foul in here." Kevan's mother scanned the main room of her son's quarters before quickly glancing toward the bed chambers. "You are alone?"

Kevan wiped his hands over his cotehardie before approaching his mother. "Naturally, I am alone, Mother. Who else would be here?" He saw how her eyes watched him suspiciously. Kevan grinned. "What?"

"All I have ever asked of you," she said, still with disbelief in her eyes, "is the truth." Her eyes pierced through him. "I know what it is you do here, Kevan. I am no fool." The queen turned her back to him. "You are all I have left."

"Come on, Mother." He approached her cautiously. "You have three other children…and father too."

"Do not mock me. You know where your father's heart lies." She grimaced as if in pain. "Cylene adores him; Orin fears him…and Lucas—"

"I know, Mother. Lucas is just Lucas. You've said it enough times that even I can't forget it."

His mother walked about the room, putting Kevan's personal effects in place. "Just look at your rooms. How often do the servants clean this place?"

The prince moved to his mother and grabbed her by the shoulder. He shook her once with just enough force as not to harm her. "Mother, you are a queen now, not a housemaid or a mere lady at court. Queen of Qev. This is who you are. You're a queen. Act like one!"

Her face fell against his breast. "How can I be queen when…when he keeps a consort who would quickly supplant me? She is young. She can bear him more heirs." She looked up at her eldest with sudden realization. "What then? What will become of us…of you?"

The visit from his mother left him exhausted. Kevan had lost the zeal to have the scullery maid back in his rooms, especially after having to confess to the presence of the girl in his rooms. He could keep nothing from his mother. The prince pondered his mother's words as he lay upon his bed. *Think on what your father would do were you to have a flock of royal bastards trailing behind you about the castle.*" Kevan closed his eyes and envisioned the future ahead. At seventeen he was considered a man, and though there was already much pressure from his father—talk of finding a wife fit for the crown prince—Kevan felt he was not ready. *If I am King*, he thought, *there should be no need to marry. A king should do as he likes. A king takes what he likes.*

## CHAPTER SIX
### *The Marula Tree*

Another two years had passed. At nearly fifteen, the Nuba boy now considered himself a man. Just the thought of what he was—what others had made him—ignited rage within him. As much as he felt he hated his teacher, Prodigal found it nearly impossible to disrespect him. Ade was harsh, but in his own way he cared for his eunuchs. The Nuba boy, as his teacher called him, had discovered the perfect place to spend the hot days. The Marula tree at the back of the garden, just by the tall stone wall, was Prodigal's place to be alone. The Marula's canopy was wide, its limbs thick, and some of its branches extended beyond the temple's wall. The Nuba boy was agile and fit; he could climb to the highest pinnacle of the Marula within moments. Now perched on one of the thickest limbs, Prodigal viewed the city from above as though he were a god. Of this he would dream each time he climbed the ancient tree—that he ruled over all the lands, brought the rain and commanded the sun to bring light.

But the Marula was also the place where the athletic eunuch usually wept. A place the Nuba boy would go to remind himself of exactly what he had become. Everyone knew what lived within the temple. Ọmọkùnrin wa ni omobirin. *Boy turned girl.* Prodigal would no longer be seen as a boy—just one of the reasons why he wept. He had been changed—made only to serve as a giver of pleasure—and this he would give to whomever he served, man or woman. There had even been a time when others threw stones at him from below as they uttered the words, ọmọkùnrin wa ni omobirin. So, the Marula had become Prodigal's friend, his protector. It never judged him, nor did it betray him by revealing his secrets. Prodigal had spent many nights atop the tree weeping for his home, his tribe, his father. He could only have done so in the presence of the Marula tree, for it comforted him so. At that particular moment, while the sun shone bright and the skies were clear, Prodigal looked outward to the busy city. From above his eyes beheld a sea of colours—various tribes came to the city each day. Again, like all other days, just for a moment, Prodigal was certain his eyes glimpsed his father only to witness the strong figure vanish into the throng. The apparitions occurred nearly every time the eunuch looked out toward the city. Prodigal hung his head, sorrowfully.

Prodigal had just wiped his tears when he heard movement upon the dry leaves below. He looked down to see Kairu staring up at him. "How long have you been there, Kairu?"

"Long enough to see you weep."

"Go away!" He did not know whether what he felt was rage or shame.

"Why do you weep, Prodigal?"

Prodigal slapped the fat limb of the Marula. "You go away, or I will come down and beat you." Immediately, Prodigal knew he should not have said that. Kairu hugged the massive trunk of the Marula in his attempt to climb up. "Do not come up, Kairu. You will hurt yourself." Prodigal shook his head, now more worried for his friend. It took great skill to climb a Marula tree. It took just moments for the black one to fall flat on his back, and seeing his friend wince in pain Prodigal swung downward from limb to limb before jumping down to Kairu's side. "Are you alright, Kairu? Why do you never listen to me…to anyone?" He wrapped his arms around his friend as if to protect him, and as Kairu's arms tightened around him Prodigal cradled his head with relief. "I am frightened for you, black eunuch," said Prodigal with a smile. "Are you hurt, Kairu?"

"I am alive." With Kairu's arms wrapped around his torso Prodigal sighed with relief. For a few moments they spoke no words until, finally, the silence resounded deep within Prodigal, stirring strange thoughts. Prodigal quickly rose from bent knees, lifting Kairu with him. Stepping away from Kairu he turned his gaze to the Marula tree. "What were you thinking, Kairu? You know you cannot climb."

"I will if you show me." Kairu walked toward the tree and pushed against the trunk. He turned abruptly and looked into Prodigal's eyes as if to search his soul.

"Do not climb the tree, Kairu. Please." The Marula was his place. He looked back into his friend's eyes until he received a nod. Prodigal nodded back. In that instant it surprised him, realizing how much Kairu had changed. His friend of the Maasai had grown. Of all the eunuchs, Kairu was tallest. The boy Prodigal had met outside the city gates that day was no more. Kairu's skin was smooth and even; his head was perfectly shaped, and his long neck, accentuated by the colourful beads, gave him the look of a Nubian king. Kairu, known by his peers as *the black eunuch,* was indeed beautiful. As Ade had foretold, Kairu was worth far more than gold…

"Why do you look at me like that, Prodigal?" Kairu's hand nervously touched the scar upon his forehead—his only imperfection.

Prodigal smiled in an attempt to calm his friend. The mark on Kairu's face served as a reminder for disobeying the rules and venturing beyond the gates of the temple. Prodigal shuddered to think of what might have occurred that night had he not followed his friend. Kairu had run so fast into the night—fast enough that Prodigal lost sight of him. "Many suns have passed, Kairu. Why do you think of it again and again?" Kairu's eyes met the ground. "You cannot blame yourself forever, Kairu. Many suns have passed. Ade said it was alright."

"But…he—"

"We must not speak of him." Prodigal looked to the Marula tree, longing for its comfort.

The boy was finally ready. Of all his eunuchs, Kairu, the black eunuch of the Maasai, was his most precious treasure; of this, Ade was certain. The teacher sat out on his terrace, the one with the best view of the city. Ade smiled, thinking of his life and travels. *Like Kairu, I thought this*—he motioned toward the city of huts surrounding the temple—*was the centre of the world.* He caressed his staff, pondering just how much he should tell the boy. Just then, Kairu arrived.

"You called for me, teacher?" He scratched the scar in the centre of his forehead.

Ade would waste no time; he would tell the eunuch what he felt he needed to know—all he needed to keep safe. "Your time here is near its end, Kairu. Your true purpose is about to begin." There was puzzlement within the boy's eyes. "Yes," said Ade. He motioned to the stool next to him. "Look, Kairu, how big the world is." He motioned beyond the city walls. "Your journey from home to me took but a short while. Your journey from here shall be long and treacherous." Ade closed his eyes briefly. "Some of you may even die, I fear. But of all my eunuchs, Kairu, I want you to live. You must live, black eunuch. Remember this, live."

The boy fell to his knees and took Ade's hand. "Please, teacher, do not send me away." The boy was afraid. "I don't care where you plan on sending us, just keep me here."

"You imprison yourself, boy. This is no prison. You cannot stay here. Now sit and listen to what I have to tell you." Kairu sat upon the stool with such grace that his teacher smiled with satisfaction. "Your purpose is to serve, yet, I see a better future for you. You will charm the hearts of many, even those of kings. I've told you this many times, Kairu. What your village did—what your father did was beyond his control. You were chosen from birth for a purpose. Your tribe remembers you for what you have done, though it was against your will."

Ade did not pause long for fear the boy would question him, as was his usual practice. "You are my best eunuch; the Nuba boy is second to you. But I know he will die to protect you." Ade greeted the black eunuch with a nod and one of his knowing smiles. "I shall do all I can to make sure you are kept together."

"Teacher, where will we go?"

"There is much more I need to tell you, Kairu. The night is still young." Ade studied the sky. A veil of darkness had begun to envelope the city, the perfect setting for enlightening his black eunuch.

Ọmọkùnrin wa ni omobirin. *Boy turned girl.* This is what Kairu had become. He had become the life his father had forced upon him, telling him it was his purpose. "I am Kairu. I am a descendant of the El Molo. I am of the

Maasai." This, he would not forget. Kairu had stood at the base of the Marula tree and watched as Prodigal cursed those who passed by and called up at him. Ọmọkùnrin wa ni omobirin, they shouted back as loud as they could, each word embalmed with hatred.

Ọmọkùnrin wa ni omobirin. Kairu would never forget the first time he heard those words. Boy turned girl. He rubbed his scar as he relived that terrifying night. The black eunuch had just affixed his beads around his neck. He had rubbed oil into his skin just as his mother had taught him. With a clear understanding of why he was made a eunuch, Kairu was determined to be the best he could be. This was his purpose, even Ade had told him so. "It must be true," said Kairu as he dressed in his shúkà. After all he had learned, all the work he had done since Ade took him in, Kairu learned he would spend the rest of his life in the service of others. A mere servant to lords and kings. His very life would belong to the one he served. Where was the good in this purpose? Why had he been cursed, bound to do the biddings of others when he was born into a tribe he loved and belonged to a family he adored?

Ade had told them many stories of his past life—tales of wars and death. He had shown them the art of sexual pleasure, ensured his eunuchs could read and write, but most of all, Ade begged them to be loyal. He had spoken with Kairu alone several times. "Make them trust you," he had said, "even more than they could ever trust themselves. Then you will have the true taste of power." Up on the balcony that night Ade had taken Kairu's face in the palms of his hands and begged him to do as he was told. "If you betray your master, your lord or king," he warned, "you shall surely die. Your beauty will mean nothing to them. Remember this, Kairu. Never lie to your master. It is forbidden. They would rather you fall upon your face before them and beg their forgiveness than for you to betray them."

Kairu touched his own face and wondered if he was truly beautiful. It was Ade who had explained the meaning of the Yoruba word *lẹwa*. *Lẹwa* meant beautiful. Kairu could hear the giant tribesman he had met in the darkened city long ago, the monster who had meant to harm him, yet called him beautiful. The tribesman had died that night. Kairu realized that he may not have survived that night had Prodigal not followed him. After that night Kairu had felt bound to Prodigal, and he had promised that his life belonged to the Nuba boy. After they realized the tribesman was dead, that night, Kairu and Prodigal had raced back to the temple and woke their teacher who sent them to bed and promised he would take care of the matter. The following morning Ade had broken his fast with the two young eunuchs and explained there would be no need to discuss the matter any further. From that moment on Ade had made certain his eunuchs were well prepared should they find themselves alone and cornered by any man who wished to violate them. As he dressed, Kairu was saddened by the realization that he would never sire a child. Kairu finished dressing and left his rooms. Ade was taking his eunuchs on a journey.

The eunuchs left the temple just before sunset that evening, completely surrounded by warriors. Fully cowled in black, Kairu was reminded of the first time he saw death. Again, he struggled with the fact that Prodigal had struck down a great warrior to protect him. The warrior had said he was beautiful; the word resonated inside Kairu's head as they walked through the temple's gates and headed through the city. Ade was carried in a simple sedan by strong, powerful tribesmen. "Where are they taking us?" Kairu asked his friend. "Ade would not tell me."

Prodigal turned to look at the sedan with anger in his eyes. He had become defiant as of late, especially after Ade had forbidden his visits atop the large Marula. "He thinks only of himself, Kairu. How could we not see this before?" The Nuba boy's smile was cynical. "He tells us only what he wants us to know, nothing more."

"But he has not lied to us, Prodigal."

"Not sharing the truth, Kairu, is the same as lying." Prodigal said no more.

A long day was over; Kairu looked upward and saw shadows stealing across the sky. As they journeyed, many people from the city stopped to gaze at the cowled figures walking into the night. From time to time the phrase ọmọkùnrin wa ni omobirin was uttered in whispers, while others shouted it aloud. Many bowed as Ade's sedan passed them.

Finally, a destination seemed to be in sight. Kairu knew at that moment his life would change this night. He could hear it in the water as waves splashed toward the shore and he could smell it in the salty air. The full moon had transformed the sea into a bed of flowing silver; the breeze was cool against Kairu's face. Astonished at the sight of nearly one hundred red tents, Kairu looked to his friend, Prodigal. "I am afraid."

His friend's look softened. "So am I, Kairu."

There was one massive white tent in the centre of the camp. Next to it was another tent of black and gold. Kairu looked around in awe as they were led toward a single hut beyond the white tent, near a rocky cliff. Within, they were fed. Ade visited them briefly. "Rest now, for tomorrow you must all show your worth."

## CHAPTER SEVEN

## *Ships*

Night had fallen. The wind carried with it a chill as well as the salty scent of the sea. Again, Ade prepared to barter that which he had created; this he had done many times in his life. However, for the first time in all his years he felt sorrow. He donned his ceremonial headdress just before he stepped upon the shore. He looked out toward the ships and smiled at the glow of light from within them. The King of men had come once more to collect the quality of his land. He passed the red tents and walked toward the eunuchs' hut. "Our final goodbye." The time had come to part with Kairu, the black eunuch—son of the El Molo, the boy of the Maasai.

Ade entered the white hut knowing he had seen all that was to come many times before. But never before had he felt such sorrow in parting with his eunuchs. His eyes found Kairu instantly, and the teacher smiled. Prodigal, the lesser eunuch, was not far from the black one's side. "My eunuchs," said Ade, "the ships have come. This night, your new lives begin." Ade pointed his staff toward Kairu and bid him to follow. He needed to give the black one final words of advice, for the horn had sounded. The King of men had come.

Outside the hut, Ade walked toward the sea with the cowled eunuch. He pointed toward the great vessels with gigantic masts. "One of these ships will take you to another world, Kairu…far away from all this. We shall not see each other again." He saw terror inside those beautiful eyes. *What I would have given to be like you, black one. If only you knew what power the Gods have bestowed upon you…*

"You shall learn," Ade said with one final smile. "I shall do all I can to see that the Nuba boy stays with you, Kairu, but I cannot promise this. He is special in his own way, men shall desire him just as they do you…but not for the same reasons, I'm afraid." The boy looked to him in puzzlement, and all Ade could do was place a hand upon Kairu's shoulder. "You will learn, Kairu." Ade's gaze returned to the ships. "This night, Kairu, you must show your worth. Everyone sees it—they know it, but you, boy, are oblivious to this. I've seen how my other eunuchs look at you…how they desire you and then hate you for it." Again, Ade lifted his staff toward the ships. "There is a king in one of those and tonight he comes to claim you for his own. You must make him desire you, Kairu. Remember what I have taught you. You have the power to choose your master. Show me you can do this and I shall not worry after you leave me forever."

The black eunuch fell to his knees and wept. Ade wept too in silence as he gave the black one final instructions.

Their day within the white tent had been a long one. Kairu sat next to Prodigal, encumbered by feelings of fear and suspense. They had not gone hungry during the wait; every eunuch had been fed. Teacher Ade, the man he once called *the shaman*, wore a colourful headdress made of peacock feathers. It was most beautiful. *Lẹwa*, thought Kairu, deeming the peacock worthy of the name. Kairu thought on his talk with his teacher the previous evening. He had seen the ships upon the sea before the other eunuchs and had promised his teacher he would prove his worth.

"You look to him," said Prodigal, "as though you expect him to save you, Kairu." Prodigal teased. "He loves us, Kairu, you especially, but that love is nothing compared to his love of gold." Prodigal kept his gaze upon their teacher. "That was all we ever were to him."

Kairu shrugged. "I am worth more than gold," he replied. "Far more!"

Prodigal laughed. "He has made you a fool, hasn't he, Kairu?"

"I am no fool," replied Kairu. He knew much of Ade's life as a boy. "He is like us, a eunuch."

Prodigal was about to respond when the sound of the horn echoed, and every eunuch turned toward the entrance of the tent. They were surrounded by dozens of armed tribesmen and told to kneel with their heads bowed low. With a wall of warriors around them, Kairu could see nothing beyond the cluster of bare feet and wooden spears.

As the white tent was filled Kairu's heart slammed against his ribcage. The time had come to show his worth. Kairu thought back to all Ade had shown him. *I must choose my master*, thought Kairu.

A fire had been lit within a circle of stones and it blazed bright, sending sparks upward. The top of the white tent had been removed, allowing white and black smoke to drift up toward the sky. With Prodigal close to him Kairu knelt as commanded and kept his eyes to the ground.

The tribesmen now lined the walls of the tent, and finally, Kairu and the other eunuchs were commanded to stand. They were brought to the other side of the fire where Ade stood before seven men. The one seated upon the large wooden chair wore a crown of gold. Kairu looked beyond Ade in utter shock, for he had never seen such men in all his life. They were different—men with pale skin.

"Eniyan ti awọn ara bia," whispered the fat eunuch. There was fear in his voice. "The man of pale skin!"

Kairu looked on, fascinated. He could not decide which should be his master—at least not yet.

"Eniyan ti awọn ara bia." Prodigal moved closer to Kairu. "Papa's stories were true," he said boastfully. "They were not fairy tales."

Ade bowed low before the seven men, and to the only one wearing the golden crown. He said: "King of Kings, we welcome you!" The king waved his ringed hand impatiently, commanding Ade to proceed.

Every eunuch was brought before this king. Kairu stood upright, his eyes fixed upon the king, for it was obvious the others feared him. His chosen master had long black hair; his eyes were the colour of the sea; set within his golden crown were precious stones of various colours. The one they called King of Kings had pleasant eyes. But he bore the ugliest scar to one side of his face and half of his right ear was missing. Kairu locked eyes with the pale-skinned king and did not look away. He did all that Ade had told him to do. The other eunuchs pushed their cowls away from their faces. Kairu untied his cloak, pushed the cowl away from his face and allowed the entire garment to fall to the ground. He stood with confidence and poise. The light of the fire reflected from his necklace of beads and his skin shone after his application of perfumed fish oils. Towering above his brothers, Kairu then lowered his chin, eyes fixed upon the King of Kings. Ade had commanded him not to smile that night, so Kairu did not. Finally, he shifted his mesmerizing gaze from the pale skinned king, slowly planting his eyes upon the sandy ground. The King looked to Ade as he pointed toward Kairu. He grunted, attempting the conceal a grin.

Ade bowed at once. "As you command, my King," he said. "The eunuch is yours."

Kairu, descendant of the El Molo, the boy of the Maasai, had chosen his master. A King.

However, a great lord rose from his seat and bowed before the crown. "But King Earvin," stuttered the plump man with hair the colour of gold. "I too wish to have this eunuch…Your Majesty." Something in the way he moved his eyes, the way he looked at the king betrayed him, for in his gaze, Kairu saw hatred.

"This eunuch is a gift," replied King Earvin. "Isn't it so, eunuch master?" He looked to Ade with piercing blue eyes.

With urgency, Ade nodded. "Indeed, Sire. A gift for you alone." Ade extended his arm with the staff, waving it as if to present Kairu to the king.

Kairu looked to the six lords, and was immediately troubled, for it was obvious they were displeased with the king. These men watched Kairu with rage-filled eyes and obvious desire.

King Earvin clapped aloud and immediately one of his servants took Kairu's arm and led him away from the other eunuchs. He then positioned him directly behind the wooden throne. Kairu looked into the servant's eyes and was astonished as he received a slight, involuntary bow.

><<<<o>>>><

The following morning, beneath the beams of the burning sun, Kairu sat near the stern of a small boat. He extended his hand over the edge and allowed the water to pass over it. *I may never see these lands again.* Kairu looked back. He had gone far out from shore but could still see Ade standing near the edge of the water. The black eunuch did not allow his eyes to meet with those of the four pale men inside his boat. He did, however, look to his right and locked eyes with Prodigal. His friend would be travelling on another ship, not the king's. Ade had done all he could do to ensure the friends stayed together, but to no avail. The plump man, Lord Theo of Qev, had won the Nuba boy. Before leaving for the ships Ade spoke with the only two eunuchs who had received lesser castrations. He had managed to ensure that Kairu and Prodigal were given to the same kingdom. As for the others, Kairu was uncertain of their destinies. "Your paths may never cross again," Ade had said. "But when it does I pray your houses will be at peace." Their teacher did not explain why he said this.

# CHAPTER EIGHT
## *"Throned"*

The youngest of the royal family, Prince Lucas detested dining with his siblings, especially his sister, Cylene. Now almost fifteen, Lucas had more freedom, especially in his father's absence. He was never permitted to leave the castle on his own; however, Lucas spent every moment he could spare with the common folk, and they loved him for it. The common folk made Lucas feel real. Now, seated with his family, he felt insignificant and bored.

"Why so quiet, young brother," said Kevan. His brother had always sat closest to their mother. "You've barely touched your breakfast."

Lucas pushed his plate farther away from him with a shrug. There were many other things he could have been doing at that moment, but there he was, trapped with those he was expected to love. Lucas grinned, eyeing his family—four of the people he should love most in all the world, yet he felt so disconnected from them. His gaze shifted to the servants standing against the walls. *I'd have more fun with them.* The sting of a corner of bread against the side of his face brought the prince back to reality. His fists clenched as he glared across the long table at his eldest brother.

"Go ahead then, say something. Do anything…if you dare." Kevan's attempts to emulate their father failed miserably. "Look at him, Mother. He sits there and taunts me, the little brute."

"Do not provoke him, dear," said their mother. "We all know how Lucas is. Let him be."

"And just how will anyone respect me when I am king if he refuses to speak to me? I demand respect!" Kevan leaned forward as his voice echoed throughout the room. "He comes to my table wearing rags—imagine, a shameful prince!"

"You're no king." Lucas had held his tongue far too long. His eyes became darts as he glared at his brother. "A true king serves his people. He loves everyone—even those beyond the castle walls." His thoughts went to his grandfather, King Bernard. "Were you and father not close enough to a good king to learn the true value of your subjects?"

Cylene tossed her napkin atop her plate in disgust. Pounding the surface of the table she screeched at her brother. "How dare you insult our father! He is King!" Cylene turned her gaze to their mother. "You would sit by and allow them to speak badly of father?"

"For all the names of the Gods!" Their mother's eyes became narrow slits. "Must you carry on so terribly? I grow sick of this constant fuss." Her gaze challenged her daughter's. Lucas watched as his mother rose from her chair and moved slowly toward his sister. The slaps to both sides of her face echoed within the room. "You will not speak to me in that tone ever again," she said. "For I am Queen."

Orin chuckled while their sister wept, shocked as she rubbed red cheeks. One glance from their mother quieted him. Cylene stormed from the room, and shortly after Kevan followed, but after eyeing their mother in puzzlement. Orin spoke only after the queen left them. "Our mother has changed…if father stays away any longer only the Gods can help us."

Lucas grunted. One could never decide exactly when to trust Orin. "I just wish grandfather were alive." There was a sudden glint in his brother's grey eyes. "What?" Lucas knew his brother well enough to know when he wished to disclose his secrets.

Without looking at the servants Orin snapped his fingers. "Leave us!" The servants departed. He must have noticed the shock in Lucas' eyes. "They are here to serve us, Brother. No need to be too respectful to mere servants. They serve us." He walked close to his brother and messed his hair. "You can't always save the world, young brother. You and I may never sit on Qev's throne."

Lucas took a step away from his brother. He seldom liked to give or receive affection from his family. "The Gods are cruel." Surely they must be, Lucas thought, since so many of Qev's subjects lived in poverty—so many deaths each day…

"Little brother, the Gods keep this whole cycle alive…we live, love, eat, fight great wars, and then we all die."

"Our brother will be the ruin of us all. Grandfather tried to teach him but Father kept him away." As his body dropped down into his chair Lucas eyed his brother. He saw that glint in Orin's eyes at the mention of their grandfather. "You know something. What have you heard?"

Orin's head tilted to the side as he grinned and played with the stem of his silver goblet. "Once," he began, "there was an old king. A good king. And all the subjects of his kingdom loved him—so much that they would have given their very lives in his honour. Remember, this king was good, but he was old, yet he was strong. But one day the king fell sick. Mysteriously sick. What, dear brother, do you think his faithful servants whisper? They say the new king is vile, a wretch. They say he loves them not. And they whisper rumours of murder. Talks of poison. They whisper of the only way the new king could acquire both the throne and crown: murder."

Lucas's heart raced, for he too had heard such whispers. To accuse a newly crowned king of supplanting his predecessor by means of murder was treason. However, it was obvious what the entire kingdom thought of his father, for they believed he had killed their beloved. "You believe our father—"

"I was merely telling a story, little brother. Our father is a good man." Orin offered a cunning smile. "Beware our brother," warned Orin. "In kingdoms such as our own, history tends to repeat itself." He glanced about the room as though they were not alone. Suddenly, Orin's gaze softened as he looked into Lucas's eyes. "We may have a duty to our family—to the crown. But we should never forget our history...or just history itself."

"I don't know what you mean, Orin," Lucas said with a shrug. "Our father is King. Some day our brother will replace him. It is what it is."

Orin's sly grin returned. "Some day?" He gave the top of Lucas's head another quick tousle as he passed him, an act he knew Lucas detested. "You should spend more time in the library, young one..."

><<<<o>>>><

Kevan paced back and forth within his sister's chambers, his mind encumbered with a thousand thoughts. He could not explain to himself why he had gone to see Cylene; however, for some reason or another he felt he needed her help. What help could a spoiled princess of nearly thirteen give to one who would soon be king? The crowned prince watched his sister carefully without uttering a word. Cylene was a true princess, Kevan thought. *Pity she was born a woman.* The prince quickly retracted that thought, as having a third brother and rival for the throne was the last thing he wanted. As far as he was concerned their mother should have stopped bearing children after his birth…or should have simply given their father a lot of daughters.

With back perfectly arched and jewels in perfect place about her body, Cylene had the appearance of a true queen of Qev, even more so than their own mother. Kevan glanced about quickly, noticing that his little sister had larger rooms than he. *This is one thing I'll change when I am king.* There was nothing within the chambers to indicate the place was occupied by a child. Cylene had been given her very own group of servants and ladies-in-waiting—another expensive gift from their father. In fact, Kevan had failed to realize that Cylene had command of nearly an entire wing of the castle. "Sister, I would speak with you." He refused to wait in silence while she stared at him seated upon that padded couch as though it were a throne. The yellow gown she wore was encrusted with tiny pearls and trimmed with the highest quality white lace.

With eyes as black as a raven's wings, Cylene's gaze pierced through, making him feel vulnerable. "Has our mother sent you to beg my forgiveness?"

Kevan nearly burst into laughter when he realized his sister had meant what she said. "No. I haven't seen Mother." The bruise to one side of her face glowed bright red. "You must understand what Mother goes through, Cylene. She feels Father no longer loves her."

"He never did." Cylene's eyes became daggers.

Kevan watched his sister, realizing for the first time how beautiful she was. Cylene had matured. The contours of her face were wonderful—a perfectly symmetrical face…

"Speak your business or leave me." She was more beautiful when angry, thought the prince.

Cylene looked more like their father. Her black hair cascaded well beyond her waist, and against her pale skin, her dark lashes and brows were striking. "I should make you angry more often, Sister." Kevan gazed at Cylene, almost mesmerized. His eyes caught the sudden heave of her chest—a sign of great impatience. "We need to stand together, Cylene. Our brothers are like poison to me…and our father. Lucas said terrible things this day. He would give up his noble birth were it not for our parents. And to say that Father is not a good king…" Kevan waited. His sister's eyes never left him as she rose from her cushion, fanning herself with one of the fans their father had given to her. *Our mother does not get these gifts.* Even her mannerisms were those of their father. *No wonder he adores her so. Father would put her upon Qev's throne if only it were possible.* The image of their father's face appeared within his mind and all the prince saw at first was a crude, ugly man. But save for the long scar on his face and a missing portion of an ear, the king was as beautiful as his daughter. The scars of wars had deceived Kevan all his life. He recalled weeping as a child whenever he was brought before his father; he heard the words of his mother inside his head, declaring how terrible and ugly his father was. *"A terrible monster,"* was what she called him. *"The ugly beast."*

"Father is all Qev needs." She finally shifted her gaze. "Father is Qev."

"Yes, Sister. This I know. But we need to help father—protect him."

Cylene laughed. "From our brothers…or from Mother?" His sister was as smart as she was cunning. She was wise to not include him. "Our mother pollutes you…Father says so." Cylene slapped the fan over her mouth as if to scold herself for betraying their father's trust. "Worry not, Brother, our father, King of Qev, shall soon return." She said this knowingly, the keeper of their father's secrets…

"Where has he gone? Our father has been away for ages, and has left his cousin, Lord Hayden, as regent. I am the crowned prince, yet he leaves the rule of Qev in the hands of a snake."

Again, Cylene laughed. "Father knows his enemies just as well as he knows who loves him…"

"Cylene! Sister. Lord Hayden Bourne cannot be trusted. You know this." Finally, a glint of weakness appeared in his sister's eyes. "Father knows this too, does he not?"

The all too confident princess lowered her eyes. "Father trusts him not, but he insists blood is thicker than water." Cylene's eyes became cubes of ice at the thought of their cousin. Kevan resisted the urge to grin. "You must speak with Father when he returns. Our cousin mustn't be regent. Hayden serves the house of Godfrey, but his loyalty lies with Lord Theo. Why does Father trust this snake?" Something in her eyes betrayed her. Cylene knew much more than Kevan expected she would.

"I will talk this over with Father when he returns." Cylene resumed her fanning.

"So, dear sister, what is it that has taken our father across the sea? What business does he have abroad that he should take a small fleet of ships from our harbour?"

Cylene's fanning ceased again. She bit her lower lip as if to cage words she did not wish to escape. "Father's affairs are his own, if you wish to know of them, all you need do is be a good, faithful son." Cylene looked toward the doors before she turned her back to him.

Kevan left his sister's chambers feeling defeated. *I have been a fool to underestimate my dear sister…*

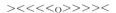

The throne room was empty. Massive columns sprouted upward from the floor to support the high cathedral ceiling. Sunbeams illuminated the entire hall through large square windows. Kevan's gait was cautious and precise, and though there was no other present, he cringed at the sound of his footsteps. The crown prince was free to roam the castle, for he was of the royal family—heir to the throne. *Qev's throne.* He was more than a hundred steps away from the one thing he coveted most, yet, as he moved toward his father's seat, Kevan's heart raced. It was almost as if what he planned to do this day was forbidden. After making it halfway to the throne the prince paused and looked back toward the door. From afar, the kingdom's throne appeared to be made of ice, for it was white. It was the most beautiful thing Kevan had ever seen. That white throne was his future, his life.

He stood before the throne for some time before circling it. Its back was high. The arms were not padded, neither was the seat. As he ascended the three stone steps and caressed the surface of the throne Kevan grinned. He took the seat and reclined. The armrests felt perfect. The prince closed his eyes and envisioned his own coronation. Kevan saw himself draped in the emblems and colours of his house; he could hear thousands calling his name, for he is king. He is benevolent. *I shall show my brothers how a king can be loved...*

"Long live the King!" The words were followed by laughter.

The prince sprang from the throne, eyes wide open. "Cousin!" He quickly composed himself, for he would not have Hayden think he feared him. "Must you spy on everyone?" Kevan adjusted his tunic and posture.

"I am regent," Hayden said. "It is my duty to protect the kingdom."

Kevan felt the urge to spit on the floor. "It is your duty to serve."

"I serve your father." The regent's hooked nose moved with every lie he uttered. His slender frame seemed to be lost among the robes of his office. However, he made certain the regent's seal was seen on his finger. Hayden motioned toward the throne. "That seat shall be yours one day." A smile exposed crooked brown teeth. "Go ahead, sit. Let us talk of your future, Cousin."

The prince hesitated. Could his cousin be teasing him? After Hayden lifted his thin brows and motioned toward the throne again, Kevan complied. Again he seated himself upon his father's throne and watched as his cousin, regent to the king, paced around the coveted chair of power.

"Many say there is but one way to the throne of Qev," said Hayden. "You, Kevan, have been lucky to be granted the first place…after your father, our king. You are Earvin's heir. But even a crown prince needs a reliable retinue."

"You speak in riddles, Cousin." Kevan's fingers dug into the hard surface of the throne. "I am Father's eldest son; naturally, his rule shall pass to me." His cousin laughed.

"Like I said, prince of Qev, Long live the King." Hayden's exaggerated bow was mocking. He backed away from the throne. Before he turned to leave he uttered a few more words in an almost musical tone. "You shall call when you need use of me…and I will be ready."

><<<<o>>>><

Princess Cylene was much displeased. Only she was allowed to enter her father's rooms while he was gone, so Cylene sat upon the king's favourite couch—the one near the window with a view of the city—and wept. In all her life she had never betrayed her father. She realized that Kevan had tricked her—beguiled her into divulging their father's secrets. The princess had changed into a gown of green velvet, her father had even given her a special necklace of green emeralds. Looking toward the sea, Cylene vowed to keep her father's affairs sacred. She would only discuss them with him. Finally, she smiled. The thought of her mother angered her once more. "If only you knew what father had in store for you."

She should never have let her guard down, not with her brother. Like all the others, Kevan was a threat to her father's rule. "You are despicable, Brother." Cylene moved from the window and walked toward the fireplace. It took several moments to push away the heavy lever, it had always been easier with her father there to help push open the door to the secret passages.

The passages were cool and dim, yet she walked them without fear. Her father had shown her the way to just a few areas of the castle, specifically the paths to her mother and siblings. Spying on Lucas and Orin had always been a bore; however, she found the happenings within the rooms of her mother and eldest brother far more entertaining. Kevan knew of the passages, Cylene was certain of this, as it was the only other way to bring kitchen maids to his rooms. Cylene had not told her father of this. The secrets of the passages were to be kept from the common folk, yet her brother had revealed their existence to young maids for mere carnal pleasures. Night had fallen; the castle was asleep, and Cylene was certain her brother would be awake again with a servant in his bed.

Kevan did not hear her enter his rooms over the moans of the young servant girl. Cylene stood in the shadows of the dimmed room and looked on as the baker's daughter gazed up into her brother's eyes, groaning with every thrust. The moon outside the window was full and as its glow caught the edge of Kevan's shoulder, his unusual birthmark became visible—a dark mark which had the look of a leaf. Her right leg was skilfully wrapped around his waist and her auburn hair cascaded over the edge of the bed toward the floor. Kevan smiled down at the girl as he gently forced several of his fingers into her mouth. The force of his thrusts increased, almost violently, yet the servant welcomed them with pleasure. *Father would be appalled, brother of mine.* More than anything Cylene wished she could say those words aloud, if only to see the reaction on her brother's face as well as his look of shame. Kevan moved both hands down the girl's chest and cupped her breasts. Cylene's mind drifted from the present to another world—where this world existed, she could not say. She saw herself in the girl's stead. But she was queen. Like the servant girl, she welcomed each thrust from her lover. The room she shared with this stranger was darkened. Cylene's body tingled; she was brought back to Kevan's rooms with the sound of her brother's climactic groan of pleasure. The princess entered the secret passages in a hurry, for fear that the pace of her breathing could be heard…

The seal of the regent could easily slip from his finger, a sure sign that the post was truly not meant for him. Hayden's belief in omens was far stronger than his own personal ambitions. The golden ring with the embossed seal of Qev's crown could never stay in place, yet although the king had suggested he have the thing resized, Hayden believed it unlucky to remove even an ounce of gold from it. Many a time he had seen eyes fall to the ring as it spun out of place on his finger. How could one exude power if the very emblem needed to wield that power betrayed him? He took the ring and placed it on the desk before him. The scribes had brought him scrolls of parchment and hot wax, ready for his seal of approval. *Small, petty decrees, these are what he leaves for me to do as regent and steward.* Hayden dared not utter these thoughts in the presence of the scribes and aides, for he knew they could hardly be trusted. Earvin and his daughter were wise. Seated behind his desk with a view of the sea, Hayden's thoughts shifted to his cousin, the king. He had not been privy to Earvin's plans—at least not the important ones…

When an aide announced the arrival of Queen Bernice's brother, Hayden resumed his duties. He allowed a drop of red wax to fall to one parchment then waited for it to set before pressing the seal into it. His visitor stood before his desk waiting to be acknowledged, yet Hayden Bourne, Regent of Qev, did not so much as lift his head. Finally, after dropping another glob of wax, Hayden looked up from his work. "Welcome, Percival. The Gods are generous to bless me with your presence this day."

The queen's brother eyed the scribes and aides as he took the chair closest to Hayden's desk. He only spoke after Hayden commanded the unwanted company to leave them. "There is talk of the king's absence," said Percival. "Many say he means not to return…that his rule will soon pass to Kevan. They say he will build another kingdom across the sea, leaving Kevan as regent. What do you know of this?"

Hayden laughed nervously and picked up the seal. "Dear Percival, are you not close enough to our king to know all his plans? After all, you are a member of his council."

"And so are you, Regent."

*My cousin is wise, I give him that.* Hayden scraped bits of wax from his ring. If what Percival said were true, where would he fit into his cousin's plans? "You think this to be true?" There was no need to pretend he had heard these rumours. Percival is no fool.

"It is near impossible to see truth among all this gossip." Percival looked toward the door again. "There's even talk of what Earvin did to acquire the throne…" His eyes glinted wickedly.

Hayden held his gaze for several moments, wondering how much the queen's brother knew. "Gossips. That is all they are." He saw a mischievous look in Percival's eyes. "You believe the king had his own father murdered in order to ascend to the throne?"

Percival shrugged. He was choosing his words carefully, for Hayden had the power to send him to the dungeons. "No. They are gossips."

"And what would you have me do to end these gossips, member of the king's council?"

"The boy is not ready," said Percival. "My nephew would use power to breed every maid as well as the wives of every lord within the realm. The boy is a fool." Hayden nodded. "For the good of the realm, Prince Kevan cannot sit as regent, even being the crown prince."

"He is of age, even to be king," said Hayden. "We both know this. I ask you again, Percival: what would you have me do?"

The queen's brother rose from his chair and paced back and forth as he pulled against his beard. "Damn it!"

Hayden shook his head in disgust. "Alright, Percival, leave it to me. I shall do the thinking; after all, I am a member of the king's council…" His words were seasoned with sarcasm. "What do the people of Qev need to quell the need for gossips? Think, Percival…think back to the coronation." He did not wait for a reply; in fact, he barely gave Percival a chance to think. "They need a celebration. Throw food and wine at the common people and they will love you for it. Alas, the gossips die. This celebration will begin immediately after their loving king returns to them." Hayden smiled, pleased with himself. "Go on, run to the council and begin your plans. The king could return any day now. All of Qev must know they shall be celebrating their king's return."

Percival nodded. "I will begin right away."

Hayden was left to ponder what he had learned from the queen's brother. Was it really Earvin's plan to share his rule with his eldest son, while he sat upon another throne across the sea? His cousin was unpredictable enough. *But surely, Lord Theo would know this if it were true.* How would the most ancient family in all of Qev feel if the king of the realm were to go to faraway lands? "There would be blood," whispered Hayden. "And there would be war."

## CHAPTER NINE
### *The Eunuch's Dance*

The absence of the sun was saddening. Kairu stood on the deck of the largest ship and watched the others behind him. A cruel tempest had raged, sinking one ship. Many had died. Kairu had remained below deck for what seemed like an eternity while waves and wind tossed the vessel to and fro, threatening to give all the souls to the sea and the Gods. The belly of the ship was the eunuch's safety; he did not wish to leave it. That morning, the king's servants had commanded that Kairu leave the safety of his small cabin. Now he stood looking out onto grey waters and a dull sky. There were no birds in sight. The sea had once again become calm; however, Kairu could scarcely think of what could have happened to him had his ship been the one to sink. Who would have had time to save him?

The great lord of the sunken ship had been saved—conveyed to King Earvin's ship with most of his belongings on a lifeboat. The three eunuchs sold to him had been lost with the vessel and now lay at the bottom of the sea. Kairu's brothers were dead. He thought of their master, Lord Ruben, a portly noble, wishing the sea had taken him as well. Surely, this man could have saved more lives instead of loading his lifeboat with personal possessions and wealth. Now, this man would journey aboard the king's vessel. Kairu was uncertain whether it was the man himself he detested or his greed. Of the hundreds aboard Lord Ruben's ship, only fifty survived.

Kairu looked to the nearest ship, fixing his eyes upon the blue flag flapping in the wind. Lord Theo's family emblem had been raised to the highest pinnacle of the ship's mast. Perfectly centred upon the flag of blue was the image of a black eagle, quite in contrast to King Earvin's emblem, a flag of red and gold bearing a wild boar. The eunuch looked upward again, ignoring the happenings on deck. The crew had become accustomed to seeing the black eunuch of the El Molo, yet some still stared as if to see him for the first time. But they dared not interfere or trouble him, as he was known to be the king's property. Suddenly, against the clang of chains and loud shouts aboard his vessel, Kairu heard the distant call of his name. He looked toward Lord Theo's ship.

"Kairu!" Prodigal was on deck across the water waving at him. "I am Prodigal of the Nuba tribe and I have survived the wrath of the sea, Kairu!"

"I am Kairu, descendant of the El Molo, of the Maasai…and I have survived the wrath of the sea!" He could not contain his elation. His friend had lived. The friends allowed their shouts to be carried with the wind from ship to ship. They spoke in their own tongue.

"Is your master good to you, Kairu?" Suddenly, a concerned look swept over Prodigal's face. "You look well…but you have lost weight." Prodigal grinned.

"My master is good to me," Kairu replied. "I do not like the sea, Prodigal." He explained how difficult it had been to keep his food down. "But you, Prodigal, have become fat." The black eunuch's comment was an exaggeration.

"Surely," Prodigal replied, "you have seen my master, Kairu. He never stops eating." He tilted his head upward and laughed aloud. "Soon, my belly shall be as big as his."

Kairu clutched his own belly as he laughed. "Is he good to you?"

Prodigal's laugh vanished. "Not so good as yours, my friend. I fear our masters do not like each other." He must have seen the look of worry sweep over Kairu's face. "My master is good enough. Do not worry, Kairu."

"I long to see you." Prodigal knew exactly what he meant. Kairu longed for that closeness with his friend, especially as they had been carried far away from home. They only had each other.

Prodigal beckoned to him. "Come to me, Kairu, descendant of the El Molo…eunuch of the Maasai…"

"I cannot swim."

Prodigal smiled. "And you cannot climb either. You fell from my Marula tree." The two eunuchs shared another moment of laughter. "Do not worry, Kairu, I shall see you this night." Prodigal explained all he had learned from being in his master's presence. "Our king holds a feast this night. All the great lords will come aboard his ship."

Kairu beamed with excitement, knowing he would have the chance to see his friend up close. He now realized why the king's crew were so busy about the ship.

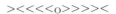

There was music up above. Kairu had remained below during most of the preparations. As he rubbed scented fish oils into his skin and donned his colourful beads, Kairu could think only of seeing his mother. His thoughts also went to the other eunuchs and Kairu bowed his head, saddened by the thought that there were only ten of them left. Ade had warned them, not all his eunuchs would live to see the lands of the men with pale skin. Kairu's heart raced. How many would die if another tempest raged? Shaking his entire body, Kairu endeavoured to rid his mind of the worry. The feast had already begun. Surely, Prodigal and his master had already come aboard. Wearing nothing but the beads around his neck, Kairu let his finger pass over his scar. He relived the pain. He thought of his father leaving him behind for two sacks of gold. What had his mother and brothers said when they saw his father return without him? The black eunuch made it his duty—a ritual—to touch that scar between his legs. His ritual served as a reminder. The Gods had taken his manhood and sent him to a new world across the sea…this was his purpose.

Kairu then touched the flaccid shaft between his legs, all the Gods had left him. As much as he pulled and caressed himself, there was no sensation. They had taken so much from him. However, Ade had given him instructions on what to do should there be a need to use what remained of his manhood. "There are herbs," his teacher had said, still holding his head high with dignity. Again, Kairu shook his entire body—a sudden quick shrug to put all unhappy thoughts out of his mind. The night was young, and his king had planned a celebration.

He left his small cabin after he could contain his excitement no longer. Kairu had promised his teacher he would follow all his teachings, and one teaching he meant to make use of this night was his timing. He had waited long enough for the king's deck to be filled with every important visitor; the shouts and laughter above, as well as the scent of roasted swine, told him his moment had come. He dressed with care, wearing only his beads and bright-red shúkà about his waist. As he emerged from below Kairu was surprised—shocked at the sight of so many of his own people. He saw warriors of various tribes, all dressed in their feathers and their beads, but his adornment of beads was far superior, at least in Kairu's eyes. The beats of the drums touched Kairu, so much that his body chilled as the rhythmic beats beckoned him forward. He had not forgotten the purpose of protocol. Earvin was King; Kairu dared not greet another before first kneeling before his master. As he walked amid the throng Kairu did not bother to search for his friend. Prodigal would see him, the other eunuchs would find him. His focus was the King of Kings, Earvin Godfrey.

Kairu walked past the blazing fire in the centre of the deck. Ahead, the king was seated upon a large chair covered with white fur. To his right, Lord Theo sat, slowly nibbling on a large cut of roasted swine. Kairu nearly laughed. The drumming slowed as he walked toward the king. All laughter and mumblings ceased as the black eunuch approached. As he looked up, Kairu was in awe at the number of bodies aboard one ship. He glanced out over the edge of the vessel to see the other ships all glowing with light. There were hundreds of men hanging from the masts, some were seated right on the edge of the ships. Now, just steps away from his master, Kairu took to his knees—not in a hurry, but with grace and poise. He locked eyes with his king, bowed his head and remained silent awhile. He still held the king's gaze. Kairu meant not to release him until he was ready to. The other lords were of little importance to him. "Great King," said the black eunuch, still holding his gaze. "Kairu, descendant of the El Molo, born of the Maasai, greets you." He released the king by shifting his gaze to the wooden deck. The eunuch did not move, nor did he find the king's eyes again. Kairu waited amid complete silence. The drumming had stopped.

The king with the ugly scar and only half an ear rose from his fur-covered seat. The deck creaked beneath his large feet. "Kairu." His master's voice was deep. The eunuch still did not utter a word. The king extended a white hand toward the eunuch. "Rise, Kairu, descendant of the El Molo, who was born of the Maasai." His hand was warm and soft. And he lifted Kairu from his knees gently. As their eyes met again Kairu's heart pounded, for there was something within the blueness of those eyes that instilled fear. How could Ade have instructed him to obey these pale-skinned men—who had such untrusting eyes? Finally, the king smiled at the eunuch. He gave Kairu's hand a gentle squeeze. "Music!" He leaned close and whispered, "Dance for your king." The king stepped away and moved back to his chair and motioned as if to present Kairu to all.

The tribesmen, all clad in loincloths of skin, began to chant their ancient songs, and as the four drummers positioned themselves by the fire and tapped their instruments with their palms and fingers, Kairu stooped before King Earvin's throne. Memories of home entered his mind as the beats escalated, bringing the eunuch back to days of his childhood, when villages would talk to each other by the beatings of their drums, sending messages over the tops of the trees and silent streams…

The beats of naked palms against stretched skin infected his entire body, even his soul. As a warrior of his tribe would have done, Kairu began his dance by jumping upward, as high as he could get, for that was the El Molo way. Kairu allowed every other thought to leave his mind. His duty was to please the king. As the drums talked to Kairu's body, he moved with grace, allowing every beat to seep through him. He used every pause between the beats to his advantage. Whatever sorrow that was within him before the drums began had since left him, and now all that seemed to exist were those beats, which had taken ownership of his limbs. Kairu, descendant of the El Molo, had become possessed by the music and chantings. He interpreted what the drums conveyed, and with every extension of his arms and legs Kairu felt a sense of liberation, for at that moment he knew that no one could move as he did. The black eunuch's only focus was his king, and as he moved closer toward the king's fur-covered throne, Kairu allowed the drumming to walk over his body—every beat seemed to travel from the inside out until they reached the very tips of his fingers and toes.

The eunuch heard nothing else but the drumming of his brothers; he saw no other but the king. Falling to his knees, he locked eyes with his new master. And he did not know how it was possible, but the music willed him to rise with his back arched and his arms outstretched. Kairu moved his hips, and as he allowed his red garment to fall away from his waist, leaving him clad in just his loincloth and his beads of many colours, he still looked to his master. King Earvin was mesmerized, enchanted. He moved closer to his pale-skinned king, realizing that for this brief moment, he had power over him. Kairu, the black eunuch, felt invincible; for a king had succumb to him—he could see it in those blue eyes, and for the first time ever, Kairu understood what Ade meant. The King sat, transfixed, upon his throne, even as the beats of the drums subsided and Kairu, the black one, descendant of the El Molo, allowed his body to halt in a kneeling position before his master. The applause, whistles and loud cheers were deafening, and all Kairu could do was kneel there, his torso moving in and out as he struggled to catch his breath…

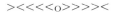

The king was surely a good master. Prodigal sat on the deck among the throng with his eyes upon the scarred king. He had studied the pale-skin's face and realized that he was not that ugly. The long scar, which extended from his forehead, just beneath his crown, to his chin, was massive. What pain he must have endured, thought the Nuba boy. On the other side of the king's face, the upper portion of his right ear had been cut away. Prodigal cringed, thinking of the agony. King Earvin had become more jovial after Kairu's dance. However, unlike the other lords, he did not drink much wine. The King of Kings was in complete control of his faculties. *This is a cautious king,* thought Prodigal. His eyes found his friend, Kairu, who had been placed not far from his master. In fact, King Earvin had placed Kairu directly to his right, squeezing the black eunuch between himself and Prodigal's master, Lord Theo. This, Prodigal saw, did not bode well for his new master. Lord Theo's eyes had become narrow slits, and even as he wiped droplets of wine away from his beard with the back of his hand he shot scathing looks toward the king's furry throne.

Prodigal's gaze shifted to his friend, who, next to the king's throne, had the appearance of someone majestic. Kairu, with his arms behind him and shoulders erect, stood with the grace of the creature he adored so much—the peacock. The beautiful coloured beads had become the peacock's fanned tail; Kairu's small, bird-like torso was much like the creature. His long, thin neck sprouted from his shoulders with elegance. "Lẹwa." Prodigal whispered the Yoruba word for beautiful several times, knowing it was indeed the essence of his friend. He could not take his eyes off Kairu, but as Kairu glanced over at his master, their king, Prodigal's insides became polluted by a gush of sudden rage. It occurred to him at that moment that Kairu had not attempted to find him. The Nuba boy rose slowly and allowed himself to be enveloped by the surging throng as the drumming and calls from the tribal warriors erupted once more.

Prodigal was free to roam the king's ship, at least the unguarded portions. He left the beating drums, the laughter and loud howls of celebration, to find what little peace he could well away from the celebrations. The Nuba boy was pleased to find a quiet, isolated area near the stern of the massive vessel. Deciding he would have a better view, Prodigal climbed the smallest of the ship's three masts. From there he had a perfect view of the other ships as wells as the blazing fire around which all the celebrants gathered. Kairu still stood to the king's right; however, as for Prodigal's master, Lord Theo, his seat near to his sovereign was empty. What had become of his master? Just as he was about to swing downward Prodigal heard heavy footsteps before seeing three figures approach the base of the mast. The Nuba boy clung to the wood and rope and held his breath, hugging the mast in the hopes of not being seen.

Lord Theo spat upon the deck. "He would place that by his throne, while I, the one man with command over half the kingdom's army, sits farther from him. How dare he!"

"My Lord, you mustn't speak such things," said an aide. "If word of this should get to King Earvin's ears—"

Lord Theo laughed. "Yes…his one good ear." But his anger soon returned. "To the bowels of hell with him," was Lord Theo's reply. Prodigal clung tighter to the mast, afraid that he would be discovered. His master looked again toward the king. "That man holds my birthright." He looked to the third pale-skin, another lord who had also taken eunuchs in his service. Prodigal remembered the man's face and his name: Lord Ruben. It was he who had lost his ship to the sea along with most of his crew and three eunuchs.

"Patience, Silas," said Lord Ruben. "We cannot act now, not without your army. Not here at sea."

"The Godfreys usurped my right as a noble king. They are thieves. And now, many years later, he still takes." Lord Theo slurred his words. "He has taken everything I've ever wanted." The great lord pointed a finger toward Kairu. "...Even that."

Prodigal clung tighter. Surely, this man, in his current state, would slit his throat and throw him to the salty waters if he realized what the Nuba boy had heard.

"I promise you"—this time his master gripped Lord Ruben's shoulders and shook him, finally displaying a smile—"I shall sit upon Qev's throne one day. Soon, I tell you. And then all the world will change. I will take back all he has taken from me."

Prodigal's heart slammed against his chest at the thought of what could happen should this man be king...

## CHAPTER TEN
### *Tamed*

His second dance was as exhausting as the first. Kairu had used that moment around the fire to find his friend, and when he spotted Prodigal among the crowd the black eunuch smiled. Prodigal did smile back at him; however, he seemed troubled. After his performance the king commanded the eunuch to return to his cabin. Inside Kairu's cabin was small and dim, but it didn't matter, as Prodigal was there with him. As he wiped sweat from his legs he searched his friend's eyes. The Nuba boy seemed sad, and, although they exchanged smiles while they conversed, there still seemed to be something troubling him. "Is something wrong, Prodigal?"

Prodigal hesitated, looking toward the shut door before he uttered a word. "There is something I must tell you, Kairu." There was fear in his eyes.

Kairu paused. "What has happened, Prodigal?"

"We learned from Ade, our teacher, that we should never betray our masters." Prodigal bowed his head low. "But I must warn you, Kairu. My master—"

The cabin door swung open and hit the wall with a thud. A member of Lord Theo's retinue stood by the entrance with legs apart and his hand upon the hilt of his sword. "Come with me, eunuch."

Kairu reached for his red cowl and covered himself, as the pale-skin's stare lingered. As he watched Prodigal leave with this man Kairu's heart quailed, for he feared his friend was in danger. What was it Prodigal wanted to tell him? There was a sudden uproar above; the music had ceased, and now all Kairu could hear were raised voices, one of which belonged to his king. Kairu disobeyed his master's command and left his cabin.

He found the ship's deck still crowded; however, hidden in the shadows, Kairu saw King Earvin and Lord Theo within the centre of the throng. The flames illuminated his sovereign's scarred face as he barked words of anger. "All night you sat with me, stuffing your belly with food and drinking your fill of my best wine. And now you say I dishonour you? You, Silas? You think me a dishonourable man?"

"S-s-s-sire." An aide to Lord Theo fell to his knees. "I beg you, forgive his folly, great King. His Lordship had much to drink this night."

"Let the man who commands half my army speak for himself." King Earvin drew his sword, ignoring the trembling servant. Kairu gasped. "All my life, I've lived to please the Gods. I've taken my father's teachings and used them as best as I could. Now he is dead and I'm King. Me, Silas, not you!" King Earvin raised his voice even louder as he addressed all the vessels. "This man says my family has wronged him." He pointed the tip of the blade toward Lord Theo, who had fallen to his knees. "Most of you are old men; you lived and fought beside Bernard, the last king. And many of you—all of you—also know the history of the Theo house. Yes, once they ruled the realm. But that was ages ago, long before even my father's time." King Earvin placed his sword upon the deck as he kneeled and placed both hands upon Lord Theo's shoulders. "We grew together as boys, old friend. Do not let the past damn our future, for it shall be the ruin of us all."

Lord Theo locked eyes with the king and, as one stare challenged the other, the entire ship fell silent. Kairu could only hear the sound of the waves colliding with the ship. Finally, the lord broke the hush. "Forgive my despair, King of Kings." Kairu did not like this man.

Many breathed a sigh of relief as the king helped Lord Theo to his feet. Prodigal was not far from his master, and as he walked behind the retinue he looked to Kairu with sorrowful eyes.

Unlike Kairu, who had been lucky to have his own cabin, life aboard Lord Theo's ship, the *Blackbird*, was unpleasant. The Nuba boy slept below deck with tribesmen, animals and the lowest servants. Many of these pale-skinned men had never seen Lord Theo's face; however, they did fear him. Prodigal, although his life aboard the *Blackbird* was harsh, considered himself lucky, as he was free to roam the ship and was sometimes required to wait upon his master. When in Lord Theo's presence, however, the Nuba boy found he did not receive the long stares which were reserved for Kairu.

This was a new day, yet Prodigal could hardly forget the events of the previous night. Much had happened, and after what he had overheard his master say before the king's anger raged, the eunuch was left even more troubled and confused. Prodigal walked the decks, hoping to see Kairu as he had the previous day; however, there was no sign of him. Again, Prodigal wished his stay aboard the *Blackbird* had been more peaceful. The

Nuba boy was expected to help with certain duties on deck, for the captain had deemed him strong. Prodigal did, however, prefer duties that kept him active rather than those of attending to his lord. He detested making beds and refilling the cups of a gluttonous master who was never satisfied.

The sun was bright this day. Prodigal walked the deck of the ship several times without anyone so much as noticing him. Being as he loved to climb, Prodigal scaled the largest mast, finally feeling free. His thoughts went back to the Marula tree at the temple, the one friend to which he had confessed his fears and woes. He had climbed high. From the utmost height of the ship Prodigal looked out and saw nothing but blueness; there was no sign of land, and for a brief moment he feared the ships would never leave the blue seas. The *Blackbird* sailed parallel to the king's vessel, *The Victor*, the largest in the fleet. Prodigal admired the magnificent ship with three masts and beautiful white sails. It was then that he saw his friend, and was about to call out to him when he realized that Kairu walked the deck with the King of Kings. *Why is he known as the King of Kings*, the Nuba boy wondered.

Kairu walked several steps behind King Earvin; however, it was not the black eunuch who hastened his steps just so they would walk side by side. The king of Qev slowed his pace, forgetting he walked the deck with a lowly servant. Prodigal hugged the mast and shifted his gaze out toward the sea…

><<<<o>>>><

*The Victor* was the fastest vessel in the fleet, which was fitting, as it carried the King of Kings. After spending much of the day walking the deck alone, Kairu felt tired and somewhat sick of seeing nothing else but the sea. He had spotted Prodigal several times climbing the mast aboard the *Blackbird*, yet they had not had the time to have one of their distant talks across the water. Prodigal was aboard another ship and could easily have visited *The Victor* by lifeboat; however, since Lord Theo's departure several days past, neither he nor any member of his retinue had returned to see the king. Even Lord Ruben had left the king's ship with all his treasures. Kairu pined for his friend so much that he became sad. But thanks to his king, the sadness was fading. King Earvin had invited Kairu to walk the deck with him several times since the feast, yet they never spoke a word to each other. Kairu could not understand why he was simply asked to walk with someone if the person had no interest in speaking with him. It later occurred to him that King Earvin may have simply been showing off another of his possessions, and this, Kairu found frustrating. He had not been given any duties, not even to wait upon the king or clean his cabin.

With no desire to leave his cabin Kairu decided to work on his words. Ade had always insisted that a eunuch was useless if he did not know how to read and write. "Your lives will belong to them," their teacher had warned. "Show them your worth and they will cherish you. Prove yourself useless and you shall die." Lying on his cot, Kairu continued his reading. Some day, he thought, the king may have need of his skills. But when he heard a soft knock upon his door, Kairu put his book away. He found Saul, the King's aide, waiting by the door. He could never forget this pale-skin— the same servant who had placed him behind the king's throne the night he was presented by Ade within the white tent. Saul was a young, tall servant with long, brown hair cascading just beyond his shoulders. As always, Saul greeted Kairu with a nod, and this time he smiled, revealing long, white teeth. "The king calls for you," said Saul. His nervous glances made him appear powerless, as he seemed to fear the black eunuch. Ade had told Kairu many times that he would be desired by all, yet this boy, who seemed to be just slightly older than Kairu, feared to utter a word in his presence. *It is I who should fear you, pale-skin,* thought Kairu. If only he could tell the boy that his purpose was to serve.

Saul brought him to the king's cabin and left him within. The spacious quarters were opulent and rich with brightly coloured curtains and woollen rugs upon the floors. The cushions upon the couches were so beautiful that Kairu feared to even look at them. He did not sit, nor did he touch a thing. The black eunuch simply stood in the middle of the cabin.

"Come, eunuch." The king's command came from behind another door.

His steps were reluctant; however, Kairu obeyed, feeling the need to remind the master of who he was. *I am Kairu. I am a descendant of the El Molo. I am of the Maasai.* But he dared not be insolent to his king, not even to remind him that though he was a black eunuch, he did have a name. He found the king seated behind an oaken desk, surrounded by maps, scrolls and ink. He did not shift his gaze from his work but simply motioned toward the bench to the right of him. "Sit." Kairu complied, with a burning desire to remind this man who he was. He sat with a sigh, his eyes fixed upon the king. His scar was horrible and the absence of half his ear nearly forced Kairu to turn away. Kairu sat with his back straight and his shoulders erect. He was wearing his beaded necklace. His skin had been well oiled and his closely cropped hair had been washed that morning. Finally, King Earvin's eyes met his. There was a slight twitch near the corner of his mouth.

Kairu had not forgotten his place. He left the seat and knelt gracefully saying. "King of Kings." He could not understand why this man was called the King of Kings. *A king is a king,* thought Kairu. At that moment Kairu wished he was free to ask the king anything he liked, for there were so many things he did not understand…so many things he had seen which puzzled him.

><<<<o>>>><

The eunuch stood there staring at him, the whites of the boy's eyes penetrating. The darkness of the boy's skin—the even smoothness, its shine, rendered the king speechless. The full lips parted again, revealing perfectly white teeth, and as Earvin watched the exotic eunuch in awe, wondering how such beauty could be granted to a man from the lands across the sea, he felt the urge to smile. To withhold the elated grin was near impossible. He could not let this mere servant realize how much he desired him. The eunuch bowed his head once more. "I come as you commanded, King of Kings." Even the tone of his voice was mesmerizing—not too masculine, yet not feminine at all. *Surely, the Gods have created this eunuch just for me…*

"Leave me." Earvin waved his hand dismissively, wondering why he had sent for the eunuch. But the boy got up off his knees and stood there for several moments staring back at him in puzzlement, neck extended like that of a graceful bird, arms held behind his back and chest outward. He was tall and lean, yet he did not appear to be weak, for his limbs were muscular and toned. Earvin studied the black eunuch's face—a perfect example of symmetry. There was no blemish upon his face, save for one tiny scar upon his forehead. Earvin felt the need to caress his long scar upon his face. Suddenly, he felt the urge to shout as anger stirred within him. He turned his head as if to hide the gash upon his face only to realize he had exposed the good side of his face—the side with the missing ear. As sudden defeat enveloped him, Earvin's fist collided with the top of his desk. Suddenly, he was a young prince again with an undying desire to go to war—to please his father, his king. *If only I had not tried so damned hard to be like him…*

The black eunuch's calm eyes persisted. He moved toward Earvin without uttering a word, yet that consoling gaze kept Earvin still, somehow abating his rage. The lean figure was so close that Earvin's nose caught the scent of jasmine. "You dare disobey me, eunuch?" Earvin looked toward the rounded window across the cabin. Something prevented him from looking into the eunuch's eyes. "I gave you a—"

The eunuch touched his scar, eliciting an involuntary cringe. Earvin shut his eyes—not even Bernice had touched him so. "I am Kairu. I am a descendant of the El Molo….of the Maasai." The words were sincere. This boy…Kah-he-ro, did not fear him. Earvin opened his eyes again as the eunuch turned his head with his other hand, still tracing a warm finger downward over his grotesque scar. Then, their eyes met. "Kairu." He lifted his dark brows. "I am Kairu, King of Kings." The eunuch looked to him with gentle eyes as he said, "Lẹwa." Earvin had never heard that word before, but he knew it was something good.

"Ka-he-roo…Kairu." Even the very sound of his name was calming.

Kairu smiled down at him. "Yes, King of Kings, I am Kairu. I am a descendant of the El Molo. I am of the Maasai." He touched what remained of Earvin's ear, and again uttered the word, "Lẹwa." Earvin shut his eyes again. "My king is beautiful. Lẹwa. Beautiful."

*He will think me weak if I weep before him. I am King.* But Kairu's touch was comforting and his words were gently pleasing. The king wept. "No, you are beautiful. I am a monster—a beastly king." He thought on the things Bernice had said throughout their lives together. He thought on the fact that his three sons had never taken a moment to look at his face—to truly see him and his scars. His entire realm had seen a ruined face, all except his beloved Cylene. And now, this eunuch…this Kairu, had chosen to look into his eyes and find his heart.

><<<<o>>>><

King Earvin was by no means a gentle man. Kairu knew this. However, as Ade had taught him, he knew his future would depend highly upon how he was perceived by his master. As Kairu caressed the scar something within him pitied the king. He had no desire to be deceitful, the eunuch simply realized that he cared for his king. Touching these long afflicted injuries helped Kairu to feel his king's pain. Yet, in a way, he somehow felt this man had a hand in the path his life had taken. As King Earvin was the one he was created to serve, Kairu saw him as the one who had inflicted such pain upon him, the man who had torn him from a life he loved and would never have again. King Earvin wielded the blade which had cut away his manhood and made him a eunuch. But Kairu could not hate the king.

"My king is beautiful. Lẹwa. Beautiful." His master was weeping.

"No, you are beautiful. I am a monster—a beastly king."

Kairu gazed down into tear-filled eyes. *This is a good man. A good king.* He could not tell what made him believe this; however, at that moment Kairu vowed to put his trust in him. To serve him faithfully.

"Lẹwa." He thought back to that dark night when he had left the temple—the night he learned this Yoruba word. But to say it now put Kairu at peace. There was no fear, for indeed, he had seen the beauty of a king. That warrior had been long dead—killed by Prodigal that fateful night, yet now, Kairu found a place within himself to forgive him. He whispered the single word over and over again, still looking into blueness. "Lẹwa." Kairu knelt and cupped the king's face into his hands, unable to stop himself. Even as he gently pressed his full lips over the king's, he felt lost, as if pushed into another world. The king exhaled. His arm moved slowly over Kairu's arms, his grip tightening. The black eunuch moved away, placing a finger over his sovereign's mouth. "I am Kairu." He looked to the king, as if to say, *I am not like the rest.* King Earvin understood. His grip on Kairu's arm loosened. Kairu pushed away the tears with his fingers before kissing the king's long scar. He kissed the king's ears, and King Earvin pulled him closer and released a burden of deep, rumbling sobs.

The master submitted to the servant, allowing Kairu to undress him first, for unlike what Ade had his eunuchs do, this eunuch made certain it was he who inspected the king, for he was giving himself freely to him. Kairu, descendant of the El Molo, boy of the Maasai, would give his body to a king. Within the king's bed, Kairu looked down at his master's smooth, pale body and saw other scars. He touched every one and the king closed his eyes in pleasure, for Kairu knew how to touch him. Finally, Kairu removed his beads and allowed his other garments to fall to the floor. The blue eyes widened with desire…

## CHAPTER ELEVEN
### *The Citadel*

Orin was by no means a favourite son, he was well aware of that fact. Yet, he sat among hundreds of his companions pondering. The prince looked around the library, knowing very well that the answer he sought would not be found in books. "So many friends," said the prince. "…When I need you most you all go quiet." He smiled at himself, struggling to dismiss the thought that he was losing his mind. "A prince of Qev all alone chatting with a library of books and scrolls. How depressing." The king's second son had always prided himself in finding answers, and although the scrolls would provide answers after days and sleepless nights of research, the puzzle of what had happened to his father was a difficult one to solve. He had even visited the aviary. No ravens had come announcing the king's return. It was customary to dispatch a bird from the ship at least three days prior to arrival, yet no message had arrived.

It was not as if Orin missed his father so much that he now pined for his return; this, he left to his sister. He just knew he would not be able to endure seeing Kevan seated upon the throne. Instantly, thoughts of a life where Kevan was second in line pushed themselves to the forefront of Orin's mind. *Would mother love me best then?* Somehow, Orin doubted she would. His mother and brother had always had a special relationship, and though she could have doted on Kevan simply because he was the eldest and first in line after their father, Orin could not see himself getting such affection. Kevan was tall and strong, while he was short and appeared weak. "My brother is a fool." He was as certain of this as the throne of Qev was white. The entire castle knew what Kevan did, for it had become a common thing for their mother to send cooks, bakers, smithies and groundsmen away from the castle, all because they had the one thing Kevan could not resist. Daughters… It had been said that Kevan had made a girl pregnant from as early as in his eleventh year. *Why then does father cherish a son who would populate a kingdom with his own bastards?*

Frustrated, Orin left the scrolls and walked out onto the library's terrace. The view from there was magnificent. To the south, he could see the hills in the distance and to the north, the caps of the mountains were white with snow. "What a world." Orin exhaled as he turned his gaze east toward the sea. No ships. He wondered what it was like to view the castle from the countryside, for Qev's castle stood upon a hill directly in the centre of the citadel. A castle of white stone climbing up into the blue sky. He had not ventured far from home. The city below was as far as the prince had ventured; however, not alone. It suddenly occurred to him that the time had come for some family bonding, so Orin left the terrace immediately.

Orin walked into his rooms unwelcomed. "How fares my young brother?" His smile was concocted.

"What do you want?" Lucas did not wish to have visitors, especially not from a member of his family. He had spent much of the morning walking the castle grounds and had even made it as far as the main gates; however, the gatekeeper and his men knew too well to let him pass. Lucas had ventured out into the real world before; however, he was always found. It was difficult being among the common folk. And they were not fools, for they always knew he was not one of them.

"You scar me, Brother." Orin's grin was menacing. "I think of you and decide to pay you a visit and this is the thanks I get? I'm hurt." He came close to see what Lucas was doing. "What have we here, little prince? Ah, a sword!" His eyes became keen. "Better be careful, Lucas…we mustn't forget what happened to father. You see, our dear father disobeyed grandfather and ran off to war—"

"I know what happened. Grandfather told me himself."

"And we both know what happened when father failed to listen. We see it every day…at least I try not to see it at all." Orin cringed. "By the Gods, that face is responsible for most of my childhood nightmares."

"Shut it, Orin!"

"If I didn't know better I'd say you wanted to be just like dear father." He waved his forefinger from side to side. "We can't have that now. You're too precious to me." Orin took the sword from Lucas' grasp. "My young brother, the warrior prince. If only our brother at least tried to wield this…or any other sword, instead of the one between his legs."

"What Kevan does with his cock is none of my business."

Orin's grip tightened around the hilt of the sword as he stepped back, shocked. "Hmm. Could my young brother have already become a man that he would speak such things?" He laughed. He returned his gaze to the sword. "Magnificent work, I must say." He looked to Lucas with curiosity. "Where did you get this, young brother?"

Lucas grasped his weapon, looking it over carefully for fingerprints. "I just cleaned this." As he had been doing before his brother interrupted, Lucas admired the sword. It was not big; however, it was quite sharp and, most important of all, made specifically for him.

"Well, are you going to share, Lucas."

Lucas huffed. "The smith! Ben!"

"I should have guessed." His brother had always made a point of knowing the names of all the servants as well as their work. "Benjamin the swordsmith."

Still admiring his sword, Lucas gave a dismissive shrug; however, as he glanced up at his brother he knew he would delve deeper. Orin had a gift for getting at the truth. "What?"

"Doesn't the smith's family live on the other side of the wall?—the countryside I think. In fact, I know he returns to his quaint village at least once every fortnight."

Again he attempted to dismiss the facts. "What of it?"

"A smith makes a sword fit for a prince…and here you are, Prince of Qev, holding that sword. Could you be friends with Benjamin…or Ben?" Lucas did not answer.

"Lucas." Orin sat next to him and lowered his voice, eyes still fixed upon the sword. "There is a reason I've come to see you. I need your help, Brother."

It took much to persuade Lucas to do what he wanted; however, in the end Orin was successful. They had little time to prepare, for what he required of his brother needed to be done that night. Orin stood outside the castle hoping he had made the right decision, for Lucas had insisted that he needed to consult with a trusted friend. *I have seen what can happen when one trusts…* Prince Orin stood in the shadow of the castle wondering whether his brother would soon arrive. From where he stood he could see guards at their posts, even up in the turrets high above. The drawbridge was also closely watched. There was a full moon that night, so Orin made certain the glow of light did not reveal him to the watchmen.

Finally, he saw two figures moving toward him. Orin pressed his back to the wall and did not relax until he recognized his brother. "Have you made certain you were not followed?"

His brother, who seldom smiled, simply shot him a cold glance then tossed a sack against his chest. "Put those on, you can't go out there looking like a prince."

Orin was about to answer him but froze with his mouth ajar at the sight of his brother's companion. "Ben…the smith." Orin looked upward into the swordsmith's face. "Lucas, you said he was to provide us clothing. There was no mention that you would bring him along."

"He knows the way out." Lucas exchanged nods with the smith.

"Yer Majesty!" Ben greeted Orin with a bow. The smith had the biggest ears Orin had ever seen on any man. He brought his large, dirty hands toward his face to cover his brown, broken teeth. Ben spoke with a lisp, which caused Orin to step back. "The young prince says I 'ave to take you from the castle, Yer Majesty."

Orin studied them both in silence; if he had not known his own brother he would not have been able to tell the prince from the commoner. He looked to Lucas and lifted the sack. "I guess I should put these on then."

"I had Ben cut them down to size," said Lucas with a snigger.

Orin looked to Ben, obviously struggling to suppress laughter. "So, it is true what you lowly folk say about me." All at court knew Orin was a short man; he could just imagine what was said of him out in the countryside.

"Forgive me, Yer Majesty…I meant no off—"

Orin dismissed the smith with a quick wave of his hand. "Where do you expect me to put my good clothes after changing?" He quickly disrobed and started to dress in the rags his brother had brought. "Where did these come from? They reek!"

"Unless you want the guards to find us here," said Lucas, "you best shut it." He grabbed Orin's clean clothes, stuffed them inside the sack and hid them in the bushes.

"Have you any idea what those are worth?" Orin nearly cried out as Lucas rubbed dirt over his face. "What was that for?"

"We've got to fit in," said Lucas.

Moments later Orin was following Lucas and the smith down a steep hill. The night had become cold and he could feel the dew upon the leaves as they swept across his face. *I was a fool to think I could spend a night outside the castle.* "Lucas." He hastened to catch up to his brother. "When we were younger"—he breathed heavily to catch his breath— "…and you would disappear for—"

"Don't be a fool, Orin. If I'd gone where we go this night when I was young, surely I would have been sold to some wayward traveller."

Orin spoke loud enough for the smith to hear. "And where exactly are we going?" Again, the prince quickened his pace. "I wanted a quick adventure, Lucas. Why must we go at night?"

The smith stopped and gazed back with an assuring smile. "Don't you fret, Yer Majesty. Ben'll take care of ya."

The older prince resumed his run as Lucas urged them to continue. Orin looked back and could barely see the castle. The lands within the confines of the walls were vast. Finally, the smith led them to the mouth of a cave. Orin entered without protest, for he had seen the looks his brother had given him since they set out into the night. It amazed him how well the smith knew the way through the darkened cave. They did not have far to go, as Orin could see the moonlit sky ahead and could also hear the sound of running water. "Who else knows of this place?" asked the prince. He had read most of the scrolls on the history of Qev's castle, yet there was no record of secret paths leading in or out of the citadel.

By the time they made it beyond the castle walls Orin was exhausted. He kept his anger under control and could hardly wait to speak with his brother in private. *I have a fool for a brother.* Orin watched Lucas, who gazed at the smith with trusting eyes.

The three entered an old tavern not far from the great wall, which made Orin nervous. Their cowls concealed much of their faces, but even as a plump alewife led them to a rickety table in a dark corner of the tavern, Orin's heart raced. The tavern was full. Never before had the prince been among so many common folk. The alewife left them and Orin quickly shuffled close to his brother. "These people would tear us apart should they discover who we are." He looked to see that Ben was busy talking with the alewife. "What do you think Father would do if he knew you mingle with them." He motioned to the common folk, most of whom seemed to not care what else happened in the small tavern.

"You wanted to get out," replied Lucas. "I got you out."

"And brought me to the pits of hell, you have." Orin lifted his chin toward the smith. "I trust him not."

"Ben is a good man," said his brother in the swordsmith's defence.

"Dear brother, you speak like a maiden. The smith may have crafted you a glorious sword. But it doesn't mean you have his trust." He saw frustration in Lucas's eyes. "A secret way into the castle could lead to our doom."

"What could they ever do to us? Our father commands an entire army." Lucas placed his clenched fists atop the table.

It took everything within him to avoid shouting. "No, you fool. Father commands only half of Qev's army—Lord Theo commands the other half…I'm sure you know the history of our houses. Even these people know." He said no more, as Ben walked back toward them with the alewife close behind with three tankards of ale.

The three spent the night in an inn much farther away from the castle. Orin was shocked by the poverty; however, amazed by the fact that these common folk could easily forget their woes. Among them, Lucas seemed at home, which more than anything else Orin had seen that night troubled him most. He had not seen his young brother smile with such ease as he had when mingling with lowly people, and whether they knew who he was or not, Orin left the tavern that night concerned, not for his brother's safety but for the entire royal family. He did not trust these people, for he was certain that at least one among them had recognized the two princes. He had even attempted to talk with his brother about his concerns as they lay upon bug infested beds that past night; however, there was no convincing him.

They broke their fasts with the innkeeper's wheaten bread and stale cheese. The ale they drank to wash it down tasted terrible. Yet, Orin ate all that was given to him and thanked the old man and his wife. They left the inn and were led through the fields of someone's farm. It was just after dawn and the sun was begging to peep from behind fluffy white clouds. "Where is he taking us now?" Orin grabbed Lucas's arm as the smith led the way several paces ahead.

"Where do you expect? Back to the castle."

"I do not like this business at all; just think what would happen if he decided to tell our enemies of the breach to the realm's citadel!"

"You're the one who asked for an adventure. You said you wanted to get out of the castle for a night." Anger flashed in his brother's eyes as he stopped and looked to Orin. "If he hasn't told anyone by now he never will…"

Orin smiled, conceding with a quick nod. But he would be a fool to believe that one, especially a lowly smith, could keep secrets for long. *The common folk can easily be bought for a price*. Of this, Orin was certain. As they left the fields of corn Orin paused and looked ahead in awe. What lay before him had to have been the most beautiful thing he had beheld since discovering the castle's library. He had never seen grass so healthy, nor had he set his eyes upon such a quaint little house. The structure before him had been built to appear as though it had sunken into the ground. The grass had grown over the rooftop—a slanted, single steep plane—and the trees surrounding it appeared to be dwarfed. Many mounds, all overgrown with this perfectly matted grass surrounded the tiny house. It was the most peaceful sight Orin had ever seen. "Magnificent! You could literally walk upon the rooftop from the ground." He moved closer to the structure. "But I see no door. How does one get inside?"

"Better not, Yer Maj…I mean good sir." Ben looked around nervously. He had come so close to address the princes as "Yer Majesties" at the tavern and later within the inn. "Ol' Walter don't like it much when others trespass, Yer—" Orin shut him up with a disdainful glance.

His brother moved to his side. "Wonderful, isn't it?" Orin nodded, still in awe. "...The perfect size for a little prince," said Lucas as he burst out laughing.

"Brother, you have grown tall, but you are still a foolish boy." Orin shook his head hopelessly as he looked to Ben. "Where's the door?"

The smith led the way to the side of the house, careful to not make too much noise. The soft bed of grass and the hilly mounds muffled the sounds. To his amazement, Orin saw a sunken staircase of stone on the opposite side of the slanted rooftop. He moved past his companions and was about to descend when the horrific bark of a beast echoed. "Who goes there?"

"Ol' Walter!" The smith gripped Orin's shoulder. "...Ain't a good idea to go down there." The beast's bark rumbled again and the swordsmith bolted. Orin followed after his brother and the cowardly smith, pushing his way through stalks of corn.

They ran until the barks were scarcely audible. Finally, Orin fell upon the ground, struggling to catch his breath. "What kind of beast was that?"

Lucas laughed. "Just a dog."

"A very big one, Yer Majesty." The smith leaned against the stump of a mossy tree. He pointed ahead. "The castle."

Orin had never been so happy to see the white turrets of the castle. The sun had pushed its way through the clouds, brightening the hue of the red rooftop. The prince longed for home. He could hardly wait to have a long hot bath—one night of filthy taverns and bug-infested beds was more than enough for the prince. Orin looked to his brother Lucas, whose eyes were not fixed upon the castle ahead, but on the distant countryside.

## CHAPTER TWELVE
### *The King's Women*

A raven had arrived two days past, but when the watchman sounded the bells to announce that ships were in view, Genesis's heart leapt joyfully, for her King had returned; the ships were but tiny specks upon the ocean, but she had seen them in the distance. She had made everything ready, ensuring that the king's rooms were well prepared. Even as she moved about the castle among the other servants her gait was confident. *Yes, fear me now…for one day I'll be your Queen.* She knew very well what the other servants thought of her, yet none of it mattered. King Earvin had an ugly face, and she was a lowly servant with beauty on her side. *It was he who called me into his bed,* Genesis said to justify her claim to him. *I did not charm him.*

She had eaten a healthy breakfast and made certain that even Queen Bernice's rooms were well tidied. As she walked through the long halls of the castle, thoughts of the queen briefly quelled her elation. And now, she was on her way to see this vile woman again, for the queen had sent for her. She had not questioned the servant who delivered the message. The queen knew she could not compete with her, for she could no longer give the King heirs; also, the years had quelled her beauty. Genesis approached the queen's doors and took comfort in the fact that she was privy to the king's plan. Queen Bernice would become a mere symbol, her queenly powers would be transferred to the king's new bride. As she approached the queen's guards she looked into their eyes and smiled at Oswald, for she had been to his bed many at time. Oswald ignored her glance, for he was a married man.

She found the queen surrounded by her servants. Her attempts to look beautiful for the king would be in vain. Genesis's curtsy was mocking. "Your Majesty." She held the queen's glance, refusing to look away first. But this woman was strong. Her piercing grey eyes became daggers, forcing the lady-in-waiting to humble herself.

"Leave us." Genesis envied the power this woman wielded, for she did not have to repeat her command nor look to the servants to see whether they would comply. Still looking to Genesis, the queen motioned toward a cushioned stool. "You may sit."

"Thank you, Your Grace." Genesis's heart quailed inside her chest, wondering whether the queen had noticed her sudden discomfort. *What is it that makes her so confident?* Queen Bernice did not shift her gaze from her; those eyes pierced through Genesis's defences, willing her to look away from the queen once more.

"The King, my husband, returns this day." The large jewel dangling from her necklace, just between her full breasts, sparkled. "I know what you are to him, but I will not have you dishonour Qev's throne for all the realm to see. I will not have you dishonour me." Her glances were enough to make the young lady-in-waiting weep. "I could throw you in the dungeons in the belly of the castle," she threatened, "yet, what good would that do either of us?" Her lips curled as if disgusted. "I was like you once—young, beautiful. Nothing lasts forever." The queen finally smiled. "Earvin is all powerful. He can use any of us as he wills, yet I have chosen otherwise. I have allowed this…arrangement you have with my husband—for the good of the realm."

Her smile vanished as quickly as it appeared. "Could you make such a sacrifice?" The queen finally looked out the window in the direction of the sea. "A mother makes sacrifices for the good of her children, and I tell you this day, girl,"—she pointed a jewelled finger at the lady-in-waiting—"you will not ruin all I have built for my son, for one day he shall be king of all Qev."

Genesis did her best to appear unscathed by the woman's threats, yet she was terrified inside. The lady-in-waiting turned her face sideways as though every word coming from the queen's mouth were a slap. "Know this, wench." The queen's words came at her like darts. "You have my blessing where my husband is concerned, for I no longer share his bed. But surely you know what shall happen when he has no need for you—after the lust ebbs and some other house maid catches his eye you will be nothing to him." Genesis met her eyes again and suddenly felt defiled by that flinty stare. "A pretty face will only take you thus far—to any man's bed. Without that you are just a girl without a dowry. But count yourself lucky, wench, for at least your pretty face managed to get you to the bedchamber of a king, as despicable as he may be." She turned her body and her gaze away from Genesis as though she were an unwanted affliction. "Leave my presence." But before she reached the door the queen said more: "You will keep your carnal dealings with my husband behind closed doors. And remember what I said, girl, you will soon see the truth. Men are all alike. You mean nothing to him."

She stormed from the queen's rooms and ran down the hall. Queen Bernice was right in all she had said. How could she have been such a fool to think that a king would want her for anything more than to warm his bed? As she left the castle and ran across the garden Genesis looked out toward the sea and could see the ships in the distance. It would not be long before they reached the harbour.

Her father's return brought joy. The princess had done all she could to prepare for this moment, yet, as she sat among several of her maids, she could not help but wonder what the return of the king would bring. Her father's cousin had managed to keep the realm in one piece; however, she could not stand the man her father had chosen as steward. Cylene had done everything to stay out of Hayden's way, for she knew he could not be trusted. The princess had warned her father too long of his viperish cousin, yet he took no heed. Her cousin seemed weak and sluggish, and was the first to sing the king's praises; however, Cylene knew what he was. She thought back to what Kevan had said and wondered whether a pact with her brother would prove fruitful. *I shall speak with father again…*

Cylene pushed all the bad thoughts from her mind. This day was one to be happy, for it would be the beginning of a three-day celebration for all of Qev. She had to credit Hayden for preparing the city, for all the realm had come to witness the king's return. She moved away from her servants and walked onto the terrace. The skies were blue; she clutched her tiny bosom as her heart leapt for joy. The ships were still far away, yet the fact that she could see them brought joy to her heart all over again. She hardly paid attention to her servants as they joined her out on the terrace and looked out to the sea.

"Do you think the king's brought you rare jewels again, Your Highness?" The lady-in-waiting giggled as she glanced over at the princess. "…Or maybe he has found you a young husband."

Another servant gasped, as if shocked. "Yes, Your Highness, imagine if His Majesty's found you a gallant prince across the sea!"

"Alva, you speak nonsense. My father would not risk his life to sail stormy seas just so he could condemn me to a loveless marriage." She spoke, addressing her maids, as though she was joking. "And you, Lyda, my father, the king, has better reason to leave Qev than a mere hunt for gems—he sends out merchants and explorers for such tasks."

"Sorry…Your Highness." Lyda lowered her eyes.

"No harm. I cannot blame you for the life you've had," said Cylene. She glanced at the four ladies-in-waiting, saddened by the fact that they possessed such empty minds. Cylene's eyes went back to the ships. She considered herself fortunate, for the Gods had given her a father who adored and saw value in her.

Moments later the princess was interrupted by another of her mother's servants. "Princess, the Queen, your mother, begs you come to her rooms." Her mother had chosen to send a beautiful boy this time, and though he was lovely, Cylene did not answer him. It had been long since the queen slapped her face before the servants and her siblings, and Cylene had vowed that it would be longer before they would ever speak again. *She fears what father will do when he comes. Let her be afraid.* The queen's messenger left them in peace.

Bernice studied her son carefully. The tailors had created garments fit for a king. Kevan was ready. She dismissed the servants and waited for the click of the latch of the prince's door. "How could they not crown you King of all Qev, my son?" Bernice stepped back, once more after adjusting the royal robes. She huffed with a smile. "The Godfrey colours…you wear them well, my son."

"Mother, these clothes look no different from the others I have." The boy lacked patience; he didn't have the heart of a king—the essence of a true ruler. But Bernice would give him all he needed. *If only you knew what I've done to give you all this…may the Gods forgive me.* The queen refocused. "The king returns this day. It would do you good to be there to greet him, as should any crown prince. You mustn't let Hayden or even your brothers get to him first." The boy watched her keenly, but his mind was elsewhere. Bernice slapped his face. "By the Gods, boy, for once, I beg you to blot out all thoughts of a naked wench." She turned her back to him. "Your sexual desires shall lead to your ruin if you do not heed what I tell you. I have got the blood of suckling babes on my hands; how many more bastards do you intend to leave behind you, Kevan?" Bernice saw tears in his eyes and embraced him. "Forgive me…please forgive me."

"I've done all that you've asked, Mother. I am already next in line; what more do you want of me? I am the eldest of Father's heirs!"

"I know…Son, I know." Bernice walked to the window. "You don't know them. They would supplant me…and even you—all for him."

"They?"

"Yes, all of them…even my own brother, whom I loved dearly has betrayed me. Hayden Bourne, your second cousin is the worst of them all, he reeks of the Theo house and Earvin cannot see it."

"Mother, tell me what to do." A wave of confusion swept across the boy's face. "You say I can't trust anyone—not even my brothers. You say I must trust no one else but you."

"And you mustn't, Son. You mustn't trust them…not ever." Bernice ran her fingers through Kevan's hair as he wept, and again she whispered her instructions: "You must be seen by all of Qev; they must see you greet him…kneel before him and pledge your service and your love. It is vital, today of all days…"

## CHAPTER THIRTEEN
### *Kairu's Song*

The king's *The Victor* and Lord Theo's *Blackbird* led the way toward the shores of Qev. Kairu would not go below deck, for already he was amazed by what he saw before him. The great citadel, bright against the sun's rays, stood upon a hill like a great shard of ice, it's red-tipped turrets gleaming. The king had told him much of his realm, yet, as Kairu viewed the vast lands across the water, he could only imagine what life in this world would be like. The black eunuch stood among many of his own kind—tribesmen and warriors from lands far behind them. Every tribesman had adorned himself with his native colours and garments; some held their spears tightly as they looked out to a world they could hardly imagine existed. Kairu, stood there in awe.

"Nothing Ade told us could have prepared us for this, Kairu." Prodigal moved close to his side. Lord Theo and the king seemed to have reconciled their differences, at least for the time being. However, since the celebrations aboard *The Victor*, Kairu's friend had not been the same.

"Where is your master?" asked Kairu. He turned to Prodigal with a gleeful smile.

"With your king." His friend's smile waned.

"He is your king as much as he is mine, Prodigal. King Earvin is master to us all." Kairu noticed a strange look in the Nuba boy's eyes." Prodigal nodded curtly and looked to the lands ahead. "You are angry that I and not you was chosen to serve the king."

Prodigal's laugh was cynical. "I am glad I serve Lord Theo…better a fat lord than an ugly king."

Kairu's anger raged. He moved away from Prodigal with haste, heading for his cabin. "Kairu! Forgive me, Kairu…" But the black one did not answer.

><<<<o>>>><

Kairu pushed his entire body against the door to his cabin, but he could not keep Prodigal out. The Nuba boy was too strong. "Do not be silly, Kairu. I am sorry." Prodigal pushed with such force that Kairu fell to the ground, his head hitting the wall. He entered the cabin and quickly shut the door. "Kairu, I didn't mean it." He fell to his knees and took his friend into his arms. His friend did not weep but eyed him with contempt…or fear. "Forgive me, I would do nothing to hurt you, Kairu."

"Your words hurt more than this." The El Molo boy's eyes looked away.

"I have seen you with him, Kairu…walking aboard this ship." The Nuba boy felt like a fool and was even shocked by what he was admitting to himself. "You want him, this king, Kairu…I see it…the way you look at him." The rough boards dug into Prodigal's knees.

"I serve him. And you serve your master."

"It's different…the king desires you, Kairu. Everyone desires you." *Even me.* The Nuba boy's heart quailed, for he was no king with power over land and people. He was just a boy of the Nuba people. A black eunuch just like the rest. It was then he looked into Kairu's eyes and saw that his friend was something more. "Lẹwa." The word escaped from within him and Prodigal knew there was no way to take it back. He became possessed after looking into those eyes. Kairu was beautiful. The Nuba boy's fingers touched the smooth black face before him and something strange swept over him. A sudden current surged through his fingertips, all from a single touch. He could see that Kairu felt it too. Kairu's fingers moved up the length of his arm as Prodigal sat close to him, still gazing into his eyes. "Lẹwa. Kairu." They were one in the same. It was evident to Prodigal that neither of them could have avoided what happened next. Their thick, full lips touched, and for the first time in his life, Prodigal felt true passion…

*The Victor* was finally anchored and everyone waiting ashore looked to see who first would spot the king. Genesis stood not far from the queen, for, as she was one of King Earvin's royal servants, she was expected to wait in place to greet her king. Earlier, she had returned to her quarters and wept, but as she glanced at the queen she was comforted, certain that the king would not seek his wife's bed. *You may hold the crown for now, woman…and carry his name. But it is I who have the king.*

Finally, a smile appeared over her freshly painted lips. Genesis stood exactly in place as her station dictated, but nothing could prevent her from standing on the tips of her toes as she watched the ship. For a brief moment she noticed the prince's eyes upon her, but the boy did not matter. Genesis needed a man, not a boy who was obviously still grabbing at the hem of his mother's gown. She studied Prince Kevan briefly and deemed him handsome, yet there was something about that look she could not stand. She could hardly decide whether the boy looked more like his mother or the king.

"Mother, listen!" Prince Kevan placed a hand upon the queen's shoulder. "What is that horrible sound."

The lady-in-waiting cocked her ears and finally heard the distant sound of which the prince spoke. Soon the entire harbour became silent, all the cheers ceased. What Genesis heard next was nothing she had ever experienced before. There was drumming; strong, rhythmic beats echoing from the king's great ship. Even Queen Bernice looked ahead with curiosity. It appeared that the entire royal family had come to see what the king had discovered on his travels.

"It seems our father has conquered the world." Prince Orin moved ahead of the others, as he was shorter than most around him. "I've read scrolls of these drums," said the prince. He closed his eyes and took a deep breath. "Fascinating."

Bernice listened as the royal family conversed among themselves, but her eyes never left the ship. At the first sight of the lifeboats her heart leapt. The sun was shining bright; the skies were clear. The sight of hundreds of lifeboats was the most beautiful sight…and then, the drumming. The music of these drums was strange to the people of Qev, yet somehow the beats flowed across the water and touched them. Genesis looked around her in awe, for no one was standing still. Then, a voice appeared, so precise and so high-pitched, but it was beautiful. Someone was chanting words in a strange tongue. The voice became shrill; then it would change. But there were other voices…deeper voices, echoing every word this woman chanted. Genesis did not know what it was that made her body move; it could have been the joy that her king had returned, or simply the fact that the sound of the drums and the chanting of that captivating voice had somehow infected her limbs. The drumming was electrifying; like everyone else in the harbour, Genesis tried her best to move her body as best as she could to match those rhythmic beats.

When the first few boats reached the shores the cheers and gasps of awe rang out at the sight of tall dark-skinned men, all scantily dressed and holding long spears and shields. For a moment Genesis felt Qev had been invaded; then she saw the scarred face of a king standing at the helm of a boat. The other boats surrounding the king were packed with these warriors and drummers. She must have been the first to see him standing directly behind the king. The chanter was dark and lean. He stood tall with colourful beads adorning his shoulders and neck. His skin shone beneath the sun, and strung about his waist was a red fabric. Her king took quick glances at this chanter…this black thing with the voice of a woman.

It took just a short while for the shores of Qev's capital to be populated with what seemed to be hundreds of these new people the king had brought from afar. They formed circles about the king and his lords; the drums played on and the boy chanted aloud. It was impossible not to see him, for it was not just his voice that commanded all eyes to see him alone—it was the way he moved. Something in his eyes compelled Genesis to want to know him…to desire him.

When the king raised both hands the drumming and chants ceased. "Citizens of Qev!" He stood boldly before his subjects; Genesis could think only of the night to come…

The king had walked by her with his band of dark warriors without even a glance; he knew she stood there pleading for acknowledgment. But when the night passed without so much as a word from him Genesis's heart crumbled. She had spent the entire night weeping. It was a new day and the celebrations throughout the city continued. Finally, Genesis was summoned. However, the call did not come from her king, it was Queen Bernice who had sent for her.

She found the queen in the middle of her breakfast. "He'll never look at you again," said the queen. "My dear child, let me tell you a few things every woman should know about men…"

## CHAPTER FOURTEEN
### *A New Court*

Kevan quickened his pace to keep up with his mother. It was his second time attending a council meeting, yet moments before it came to a close the queen stormed out. "Mother, wait!" Finally, he slowed his mother by grasping her arm. "Mother, please!" The long hallway ahead of them was empty. "You say I must show my presence at the council meetings and now you walk out…"

"We have a big problem, Kevan," said his mother. "And you are a fool for not seeing it." His mother poked his chest with a ringed finger. "I can only teach you so much, boy! You must start using your head."

The prince looked at her, puzzled. "Father's come back, Mother. I did all you said and he was pleased with me. And now you call me a fool after only following your instructions." Kevan had had enough; he slapped his mother's hand away. "One day I shall rule all of Qev. Please, Mother, don't poke me. What if the servants—"

The slap to his face burned. Kevan clutched his face, shocked. His mother's grey eyes cut through him as if to make hateful gashes to his soul. His mother had looked at the king that way, but not him. "A king never says please to a servant, dear son." She turned away from him and resumed her brisk gait. "Have I taught you nothing? All the work I have done to prepare you—all the sacrifices—shall all be in vain if you do not use your head."

They entered his mother's rooms and she immediately ordered the servants to leave them. "Tell me what you saw today." She looked to him as his tutor had when he was a child. However, his mother did not wait for his reply. Kevan watched her, now curious. "He's changed things," she finally said. "Everything is different now." His mother looked off into nowhere as if he were not present, speaking to the empty room. "Your father has changed court. He has replaced his royal guards with these...these coloured warriors. They would all die for him."

"And they will gladly give their lives for me too, Mother...when I become king."

She shook her head. "You disappoint me." Then she sighed.

The prince's shoulders drooped. "I...I don't know what to do, Mother." Kevan thought of the servant he had in his room earlier that morning. *This was supposed to be a good day.* All days would be good for any man if they began with the butcher's daughter...

"Are you listening to a word I'm saying, boy?" Her voice dragged him back from his world of passion.

"Yes, Mother." The prince nodded.

"We shall be wise," she told him. "We must deal with the problem."

"Mother, they are but a few dark warriors with sticks and wooden shields." Finally, Kevan laughed. "They are no match for the royal guards."

She sighed again. "They have become the royal guard. Have you not heard what I've said, boy?" His mother's eyes lowered to his codpiece. "It seems you've used the wrong instrument for thinking. I will explain what I've seen at the council to you just once. Earvin has brought hundreds of these black things to pollute our realm; only the Gods can tell how many more shall come across the sea—"

"Mother, they are nothing—these tall beasts are mere fighters; that is all they know. I would be shocked if they can be taught to read or write." He laughed aloud.

"One of them can." His mother looked away, obviously displeased.

"What do you mean, Mother?

"You must learn to open your eyes to your surroundings, boy. A good king knows this. Your father has even acquired a new amanuensis—this black eunuch." Her grey eyes were accusing. "Yes, I saw you looking at this…this darkened beauty. A half man. A eunuch whose presence in a room strips all men of good sense and wisdom."

His mother spoke true, yet Kevan had to show some sign of resistance. "Nonsense, Mother."

"That abomination was the only thing you saw in that room, yet you failed to notice that he is able to read and write. This black eunuch…this…Kah-he-ru…shall become your biggest problem. Mark my words." She did not allow Kevan to utter a word. "Your father could hardly resist his precious lady-in-waiting before leaving on his voyage; now, upon his return with this black eunuch, who is able to read and write, he has spurned the girl."

Kevan looked up with interest. "Father must have sent for you." He thought of Genesis's beauty…her full bosom…

"Why would he have need for the girl when this black eunuch, who has obviously enchanted him, now shares his bed?" She moved closer to her son. "I have done all I can to prepare you for a long rule…but I fear it shall not be easy. I can feel it in my gut. Kevan, from this moment on you must heed every word I tell you." His mother's eyes were like two flint spheres; they were fixed upon Kevan's head of curls. "Now," she said, "you will do as I tell you, for I am the only one who truly loves you…the only one who can put the crown of Qev atop your head."

The night was cool and the wind brought with it the scent of the sea. The city's celebrations had been long over; however, a sense of peace and prosperity lingered within the hearts of the people. A cowled figure travelled fast through the thickets to meet someone in secret. Finally, at the mouth of the darkened cave, the cowled figure waited in the dark, watching to ensure no one had followed. *Of all the bloody nights*, the cowled figure thought, *he chooses to send me on this errand of his…and to this place*. He looked around in the dark until a sudden grip to the shoulder elicited an involuntary yelp. "How do you do that—sneakin' up on folk without makin' a sound?"

"I could hear your breathing twenty paces away, dog." He revealed his face by pulling back his hood. "You are late."

The cowled figure kept his face concealed. He looked in the direction he had come. "…Had to make certain I wasn't—"

"Yes, that no one followed you." He was in haste. "He has become a big problem, our king…some say he is the King of Kings—maybe once, but not now. That title has long been changed, yet he keeps it for himself. This king must pay for his deeds."

"The king…," said the cowled figure in a shaky voice, "filled the whole castle with dark men, he has."

"We know."

"What says he of this, yer good master?"

"What he thinks is no business of a mere servant," said the other. "Deliver your message and be gone, fool."

The cowled figure bowed, accepting his station. "As you say." He handed the sealed parchment, wondering what secrets had been scribed upon it. Had he been able to read he would have read the words, as he had stood over the person who sent him on this errand.

"We meet here again. You know when." The other messenger produced a glistening coin and the cowled figure's smile appeared.

"As you say…" The coin was tossed to the ground and the cowled figure fell down and grabbed it. He admired the silver briefly before looking up again, shocked, for the man who tossed him the coin had left him as quietly as he had come.

><<<<o>>>><

A caravan of horses, wagons and opulent carriages had left the citadel shortly after the celebrations ended, and in one of the wagons, Prodigal had surveyed the lands around him with widened eyes. This place, Qev, was not the same as his own lands, where the mornings were long and lands flat. Now, with the citadel far behind, the Nuba boy found himself a lonely eunuch with a castle to call his home and a master who never failed to look at him with contempt.

The Nuba boy sat alone upon his cot eating a meal of a small maslin loaf, stewed beans and a flagon of ale. Unlike Kairu, Prodigal was not permitted to dine with his master. In fact, he would not have wished it any different, for every look from Lord Theo carried not only hatred for the king, but lust for Kairu, descendant of the El Molo. Lord Theo desired

Kairu as he desired King Earvin's white throne—Prodigal had seen the king seated upon it. After wiping away every trace of the beans from his bowl with the last crust of bread the muscular eunuch walked to the window and looked out to the vast lands that belonged to one man. He found it strange, the way these pale-skinned men coveted property, crowns and places to sit. The Nuba people lived as one within their tribe, and though a chief was set above them, the place was earned.

Lord Theo's castle was by no means as grand as the king's; however, it was massive. Many others served his master, for there were villeins who paid this already rich lord for use of his lands. Why would this great lord, a man said to command half the realm's army, then wish to have more? Why would he covet all the king's possessions? Prodigal was puzzled by this.

His thoughts went to Kairu and he was saddened, for he barely had had the chance to say goodbye. Kairu's rooms were not far from King Earvin's, and while the king dined, he did not keep his prized eunuch far from him. Lord Theo's lands were some distance from the city, yet it was not far. Prodigal thought of the journey from the king's castle. *If you leave the king's castle at sunrise by wagon, you reach Theo Manor at sunset.* He could make the journey short if he went by horse. Prodigal thought of the wild beasts with fear, for he had ridden a horse.

The eunuch had lost himself to the thoughts of his riding a horse, unaware that he had a visitor. The moment the door shut behind him Prodigal turned abruptly. It was his master's son, Cedric. As he had been taught, the eunuch bowed. He did not speak, for there was something in Cedric Theo's eyes that willed him not to utter a word.

"So this is the eunuch Father speaks of so often—the one he got stuck with." The young lord of Theo Manor was an exact replica of his father, with the exception of a younger face and more hair. He was stocky, yet not fat. His eyes, which were small and too close together, were filled with mischief, enough to install fear in the brave Nuba boy. Prodigal had only glimpsed the young lord of the manor but had had little interest in meeting him. "I have seen you about the castle." His grin did nothing to soften his appearance. "You do speak, do you not? Or has father bought himself a dumb mute."

"I am Prodigal of the Nuba Tribe." Lord Cedric's eyes widened; it was as though he expected some other response or sound.

"Prodigal." He moved close to the eunuch, eyes fixed upon him. "I saw the other one—the nicer eunuch." As Prodigal's eyes met his he laughed. "Yes, the eunuch that usurper stole from my family." Prodigal looked to the floor. Lord Cedric motioned toward the window, as if to point a finger at the king. "The Godfreys are all thieves, every last one of them. For years they have taken…and taken. When will they ever give back?" The angry young lord did not expect an answer, and for a moment, Prodigal wondered why he had come to see him. "I shall be happy when that king is dead. I shall fuck his wife." His eyes became enlarged, as if his own words excited him. "And his daughter, Cylene, will bear me heirs…for I will be prince. I'll be the king of Qev when my father is dead."

Prodigal thought of his own father and would have given anything to see him—to simply say, *Papa, you are forgiven*. Yet, this young lord would speak of his father's demise as though he longed for it. Lord Cedric studied Prodigal's face before he poked a finger into his cheek.

"Already, they say that eunuch—the nice one—they say he shares the king's bed—that he has even spurned his mistress. Some say the king has been enchanted by his black eunuch." His thumb moved over Prodigal's lips. "Is this true, boy? Would he cast such spells over me were I king?" When the eunuch did not answer, his eyes narrowed. "Tell me, black thing, my dear mother is long dead and my father is without a wife. Have you been to his bed?" Prodigal stepped back. Lord Cedric suddenly gripped his neck and squeezed it.

Prodigal's back collided with the stone wall, but he showed no sign of pain; he would not be weak. The eunuch glanced toward the door; it had been shut. There was no hope, no help. Should he attempt to fight back, Prodigal was not certain what would become of him, for Ade had warned all his eunuchs: their very lives belonged to their masters. Even as the young lord tore away his loincloth and groped at the gash between his legs, Prodigal remained silent and still. However, he held the young lord's gaze.

The door to the room opened suddenly, and the eunuch's saviour looked in. Prodigal would never forget his face. He was another pale-skin. His dark-brown hair was cut evenly just above his shoulder. It was the gentle look in his eyes that rescued Prodigal. "By the Gods, Cedric, where have you been? Your father calls." His eyes fell upon Prodigal's nakedness; however, the pale-skin walked into the room with a pleasant smile and bowed. "Greetings. You must be Prodigal. Lord Theo has spoken of you."

The young lord appeared surprised. "You know this servant's name?"

"I pay attention, good friend." He retrieved the eunuch's loincloth and tossed it to him.

"Has my father sent my best friend, the good Ayden Thorne to fetch me out of trouble again?" A spark of anger flashed in his eyes; however, a look from his friend quickly calmed him. Young Lord Cedric grinned.

"Lord Theo has important guests this night, and the first few have just arrived. It would make much sense if the second lord of the manor were there to greet them." Ayden's smile was not easy to resist.

Lord Cedric shrugged dismissively. "My father mingles with traitors. I have no need to dine with them."

"Consider how it will look if a son is not present to stand next to his father, especially in times such as these."

The lord's son sighed. "Very well, friend." He placed a hand on Ayden's shoulder. "You always know best. When Father takes Qev…and I am prince…I shall always need you by my side."

Prodigal reached for his loincloth and quickly covered his nakedness.

## CHAPTER FIFTEEN
*The King's Command*

The summers of Qev were long and hot—nearly six sidereal months. Kairu walked the castle garden alone, fearing what would become of him when this season the pale-skins called winter arrived. Lord Alton Rowe, King Earvin's trusted friend, loved to watch the stars. It was he who had shown Kairu the ways of Qev. The black eunuch pulled his cloak about him, for the days were becoming cooler. He looked to the trees, finding it peculiar that their leaves had transformed from bright green to shades of brown, red and yellow. Kairu had learned from the old lord that the king's ships had arrived at the shores of Qev near the end of a long summer. Winter was coming. Kairu wore nothing but his beads and a loincloth beneath his cloak; however, he knew he would not be able to endure the frigid temperatures, even if this chill the pale-skins called winter would last just three of their months. After the short chill, the rains would come. Kairu hugged himself as he attempted to recall how long the rains would last. "Many months," he said to himself.

From the garden he had a clear view of the ocean, and as Kairu looked in the distance across the sea he thought of home. *What has become of Ade?* He was suddenly enveloped by sadness at the thought of his happy village; the safety of the wooden wall surrounding his tribe was nothing compared to the stone wall which guarded the king's castle. *Papa, why did you leave me? Why did you give me away for two sacks of gold?* As much as it had been explained to him by his teacher, Kairu still could not justify what had been done. *They did not love me…did not want me…*

Kairu, descendant of the El Molo, boy of the Maasai, had been given a new life—an advantaged life, for here in Qev he dined with a king. After pausing before a tall tree, which had not lost its colour, the black eunuch ran his fingers over the rough bark before touching the green spikes. There were peculiar things in this world, Qev, and peculiar people. He hugged the trunk of the tree as memories of Prodigal perched on the large branch of the Marula tree filled his mind. Kairu smiled before another wave of sorrow washed over him, for he had not seen Prodigal since he left the citadel with his master. Much had occurred since the king's return to Qev. King Earvin had come to mistrust those around him, save for a few in his retinue…and Kairu.

"Your love for nature is refreshing, Kairu."

The eunuch turned from the pine with a smile, for he knew the voice of the king's old friend. "Lord Alton Rowe." Kairu bowed. "I did not hear you come." He moved with haste to assist his new friend, offering his arm.

"Thank you, my boy." There was no sign of shame in his green eyes. "I walked this world but four winters before our king was born, yet I feel no younger than his dear father…the Gods rest his soul." Kairu studied Lord Alton Rowe's pleasant face. His neatly trimmed beard was silver and his brown hair streaked with grey. "Got my staff to lean on, Kairu. You mustn't rob an old warrior of his dignity, my boy."

Kairu obliged and the two walked the paths of the garden together. Kairu greeted his brothers with quick nods as he passed them along the paths. The king had heeded his advice to allow the tribesmen and the royal guards to blend their forces, thus showing unity. However, Kairu felt it was too late, as the initial decision to remove the royal guards completely from the king's side had already caused division within the castle. This troubled the eunuch. Much had changed since the king from across the sea brought him to this new land. "The queen visited my rooms," said Kairu.

Lord Alton Rowe dismissed his comment with a quick wave of his hand. "Never mind her, Kairu. Queen Bernice is not with the king, though she is his wife and the mother of his children."

The eunuch had heard the gossips within the castle and had made a point of getting to know each member of the royal family. Kairu looked to the gloomy sky, pulling his cloak closer around him. "The king commands this world but trusts no one. The Gods have given him a family; yet, he is alone. I do not understand this, Lord Alton Rowe."

"Being king of the realm isn't easy, my boy. To be king is to be alone."

"King Earvin does not want this wedding."

"The Gods curse this union. And I spit upon it," said the king's good friend. "A betrothal of the worst kind—mistress of the king to Qev's crown prince." He pointed a finger at Kairu. "This is part of something…something evil, I tell you…some part of a plan devised by a vicious woman. Queen Bernice despised that lady-in-waiting, and now she plans to bind her to her son and to Qev's throne." His wise eyes brightened beneath a frown. "Always remember, my boy—women do not wield swords and vanquish their enemies with brunt force as do men." The once valiant warrior lifted his bearded chin. "They use another weapon: cunning."

Kairu nodded in agreement. "The queen visited to ask that I dine with her and the prince this night."

"Be careful, my boy. If she does not bed you herself, she shall give him the task." Lord Alton Rowe nodded with a grin. "…And the last thing ya need is to succumb to her wiles."

As Lord Alton Rowe walked on in silence Kairu thought on the queen. Why had she come in person to formally welcome him to Qev after so long? But most of all, Kairu wondered why she had begged him not to utter a word to the king?

He was suddenly brought back to the chilly world around him and the dullness of the garden when Lord Alton Rowe playfully jabbed him with his staff. "My boy, I do believe you've yet to walk the streets of the city since you stepped off Earvin's *Victor*. Am I correct, Kairu?" He jabbed Kairu again.

The black eunuch had observed the city from the terraces of the castle, but he had not ventured outside the walls of the citadel—something he was well accustomed to. It brought much sorrow to think of the night he left the temple and was accosted by a tribesman in the dark of night…

"Speak, boy." Lord Alton Rowe issued a third jab to Kairu's side. "Have you left this damned castle and experienced life outside or have you not?"

He admitted he hadn't with a quick shake of his head.

"Well, I can remedy that!" Lord Alton Rowe's pace quickened; it was as though a sudden surge of life had entered his body, for he moved as though there was no need for his staff. He then turned abruptly, waving the staff. "Come on then! We haven't got all day, lad!"

Kairu had not expected the walk through the streets of Qev's city to be so refreshing. With just one guard several paces behind, Lord Alton Rowe and the elegant black eunuch walked slowly among the common folk, though many gawked at him. However, Kairu felt no different from them, for he was not of noble birth. Many had not seen folk as dark as he, at least not up close, for King Earvin had kept his eunuch and his tribesmen behind the gates of the citadel. Lord Alton Rowe was known by many; he was greeted with reverence—even fear. The former captain of the king's guards had a reputation for fearlessness.

Winter was near and the wind brought a chill with it; however, as they walked the city the sun did show its golden face through fluffy white clouds. Kairu had stopped to admire the various items sold by shopkeepers; he even had tastes of a variety of unique foods and treats, but most of all he enjoyed the sweets. He had just eaten the last bit of sugared ginger when Lord Alton Rowe gently touched his arm. "No need to be alarmed, my boy," said the old captain. "I do believe we are being followed."

Kairu waited some time before turning casually. He saw nothing strange—no sign that anyone was watching him, for as far as he could see, the entire marketplace looked as it would on any other day. He saw hagglers bargaining over costs of items; the aisles between the stalls were busy with customers stretching over each other to get the best their coins could buy; and the loud echo of children at their mother's feet as they played filled the entire world in which Kairu stood. He saw nothing conspicuous, no one person appearing as though he or she did not belong. "I see no one, sir." Kairu turned his attention back to a stall where a merchant presented his finest silks.

"A woman followed us from the moment we entered the market," said Lord Alton Rowe. "Only the Gods know how long she's trailed us." He tilted his head as if he were a dog attempting to listen keenly or to catch a scent. Then he grunted. "Something is amiss."

"You might have been mistaken, Lord Alton Rowe." The eunuch scanned again for any sign of a woman, but there were so many women in the marketplace.

"She was not young," said the king's friend, "and not fat. Her coif was white, and from beneath it I saw a lock of grey hair."

The black eunuch widened his eyes in awe, impressed that Lord Alton Rowe had gleaned so much from quick observations of someone else whose intent was to be discreet. "Why would a woman be following us?" Kairu questioned. "Do you think—"

There was a shrill scream. Something collided with him, and before he knew it, Kairu had the body of a woman in his embrace. The woman had bulb-like brown eyes—eyes glowing with terror. The woman wore a white coif, which had been pushed back off her head, revealing greying, curly hair. The woman clung to him with all her might, those large eyes pleading with him, but for what, Kairu could not say. Blood dripped from her mouth. Her hold on him was weakening.

"Set her down, laddie," commanded Lord Alton Rowe. "Gently." He gripped the hilt of his sword as he barked aloud his command that the bystanders back away from the scene. The tribesman spoke in the tongue of his tribe, brandishing his long spear.

As Kairu laid the woman down his eyes fell upon her bloodstained kirtle. Her eyes rolled in the direction of Lord Alton Rowe, and as weak as she seemed, the woman beckoned him closer. Her words were but a whisper. "The…the…king…"

Lord Alton Rowe leaned closer and so did the eunuch. "What of the king?" asked the old captain. "Speak woman!"

She shook her head several times. "…Son…The king's son."

"What is the meaning of this, woman. What news have you of Prince Kevan?"

"Dorcas…she got the king's son…" She shook her head, looking wide-eyed at Lord Alton Rowe. "No…not the son…but the other…the mark…" The woman's eyelids partially veiled her large brown eyes as she took one last breath.

The King's old friend remained composed, though he was obviously angry that the woman had died. "Not a word of this to anyone, Kairu—not even to the king himself."

Kairu gave his word right there as he stooped over the woman's corpse with blood stains on the front of his cloak. Lord Alton Rowe inquired of the bystanders if anyone knew the dead woman, but no one came forth.

They returned to the castle immediately after the body was removed, and within the privacy of Kairu's rooms, Lord Alton Rowe spoke of what had occurred in the market as Kairu cleaned blood from his hands. "What sense do you make of this, laddie?" The old warrior tapped his staff on the floor.

Every word the woman uttered before her death was vivid in Kairu's mind. "She mentioned the king," he said. "And then she said, *the king's son*."

"Well, I know one thing for certain, my boy," said Lord Alton Rowe. "This woman spoke of another son, not Prince Kevan."

Kairu nodded. "That was clear. Said there was another…and she mentioned a woman, Dorcas."

Lord Alton Rowe grinned. "Obviously the mother," he replied excitedly.

The eunuch scratched his chin in puzzlement. "And what of this mark of which she spoke?"

"Nothing of consequence," replied the old lord. "'Twas a dying woman's last word, nothing more." He tilted his head backward and smiled again. "The Gods are good, I tell you. Somewhere out there, Earvin has a bastard, and it may well be this bastard that claims the white throne."

Kairu did not agree. The woman's intent was to say as much as she could before she died. But it was not to be. As they parted, Kairu again promised Lord Alton Rowe that he would not utter a word of what was said by the unknown woman. However, they did agree that somewhere out in the city, King Earvin had an older heir, an heir with all the rights to the throne of Qev.

The king of Qev shoved the contents off his desk in sudden rage, for he had lost patience with the world, as he himself had put it when he left the council. "What good is power to a king if he cannot wield it?" He was alone in his offices, yet he spoke aloud as though the council still surrounded him, all wide-eyed and silent. "Is a council not expected to speak?" He looked around the room as if something or someone should produce responses to his questions. With a sigh, King Earvin refilled his goblet with wine. He had sent all his servants away, for he needed no one near him. "Useless lot." After drinking half the contents of his goblet he dragged both hands over his face. "In the name of the Gods, where is Hayden Bourne, regent of Qev and cousin to this man called King!" He had sent for his cousin long ago. Why was he still waiting? When the door opened slowly the king felt sudden satisfaction, for indeed the warriors and aides outside his door had heard his angered cries. But it was not his cousin who bowed loyally at the door's entrance, it was Kairu. Immediately, the king's anger ebbed. "You." He turned and looked away from the eunuch.

"Great King." Kairu's soft, gentle eyes showed no fear.

"I don't recall sending for you."—he could not look into the eunuch's eyes for too long—"…or else…"

"I have come to make sure you are alright, King of Kings." There was a terrified look in the eunuch's innocent eyes; something troubled the black one, but he shifted his glance as if to hide his eyes and immediately began to collect the items strewn over the floor.

The king grunted. *Why do I desire this eunuch so? Why am I so weak?* Just seeing the eunuch ignited thoughts within him…lusts, even rage. Kairu made him feel real. He did not see himself to be the monster his own wife saw when she looked at him. "Tell me, eunuch, what say you of this union—this betrothal between Genesis and my son?"

Kairu bowed. "Great King, I am Kairu."

"Yes, yes. I know who you are." *He still insists on making me bow to him…to make me weak.* King Earvin had admitted to himself that he desired the boy, for he had only called him by his name in the height of passion. "I say your name when you warm my bed. What more do you want of me?"

"King of Kings." He placed the last of the items atop the desk before kneeling at the king's feet. "You are Earvin Godfrey, king of Qev. Your title I give to you willingly. I serve you. You rule an entire realm. But I am just Kairu—my name and my beads are all I have left of my world." He pressed his palm against the colourful beads. "It is important to me." Those eyes looked up to him and the king was humbled.

"Kairu. Black one," said the King. The eunuch smiled with thanks before kissing his golden ring.

Kairu's eyes sparkled with wisdom. "I have not seen the prince and the lady—"

King Earvin stopped him with a wave of his hand. "Lady?" His blue eyes seemed to lose some of their colour. "She is just a wench."

When the door opened and Hayden Bourne walked in, Kairu stood and turned his body slightly toward the door. "Cousin"—King Earvin cleared his throat nervously and shifted in his chair—"how good of you to hasten to my call; after all, I am king."

His cousin grinned at his sarcasm. "Forgive me, Your Majesty. I was detained."

King Earvin shrugged. "Tell me, Cousin, has the council decided on this wedding I am so strongly against?"

"Yes, Your Majesty. The council has decided that it would be wrong to prevent the couple's union, as they are in love." His cousin's eyes betrayed him.

"Love!"

"Yes, Your Majesty. The prince swears by the Gods their love is true. He says they courted while you travelled across the sea."

"You know as much as I do that it was that woman who put him up to this. The only thing my son loves is his cock!"

Kairu stood there, silent, even as the king's cousin shot him unwelcome glances. "Your Majesty, I would speak with you in private, My Lord."

The king motioned to Kairu. "Don't mind him, the black eunuch is my trusted amanuensis. You may speak anything in his presence." His cousin cleared his throat uncomfortably. "Well, go on then."

"Yes, My Lord. You see, the girl…said things, Your Majesty. She told the queen of your intent to…"—he glanced at Kairu before continuing—"…that you meant to build a harem, Your Majesty. I've told the queen this could not possibly be true." Hayden Bourne's left eyebrow arched when the king made no response. "Certainly, Cousin," he said more casually, "you didn't mean to do such—"

"Of course I did. Am I not king?"

"No, Your Majesty." His eyes softened when the king's eyes met his. "...I mean, yes, Your Majesty. But surely you jest." The right eyebrow raised above the left after the king nodded. "And the concubines?"

"All true." He looked to Kairu, who may have been shocked. The eunuch's eyes darted toward the sea. "But I have changed my plans." He motioned to Kairu. "I got him for a purpose, you see—*Chief of the Girls*. The king watched his cousin as he studied Kairu with a sidelong glance.

"Your Majesty, the prince and his betrothed have decided to wed after the rains." His cousin's face bore a half smile. "They seek your blessing."

"A summer wedding. The winter has not yet begun." He turned his back to his cousin. "If Kevan intends to marry the wench I once bedded then let him do so now." He turned abruptly when Kairu spoke.

"King of Kings"—Kairu bowed, keeping his eyes to the floor—"you should grant the prince's request…for the winter, Great King. But after winter come the rains—the two may grow weary…and apart."

King Earvin smiled. "Your master, the eunuch Ade, said you were worth more than gold, and he spoke true." The king looked to his cousin and then to the door. "Go on." He eyed his cousin with a grin. "Run to your queen and tell her she has my blessing."

><<<<o>>>><

The black eunuch did not expect an audience when he entered the royal dining hall, for after the events of the day, the company of the royal family was the last thing he needed. Queen Bernice wore a gown of blue silk, and around her neck dangled the most beautiful pearls. Kairu had decided to wear a white tunic made of silk, given to him by the king himself. The large dining hall with high ceilings was illuminated by many candles and the dining table was well spread. As the servant led him to the chair opposite the queen, Kairu quickly took note of the other guests. Prince Kevan and his betrothed were seated to his left. Seeing the prince, Kairu could not wipe the image of the dead woman from his mind. Who was this woman, Dorcas? How would the presence of an older son of the king change the realm? The eunuch avoided the prince's stare, fearing the truth of what he knew could easily be discerned.

The king's daughter, whose presence Kairu found peculiar, sat directly to Kairu's right, while the queen's younger sons, Prince Orin and Prince Lucas, sat next to the lady-in-waiting, Genesis. Kairu recognized the queen's brother, also of the king's council, Lord Percival. But it was Lord Hayden Bourne's presence at the queen's table that puzzled Kairu most.

The queen spoke of various issues as they dined. She questioned Kairu of his home across the sea and how he lived there; she asked him how he liked the rooms he had been given, being as they were located not far from the king's. These things she asked with cheer, as though she and Kairu were old friends.

Queen Bernice also questioned Kairu on the art of creating a eunuch. "Tell me, Kah-he-ruh…" She smiled, resting several fingers upon her bosom. "I did say it right, did I not?" He bowed in acknowledgement, though she pronounced his name much too slowly. "Kairu, how did you come to be…how did they make you what you are?" All eyes within the dining hall turned to the black eunuch, even the servants.

He would not let them see his discomfort. Kairu rejected the urge to move uncomfortably in his chair, keeping his gaze locked with the queen's. "I was a child when I was cut." He noticed from the corner of his eye that Prince Orin, the small prince, leaned forward.

"Do you remember it well?" Already, the studious prince seemed to relish the conversation.

Kairu's thoughts went to the vision of his father leaving him; he would never forget the fact that his papa never looked back once. "How could I forget what was done to me against my will?" asked Kairu. "My prince, I do not believe you would forget the events of the day, should our king sell you to be transformed against your will…into this." He spread his arms.

"Mother, must we endure such sad things?" Cylene shot the queen a scathing glance, confirming there was still friction between them.

"I am merely getting to know the eunuch," said the queen.

"Why have you come?" Prince Kevan eyed the princess with contempt. "You've not spoken to mother since—"

"I will gladly leave." Princess Cylene gathered the folds of her flowing gown as she rose.

Kairu could not stop himself from resting a hand upon her shoulder. "Please stay, Princess." The anger which burned in her blue eyes faded. The black eunuch was astonished by her resemblance to the king.

"I invited you all here with the intent of having a peaceful meal," said the queen. "Must we allow our honoured guest to believe the royal family of Qev cannot dine peacefully?"

Lord Hayden Bourne lifted his goblet. "Very well said, Your Grace."

Kairu looked about the great hall, somewhat confused by his surroundings. It was evident that there was no peace at the queen's table. The queen's brother had not uttered a word since the dinner commenced, nor had her youngest son, Prince Lucas. It seemed as though the young prince had more important places to be. As for his uncle, Kairu could not understand him, for even as their eyes met briefly, Lord Percival, a member of the king's council, had a face that was impossible to read. His countenance was neither joyful nor sad, for his impenetrable grey eyes gave nothing away.

The lady-in-waiting, Genesis, whenever she looked to Kairu, had eyes like daggers. She sat next to her betrothed, obviously saddened by her imminent wedding. Kairu was certain there was no love between Prince Kevan and the wench Genesis.

Finally, the reason for the queen's invitation came to light. "Tell me, Kairu." Queen Bernice sipped from her goblet gracefully. "There has been talk—rumours—of a harem my dear husband and king plans to create." She turned her gaze toward Genesis. "My dear Genesis has told me this. Even Lord Hayden, regent of Qev, has brought me news of this abominable act."

"My queen." Lord Hayden Bourne jerked upward, astonished that the queen implicated him, for his skin paled. "My cousin is king and has the right to do as he pleases."

"Father means to secure his place in history," said Orin. "What good is a king without heirs." He smiled cunningly. "And what other use other than pleasure would a harem serve if not to spawn heirs for a kingdom."

Prince Lucas pushed his plate away from him. "You are sick."

Prince Orin shook his head. "And you, dear brother, are still a virgin. Speak with our brother, I am sure he may be willing to offer some tips on how to bed the help."

Prince Kevan slapped the top of the table with his palms. "You bastard! You will live to regret those words."

Prince Orin's smile never left his face. "Yes, Brother…when you are king. Long live the King! It seems we have forgotten why Mother called us all here." His eyes jabbed into Kairu. "Our father has turned our worlds upside down, and we all feel Kairu is the key—the only one able to sway our king from squandering our birthrights by building a house of whores. Let's not fool ourselves. We need this black eunuch's help."

The silence within the dining hall whispered to Kairu—what the young prince said was indeed true, for the others looked in his direction, waiting. Kairu, descendant of the El Molo, boy of the Maasai, thought of his father. *Papa.* He would not forget who he was. *All things happen for a purpose...* The image of his teacher's face appeared in the forefront of his mind. Ade had taught him to always honour his master. He would not plot against the king. "The king no longer plans to build a harem." Kairu looked to Lord Hayden Bourne, for he had been present when King Earvin said this.

Kairu slept with the window open that night, allowing the chill inside. One single evening with the queen and her children had brought much stress. He lay in bed that night with his eyes fixed upon the night's moon. His master and king was oblivious to the fact that another heir existed. And Kairu knew that if this were to be known by the queen, this bastard son would be in grave danger; this, Lord Alton Rowe had said. The eunuch could not abate his worries, for he was convinced King Earvin was not loved by many. Kairu did not know why; however, the king's safety, as well as his own, were at the centre of his thoughts that night.

## CHAPTER SIXTEEN
### *Summer*

A cold, frigid winter and dull raining season had passed. Summer had arrived at last. Cylene felt alive again. As she walked the halls of the castle, the princess looked to the bright sky and welcomed the rays of the sun. However, she could hardly endure the fact of what the arrival of summer brought. All of Qev was abuzz; the marriage of her brother to Lady Genesis Skyers was close at hand. Cylene grabbed the folds of her gown with aggression, for she had finally been granted audience with her father, the king.

When she reached the throne room, Cylene, princess of Qev, found she had to wait before closed doors with four dark tribesmen eyeing her with suspicion. This infuriated her. She watched the strange men, knowing she could not command them to move away. Only after the tallest of the scantily clad warriors tapped his spear against the doors did she get access to the throne room. It was Kairu, the black eunuch, who greeted her with a bow and bid her in. "Princess of Qev," said the eunuch, "my king shall see you now."

His king, *he says. Last I checked, the king of Qev was my father.* Cylene eyed the eunuch scathingly; however, she could not help noting how beautiful he was. *It is something in his eyes,* she thought. *But then it is something more…* She swept by him as though he were nothing, but the princess knew what the black eunuch had become. Her father had elevated this servant much higher than his station—too high, concluded Cylene. Kairu, this dark thing from across the sea—this…descendant of the El Molo, of the Maasai, had been given the title of Royal Advisor and now had a seat upon the council. The black eunuch was able to read and had taken to spending much of his time within the castle's library. The entire castle was abuzz with rumours that every decree passed by the king were carefully scrutinized by the common black boy.

Seeing her father seated upon the throne, Cylene stopped abruptly and curtsied reluctantly, for the thought of the days when she would run into her father's arms, into a joint, welcoming embrace. Gone are the days when she could hold her father's hands and he would tell her how beautiful she was…and that she would one day rule over all Qev. But as Cylene looked into her father's eyes she realized that he had lied to her. "Father." She did not move any closer to him; instead she stood about twenty paces from the white throne, a seat that would forever be out of her reach.

He had the nerve to smile at her after spurning her for over two seasons. "My beautiful Cylene." For the first time in her life she really looked at his scar.

More than anything, Cylene wanted to rush to her father and kneel before him. She longed to rest her head upon his lap and tell him all her troubles. But things had changed. So much was different now. Cylene saw him from the corner of her eye, the black eunuch. He hovered not far from her father's throne, but she would not look at him. She would not give him the satisfaction by making him feel he was anything important. "I must speak to you alone." Her tone was more demanding than she had intended, yet Cylene kept her gaze upon her father. *If ever you loved me, send this black thing away.* She saw her father's right eye twitch a little. And then, as if he had seen what he wanted in her eyes, he spoke to his eunuch…his *Chief of the Girls*, according to Hayden Bourne.

"Leave me with my daughter, Kairu."

Cylene's shoulders lowered only when the eunuch had left them; she sighed. "Father, you dishonour us by openly bedding a eunuch," said Cylene. "It vexes me." Her father's eyebrows lifted, as if surprised. "Can this eunuch give you heirs? Can you put Mother, your wife, aside and place him beside you as queen?"

Her father shook his head. "You disappoint me, little girl. I seriously believed you knew me—understood me." Earvin Godfrey, king of all Qev, pulled the crown from his head and placed it upon the throne. As he stood next to the throne and crown he pointed to them. "There are some who would kill their own flesh and blood for that—iron and wood." He smiled. "But it is the power they wield that makes them desirable. Never forget that."

Cylene did not wipe away the tears that fell from her eyes. "You lied to me—betrayed me. You knew I could never be queen."

"You are my daughter. My flesh and blood. You know the protocols of our realm." Her father turned his back to the throne. "I have always been true to you, my daughter. If I have done anything to offend you, I am sorry. But I am king. And if a king values his life and his family he has to make sacrifices—keep his plans inside his head. Cylene, I have taught you this. I spoke truth when I said I wished you had been born a boy, for when I look at you I see myself. You are strong!" He twisted his ring with the royal seal around his finger. "After Father's death all of Qev whispered lies—rumours that I had him murdered so I could ascend. My father prepared me to be king, and I loved him for it.

"So after Father died and I got the crown I followed through with my plan—Father's plan. It was he who suggested I change the ways of the realm." He must have seen the shock in her eyes. "Yes, Cylene, Grandfather commanded that I build a harem, only to protect the Godfrey name."

Cylene heard the door open and turned abruptly. It was the eunuch, Kairu. "What do you want?" The princess clenched her fists. Kairu merely bowed.

"Enough, Daughter, I trust Kairu with my life."

She would not hold her tongue, not anymore. "Father, I cannot bear to see him, this reproach to our realm and ways."

"Princess." The eunuch did not request permission from her father to address her. "I am bound to serve your father, our king. I serve him alone. If you are true to your father, the king, you too shall have my allegiance."

"Father, I am confused." She looked from the eunuch to her father. "You speak as though something dreadful is about to happen."

"Do not worry, Cylene. All will be well. Just remember that I have always loved you."

"King of Kings," said the eunuch, "please permit me to explain." Kairu continued after her father nodded and walked toward the window. "Princess, what I tell you now must never leave this room." The eunuch's long, toned arms were gracefully held behind his back. His shoulders were straight and his elegant neck erect. The many colours of his beads complemented his dark skin beautifully. Her father's black eunuch was indeed majestic. As Cylene watched the fullness of his lips and the whiteness of his straight teeth, she could not resist the thoughts of Kairu's full lips against her own…

"Princess Cylene, your father, the king, has reason to believe there is a plot to supplant him." Kairu locked eyes briefly with her father before continuing. "We do not know how or when this will be done, yet we believe your own mother has planned to place your brother, Prince Kevan, upon the throne."

Cylene shook her head. "You are a fool, eunuch. I am told you are able to read; however, you may wish to read the laws of our realm…or speak with my brother, Orin." She actually laughed. "Kevan can only ascend to the throne when…" Cylene paused. Her eyes widened. "Father, surely you don't mean—"

"Yes, Cylene, Kevan will only ascend to the throne upon my death." Her father's eyes became sad. He picked up his golden crown and sat upon the white throne. "My three sons would rejoice, were I to fall. I have failed them. I have failed you, Cylene."

She raced to him and threw her body upon him and the throne. "Oh Father, forgive me." She wept. "You were gone so long…I thought you had left me forever—left me with Mother. I have no one, Father. No true friends, no betrothed…and then you return with him. You love the black eunuch and have left no place for me."

Her father laughed. "Worry not, Cylene. I will keep my promise; my daughter shall choose a husband she loves." She breathed a sigh of relief as his strong arms enveloped her. "And I will have you know, Daughter, I do not love Kairu; he loves me as his king, for it is I alone he must serve until the Gods take me from this world. It is his duty—his purpose."

"Forgive my despair, Father. I failed you." She buried her face against his chest and wept silently.

The lowly servant had been sent through the thicket again on an errand, cloaked in a dark woollen cowl on the darkest night of the long summer. He had moved quickly through the forests after leaving the castle and was soaked in sweat, but most of all tired. Leaving the castle that night had not been easy, for again, the castle of Qev, as well as the entire city, had become busy. Many had come from afar to attend the royal wedding. The servant had not seen so many nobles in one place before; not even for the king's coronation did so many sweep through the city gates. The markets too were busy; every stall was stocked with trinkets and souvenirs, all mementos for those attending the capital city for the wedding of Prince Kevan and his betrothed, Lady Genesis Skyers.

The servant finally arrived at the meeting place. He did not wait long at the mouth of the cave before that familiar voice spoke in his ear. "You smell, dog." He turned abruptly, startled, though he had expected the same stealthy appearance.

The servant smiled as though he had come to meet with a friend. But this was no friend, of that he was certain. Though he had seen the face many times at that very spot, he did not know the name of this man who had always come dressed in black and armed like a warrior. "…Was sent to deliver this." He handed over the parchment bearing a red seal, his eyes quickly noticing the glistening hilt of the warrior's sword.

"My master commands that we act now…Tell this to the one who sends you." His eyes were intense. "It must be done before the prince and his wench are wed."

He knew exactly what was to be done, for it was he who would carry out the task. "…It ain't the right time…not with the whole city swarmin' with noble folk."

"And no one will know exactly who would want him dead." His lips tightened. "This must be done. Do not delay." He turned to leave but paused as he gave one last command. "We meet here after he is dead."

The servant moved with haste through the night, for he needed to report to his master, and prepare his instruments for taking a life.

## CHAPTER SEVENTEEN

*Arrows*

"You have done well, Kairu." Prodigal placed both hands upon his shoulders before embracing him. "Our teacher, Ade, told us you were destined for an advantaged life, Kairu. He never said you would be the closest person to a king." There was a beam of joy in Prodigal's full eyes, or it may have been awe.

Kairu smiled back. As they left the library and walked the halls to Kairu's rooms he watched as his friend's eyes again were filled with awe. "I have done all Ade said," he replied. "And I have been rewarded for my loyalty." Even as servants and aides passed them Prodigal's mouth fell open as they greeted the black one with a bow. Lord Theo had arrived days ahead of the prince's wedding and Kairu insisted that Prodigal stay with him, for they had not seen each other since Prodigal left the citadel. "And what of your life with Lord Theo?" Prodigal had spoken little of his life with his own master.

Prodigal's eyes strayed briefly and his nostrils flared slightly as he quickly exhaled. "My master is good to me," he replied "but I have found a woman, Kairu!"

The black eunuch felt his heart quicken its pace. "A woman?"

"Yes, Kairu. She too is like us. My woman is Nadira." The emptiness within his eyes quickly disappeared. "Lord Theo gave me a woman. Life has not always been bad with my master…even before we came across the sea, Kairu." He clasped his hands as if to plead with his friend.

Prodigal's glee left Kairu speechless. There was nothing to say, so Kairu did the only thing he could. He smiled.

"Does this make you unhappy, Kairu?"

Kairu thought of the time their lips had touched…the embraces they shared. "I am happy for you, Prodigal." Thoughts of what their lives could have been, had they not been made eunuchs flooded his mind. However, Kairu was certain that the feelings he had for Prodigal would have been the same had they met under different circumstances. He had felt connected to the Nuba boy from the moment they met outside those massive stone walls…beneath the pelting sun.

"You say you are happy, Kairu. But I do not see happiness in your eyes…" Prodigal's eyes suddenly hardened. "My master gives me a chance to love, Kairu. But yours gives you titles."

"I am sad."

"And I was sad when you gave yourself to that cruel king." His eyes blazed with rage.

Kairu looked back at Prodigal, shocked. "We were taught to serve. I served my king."

"Do you serve him still?" Kairu knew exactly what was asked. Prodigal suddenly turned away. "Do not worry, Kairu…we need not talk of this…"

"I sleep in my own bed. King Earvin has taken concubines but shall build no harem. I am also called *Chief of the Girls*." Kairu did not know why he revealed this information, for he had never before discussed the king's plans with another. He knew his friend would not betray him. "Prodigal, the king means to produce new heirs; already he has sown his seed and now two concubines have swelling bellies." The relief that came from sharing just a portion of the king's secret brought relief. But Prodigal showed no sign of interest; he simply tuned his gaze out the window.

"Kairu, let us walk through the gardens…like we did at the temple." Prodigal smiled wide. "Come on, Peacock! Maybe I can teach you to climb."

Kairu's thoughts drifted back to the moments spent watching the beautiful peacock in the temple's garden. Nodding, he took Prodigal's arm as the two left his rooms. "There is no Marula tree in the garden of Qev," said Kairu. The black eunuch threw his arm around Prodigal's neck as they walked down the hallway.

><<<<o>>>><

It was the perfect day to walk the gardens of the castle. Kairu embraced the warmth of the summer's sun, as it reminded him of home. The sky was bright and all the plants of the garden were in full bloom. As always, he was amazed by the neatly manicured hedges and the stone walkways. The trees were at their greenest. "This is my favourite place to be," said the boy of the El Molo to his friend. "I would spend my nights under the stars, Prodigal, but the king forbids it."

They were about to walk into a cluster of trees, just near the forest, when Kairu heard a familiar voice call out to him. "Kairu, my dear boy. I have been searching the castle for you."

A smile appeared even before he turned to greet his old friend. "Lord Alton Rowe." The eunuch bowed with grace. The king's faithful friend moved as quickly as he could, his gait slightly laboured. Although he required a staff to support him the old warrior still wore a sword belt. The weapon was magnificent; Kairu had seen it—held it with his own hands.

Lord Alton Rowe looked at Prodigal with quizzical eyes. "And this must be your good friend…" He brought his free hand up to his bearded chin as he pondered. "Ah, Prodigal, is it?"

The Nuba boy nodded, yet his eyes were unwelcoming; it was as though he knew the old lord. Kairu rested a hand upon the old man's arm. "Please walk with us, Lord Alton Rowe."

"Gladly." Lord Alton Rowe seemed not to notice Prodigal's slight. "I have been to see the king," he said, "and he has convinced himself that this wedding will be exactly what the realm needs." His sudden grimace was a sure sign of his disapproval. "That boy cannot hold a candle to the greatness of his father. How many battles has he led to victory? In fact, how many battles has he seen at all? He is nothing like his father, I tell you! I've told Earvin a thousand times—there's something amiss."

Kairu looked to Prodigal, somewhat apologetically, for it appeared Lord Alton Rowe had disrupted their visit to the garden. "Let us talk of this, Lord Alton Rowe." He said this as gently as ever. And the old man smiled casually.

"Certainly, my boy." He had his eyes fixed upon the thicket as though he had seen or heard something among the trees. "Have you done what I asked of you, clever one?" Lord Alton Rowe asked. Kairu nodded. Lord Alton Rowe briefly glanced toward the trees again before continuing on with Kairu walking close to him. Prodigal, who had distanced himself from the two, was studying a large tree, which had the look of the great Marula.

"I have asked Earvin—begged him—not to allow this wedding, yet now the citadel bursts with nobles and common folk from all ends of the realm."

"Lord Alton Rowe, if we speak with the king—" The old warrior dismissed him with a wave.

"No, my boy." He looked to ensure Prodigal was well out of earshot. "The king will not displace a rightful heir to throne and crown with a simple whisper of a woman's name…"

"But the king may remember this woman," said Kairu.

"Bah." Lord Alton Rowe shook his head. "Earvin needs facts; he has to see the boy with his own eyes." The old man turned to Kairu with a steadfast look in his eyes. "The winter and rains have passed; another long summer has begun, yet we have not found this son of the king. And we know nothing of the woman who died to get word to me." He gripped Kairu's arm. "My boy, at least one person knows of the message that woman brought, and that one person may also know that we are privy to it."

"And if none of this is true?" Kairu had always hoped the death in the marketplace, as well as the news the woman brought, would somehow be forgotten. The eunuch had tried everything to discover the identity of the poor woman, a woman long dead. But the wise Lord Alton Rowe returned for the body that day and commissioned an illuminator to capture the woman's likeness as she lay dead. The black eunuch and his old friend only had the name, Dorcas, and a face in ink on a piece of parchment.

"A woman dead in light of day, all over a lie?" Lord Alton Rowe shook his head. "The existence of this boy would change everything within the realm, Kairu. Besides, the boy may be in danger. We must find him."

The black eunuch nodded. He turned his gaze to Prodigal, who seemed to have forgotten he was not alone in the garden. Kairu smiled, for he understood Prodigal's need to be among trees. Suddenly, an object zipped by Kairu's head. His first instinct was to look behind. But another arrow came, and then another. The black eunuch immediately fell to the ground but not before he felt a sharp pain to his shoulder. And as he lay there grimacing he looked for his friend. He did not see Prodigal. Lord Alton Rowe had fallen to his knees with his hand on the hilt of his sword and his staff on the ground. "Lord Alton Rowe!" Kairu attempted to move but his old friend bid him stay with only a cautious stare. Kairu looked to his shoulder to see that he had been grazed by an arrow; it bled profusely. The king's good friend had taken an arrow directly to the chest, and even as he fell he kept his gaze locked with Kairu's. "Find my king's son, Kairu…descendant of…" He took one last, long breath before he lay still. The eunuch crawled toward his dead friend, and just as he reached him, Prodigal ran out from among the trees.

"Come with me, Kairu. It is not safe here." It was Prodigal's loud calls that summoned the king's guards, for Kairu did not have the strength to rise. Soon they were surrounded by guards and tribesmen, while Kairu, the black eunuch of the El Molo, clung to Lord Alton Rowe, and for the second time in his life, Kairu wept over the dead…

# CHAPTER EIGHTEEN
## *The Council*

"Speak, eunuch! I command it!" The king had fierce, sorrowful eyes. Seeing him seated upon the white throne filled Prodigal with fear, for mingled with the fierceness and the sorrow, was rage. His blue eyes pierced through Prodigal's defences, forcing the Nuba boy to shift his gaze. To the king's right stood Kairu, advisor and member of the council, before which Prodigal now stood. There were several tribesmen guarding the doors, and they far outnumbered the king's regular guards. Prodigal pivoted, as the king's blue gaze enveloped him with a feeling of vulnerability he had never experienced before. And all the while, his faithful servant, Kairu, descendant of the El Molo, the boy of the Maasai, stood there in silence.

His nervous gaze shifted from his friend, Kairu, to his own master. "I saw nothing, Your Majesty." He could not avoid his master's frown.

"I haven't asked your master the question, boy. I am your sovereign—your king!" The king's fists pounded the massive armrests of the white throne. "You say you climbed the tree, and that you saw the arrow strike down Lord Alton, and yet you say you could not see the bowman. Do you take me for a fool, eunuch?" He then leaned forward. "Speak!"

"Your Majesty," said Lord Theo, bowing just slightly. "I've questioned the eunuch myself, and he's said—"

"My friend is dead!" The king's voice echoed within the hall.

Prodigal quivered, for he knew this pale-skinned king could command that he be put to death if he wished it. The queen stood in the far corner of the throne room, her son, Prince Kevan, not far from her side. A thin smile quickly appeared over her usually stern face before she whispered to the prince. The regent, Lord Hayden Bourne, lingered, for he paced the great hall with catlike skill.

"If I may suggest one thing, Your Majesty." Lord Percival, the man Kairu had identified earlier as the queen's brother, moved forward and bowed with reverence. "The eunuch may speak true. The archer would have had a perfect vantage point; it is natural that he would have used the foliage to conceal himself. This culprit may very well be among us right here within the citadel; after all, it could be anyone. With the royal wedding close at hand, the city is filled with travellers, both noblemen and common folk alike."

"I do not like what you say, Lord Percival." Prodigal saw contempt in his master's eyes. "My own son has gone out himself to search the woods. There is no trace of either archer or arrow." Prodigal was filled with rage as the young master, Cedric, stepped forward and knelt before the king. This, Prodigal could hardly endure, for he knew too well how much his masters despised the king. He had considered warning Kairu about these two, yet Ade's teachings had always prevented him. A eunuch was bound to obey his master; to betray a master's trust was punishable by death…

"I meant no offence, Lord Theo." The queen's brother spread his arms and gave a look as if to atone for his words. "I was merely cautioning the king. Who else will this fiend strike down?"

"My brother's concerns are justified, My Lord." Queen Bernice walked out before the throne, and with a mere look, she commanded Prodigal out of her way. "We may all be in danger with this killer roaming the forests."

King Earvin listened attentively as Kairu moved close and whispered in his ear. The queen's countenance changed instantly. The king nodded. It was then Kairu began to speak. "Lord Alton Rowe is dead," said Kairu. "He was my friend and friend of the king. The king has commanded that I find the bowman." He looked to Prodigal. "And I need you, Prodigal, to help me find him."

"But Your Highness." Lord Theo frowned as he bowed to the king. "My servant…the eunuch, has duties—"

King Earvin leaned forward. His scarred face appeared even more deformed in his sorrow. "The eunuch will serve me until this mess is done with. This, I command." He waved his ringed hand several times with finality. And did not recline until Lord Theo nodded and gently backed away. The queen had already rejoined her son, Prince Kevan, who had not shifted his cold gaze from his father since walking into the throne room.

Later, after his master was forced to leave the great hall without him, Prodigal stood before the king with Kairu by his side. The king's eyes had softened now that they were alone; however, they were still laden with sorrow. Even the royal guards had left them. Prodigal was torn. He stood before King Earvin, a man he too had come to hate, for how could he not hate this man who had taken Kairu from him—this king who was nothing but a usurper. He had heard his master say this; it was the belief of all who served Lord Theo. The Godfrey house had taken the rule of Qev from the Theo house by mere marriage, generations before, and after all those ages the conflict stayed strong and was now getting stronger. For it was Lord Theo's intent to reclaim his birthright.

"We are ready for you to command, King of Kings." Kairu bowed with grace. Prodigal watched him, the way he looked to the king, and again he felt that rage. Had Kairu lied to him when he said he no longer shared the king's bed? Prodigal had deduced much in the way they interacted—something in the way they looked at each other.

"Find this dog before he kills again." Again, the king's eyes blazed with rage. "Alton would never have wanted to die by a coward's bow. He was too valiant a warrior." The king smiled. "My old friend would have wanted to die looking into the eyes of the man lucky enough to deliver that last deadly blow...instead..." He hung his head in sorrow. "Leave me."

"Yes, King of Kings." Kairu led the way out of the great hall, and Prodigal followed. But as they walked away from the throne room Kairu examined their surroundings before he spoke as softly as he could, making certain they were well out of earshot of the guards. "How can I find a bowman, Prodigal?" said Kairu. "I have nothing…"

"But you do have something, Kairu." Prodigal smiled. "You have the bowman's arrows! What have you done with the arrows, Kairu?"

He had asked his assassin to meet him secretly, but not before night had fallen. It would be too risky to be seen with the fool. The master had packed the reward carefully—a sack of gold, stashed ever so carefully inside the folds of his cloak. The night was warm and the moon glowed above the citadel. With his hood concealing his face the master walked the narrow pathways of the citadel with ease, for he knew it too well. He finally arrived and could see a dark silhouette leaning on the old shack. He glanced behind quickly before quickening his gait. "You fool," said the master when he stood before the servant. "I told you to wait inside." He swept past the servant. "Get in now!"

"…Couldn't get them both," said the fool. "'Twas the other eunuch that threw off my aim." His uneven teeth glistened as he moved close to the candlelight.

"I wanted them both dead," barked the master. "You had enough arrows…and missed the mark. The black eunuch should be dead." He tossed the sack of gold to the table. "You don't deserve this, but I shall keep my word."

The servant bowed. "Much obliged, master." He grabbed the sack of gold with one hand and tugged at his large, floppy right ear with the other. His greedy eyes widened at the jingle of the coins. The master saw his chance and took it. As quickly as he could, he unsheathed the dagger he had carried specially for his other task and plunged it with force into the servant's chest. The enlarged eyes shifted from the sack of gold, shocked. However, his grip on the satchel tightened. "Master?"

"Fool. Did you really believe I would allow you to live, knowing what you know?" The master grinned as he twisted the dagger, still looking into the fool's eyes. "Do not look so surprised. You were dead the moment you accepted my offer…"

The body had fallen to the ground with a thud, but not before the master grabbed back his sack of gold. He left the shack with haste after wiping warm blood from his hand.

><<<<o>>>><

"He has taken everything that did not belong to him!" Lord Theo sat before his retinue with his son standing to his right. "Too long have I served this thief…this false king."

"And he continues to take," said Cedric. "Let us seize the throne now, Father. It is ours by right. We are right here within the citadel!"

Ayden Thorne watched his lord and friend in silence, for it would be unwise to speak, being the son of a dead warrior—that was all he was, especially while surrounded by the members of his lord's council.

Lord Theo eyed his son with scorn. "Don't be a fool, boy. One does not take a citadel with a mere fifty men. We come as guests to Earvin's domain. We shall have our day…but that day has not yet come." The great lord gave his son a sidelong glance. "We stick to our plan—the best chance we have."

"But you command half the army, Father." Cedric slapped his thighs with his palms.

Again, his father glared with impatience. "You best hold your tongue, boy, at least until you win your first battle." Others of Lord Theo's retinue laughed. Lord Theo directed his next words to the captain of his guards. "Lord Byron, what must we do about this eunuch?"

Lord Byron addressed his master as though he were king, taking to a knee with his right hand upon the hilt of his sword. "There is no telling what the eunuch will disclose, My Lord."

"And who is to say the boy is truly loyal, My Lord," added another noble.

Lord Theo nodded with a laboured grunt. "Earvin, you've taken my crown and my lands…now my eunuch—the very same one you rejected across the sea."

Ayden Thorne could endure it no longer. He knew what Lord Theo would say next. "Prodigal is loyal to you alone, My Lord. I have no love for the false king, and I see flames of hate in the eunuch's eyes. It would be wise to wait—see what he learns from the other beautiful one." He thought of the false king's black eunuch and wondered what it would be like to see him close. Prodigal had spoken much of this unique eunuch, Kairu, leaving Ayden Thorne intrigued. *I would kill the false king,* thought Ayden Thorne, *if only to claim his black eunuch as my prize…*

"And why, ranger, do you think this eunuch would forsake his friend and be true to us?" Lord Byron turned to Ayden Thorne with an unwelcome frown.

Ayden remembered well what his father had told him as a child of this man, a ruthless traitor who could easily be bought. *Father has told me all about you, Lord Byron. I know you too well.* The tall, lean captain of battle had obviously remained in Lord Theo's service simply for his own gain, for this was his way. Lord Byron would quickly betray all his oaths to join the winning side.

Ayden Thorne bowed, his thoughts only on what he had learned about Prodigal from the time he spent with him. "The eunuch is faithful, My Lord."

Lord Byron sniggered. "He owes us nothing." He turned to Lord Theo. "We cannot put our hard work at risk on the hope that a eunuch may or may not remain loyal."

Ayden Thorne bowed his head in defeat after seeing the look in Lord Theo's eyes.

## CHAPTER NINETEEN
### *A Dead Man Speaks*

Although the royal wedding was close at hand it was known by most that the two black eunuchs, by command of the king, had been given the task of discovering who had killed Lord Alton Rowe. A veil of darkness had descended upon the city, and all Kairu could think of as he lay in bed was the fact that he knew why the king's closest friend had died. It was evident that Lord Alton Rowe and the woman who had been killed in the marketplace had died at the hand of the same individual; however, Kairu knew this person killed at a master's behest. The black eunuch could not free his mind and had turned constantly in bed. After tossing the linen from his naked body Kairu walked to the window, pondering what he had discovered thus far.

The woman at the marketplace had come to Lord Alton Rowe with an urgent message, one which would obviously change the future of the realm. But she had taken her last breath, only after uttering words which made little sense. This occurred at the start of winter, and although Kairu and the now dead Lord Alton Rowe had captured an image of the mysterious messenger's face after she had died, no one recognized who she was. Then, after the rains, Lord Alton Rowe was struck down in the royal garden. Kairu shivered at the memory of how his friend had died, for he too would have died, were the Gods not on his side...

Now all he had to end this trail of death were five arrows, one which had been removed from Lord Alton Rowe's chest, an illumination of a dead woman's face, and shards of the message she had brought. The prince's wedding to the Lady Genesis Skyers would take place in just three suns. Kairu was determined to discover as much as he could before the royal wedding, for he feared the killer and his master would soon leave the citadel if not already. The black eunuch walked out on the terrace after deciding against awaking his friend. Prodigal had been offered his own rooms; however, he convinced Kairu to permit him to spend his time in his anteroom. Kairu looked in the distance and admired the calm surface of the sea. Beneath the moonlit sky, the sea glistened as though it were a bed of silver. *Ade, I claimed my master as you said I should...but I claim also his sorrows.* So far, Kairu's life had been advantageous—just as his teacher had foretold, yet, at that moment as he watched the sea, the black eunuch wished himself back at the temple behind the stone walls. He wished himself back behind the wooden defences surrounding his tribe, and he longed to feel his mother's touch as she massaged fish oils into his body. At that moment, Kairu would have traded his new life just to be back with the father who had sold him for two sacks of gold coins.

Kairu, descendant of the El Molo, the eunuch of the Maasai, closed his eyes as if to wish away his current life. But the only thing which changed was the realization that a pair of warm arms had enveloped him from behind. He felt Prodigal's face pressed against the smoothness of his back. Kairu wept. Even as Prodigal's arms tightened around him, Kairu kept his eyes shut. And when Prodigal moved around to face him and pressed his mouth against his, Kairu's lips parted willingly, for the sudden passion had somehow pushed the worries from the forefront of his mind. The night was warm, and except for the glow of the moon the night was dark. Kairu's naked body tingled all over as Prodigal pulled him closer…

It was the bright glow of the sun that woke him. Kairu lay facing the window, his body wrapped in Prodigal's muscular arms. *What have I done?* He knew he shared something unique with Prodigal, something special, yet, they were expected to work together to find a killer.

"Good morning, Kairu…Lẹwa…"

Kairu cringed at the utterance of the word, for it was bittersweet. He felt grateful that Prodigal thought him beautiful, yet he clutched his body, suddenly enveloped by sorrow. Kairu, the black one, could not erase the memories of the warrior Prodigal had slain the night he left the temple. Now, he could not help feeling bound to his eunuch brother forever… "Good morning…Prodigal." It would have been dishonest to repeat the word to Prodigal, though he too was beautiful. "We must do as much as we can today, Prodigal. The king wills it."

Prodigal's hold on him loosened at the mention of the king. His friend released a soft grunt before rolling his body to the opposite side of the bed. "Then we must do it with haste," was Prodigal's reply. "We must not disappoint the king."

Kairu paid little attention to Prodigal's tone and the change in his demeanour. "We must first see the artilliator," said Kairu, rising from the bed. When Prodigal looked up at him, his large eyes filled with puzzlement, Kairu explained: "A maker of bows." It suddenly occurred to him just how much of his new life he took for granted. "We must also visit the fletcher," added Kairu. "He makes—"

The Nuba boy frowned. "I know, Kairu. He makes arrows."

The two bathed and dressed before breaking their fast with maslin loaves dipped in honey, cheese and ale. After they finished all that had been brought in, the servants returned with a large tray of fruit. "Are you alright, Prodigal?" questioned Kairu after seeing the way he was being watched.

"You live like a king, Kairu." There was something sad in his eyes.

Kairu pushed the tray of fruit away from him. "I serve a king. I am not one."

"I would be careful, Kairu. Do not be a fool to think your king will live forever…" Prodigal suddenly closed his mouth, shaking his head.

"Prodigal."

His friend pounded the top of the table. "I am only concerned about you, Kairu. There is a killer running loose…if he should…" Again he broke off in silence.

"Come, Prodigal. Let us get to the artilliator's shop." As the two made their way from the castle in silence Kairu could hardly avoid the feeling that his friend knew much more than he said. He reacted to every mention of the king with disdain, yet he showed little respect for his own master. Then it occurred to him why Prodigal was troubled. The Nuba boy knew his master had no love for the king. But it was the fact that Prodigal too despised King Earvin that troubled Kairu most…

Prodigal walked with Kairu, but in his head he heard the words echo over and over again. Ọmọkùnrin wa ni omobirin. *Boy turns girl*. The Nuba boy had spent countless hours wondering what his life would have been like if he were at home with his tribe. It filled him with sorrow, even guilt, when he came to one conclusion: if he had not been transformed, one thing would be missing in his life: there would be no Kairu. The golden sun blazed against a bright blue sky, thus Kairu walked the grounds of the castle clad in his colourful beads and a short red shúkà about his waist. Servants and noblemen alike watched them as they walked toward the castle gate; however, their stares lingered on Kairu. Prodigal heard whispers.

One young boy pointed at the black eunuchs. "Look, Mama…it's Kairu!"

And then the young girl next to the boy smiled wide. "It's the black eunuch," she said.

Kairu nodded toward the children with a smile. "Those children," he explained, "are the grandchildren of the castle's gardener, Prodigal. But we must not stop." The two quickened their pace toward the gate, and as they neared the massive white gates of the citadel four members of the king's guards fell in behind them, for Kairu was forbidden to leave the castle alone. This too was King Earvin's command.

The eunuchs decided to pay the fletcher a visit first. Prodigal entered behind Kairu, with the arrows wrapped in a length of linen. The maker of arrows keenly examined the shafts presented to him before offering an acknowledging nod. "Made 'em miself" said the fletcher. "An I made 'em right…ta go quite a distance, I did." He moved his fingers over the black feather of a raven. When asked whether he could recall whom he had sold such arrows to, the corner of the fletcher's mouth twitched. It took several moments pause before he provided the answer, as well as a reminder that the eunuchs were there to see him at the command of the king. "The bower's always a regular customer…," said Gawayne, the fletcher. His plump face displayed no sign of deception, but there was a glint of sadness in his small eyes. Again he lifted the arrows. "These here be longbow arrows."

The artilliator was not as forthcoming as the fletcher. Prodigal watched the maker of bows and saw contempt within those grey eyes. "Don't sell arrows," said the bow maker.

"But you sell bows," replied Prodigal. He presented the arrows again. "The fletcher told us," said the Nuba boy, "that these arrows are made for the longbow. Tell us who owns a longbow—in the name of the king!" Prodigal felt himself cringe at the mention of the false king's name. He had said nothing to Kairu of what he had learned from the Theo house—what he had seen with his own eyes in the book of the clan's written history. There had indeed been a time when the Theo house ruled over all of Qev. The Nuba boy had made a decision not to betray his master, for he also believed that King Earvin was not the rightful king of the realm.

It was Kairu who eventually convinced the maker of bows to speak. "I shall speak with King Earvin myself," said Kairu. "Your aid in finding the killer of his dear friend, a faithful warrior who defended you and this citadel all his long life, shall be appreciated."

The king's black eunuch caused the maker of bows to smile, and with a gentle nod, he gave just one name. "'was the smith, Ben," he said. "Showed up here several nights past—woke me in the middle o' the night askin' fer them." He motioned to the bows. "Had coin enough fer a new bow as well." The artilliator lifted a longbow from the wall and gently handed it to Kairu. "Like this one here." He smiled as he presented another bow. "Keep 'em if you like." His smile widened.

Prodigal moved closer to his friend. The bow was magnificent. As he touched the bow the Nuba boy noticed how the maker of bows gaze lingered upon him; the smile with which he greeted Kairu had vanished.

They left immediately for the swordsmith's shack with the bows given to them. "The swordsmith does not earn enough to afford such a fine longbow," said Kairu.

"Someone must have given him the coin, Kairu."

Kairu nodded. "The one he serves…and the one who would see me dead." There was a sudden look of determination in his friend's eyes. It was at that moment the Nuba boy realized there was much more his friend had not shared with him.

><<<<o>>>><

The midday sun had reached its zenith, and the fact that the door to the swordsmith's shack was found shut was a sure sign that something was amiss. Kairu stood before the large wood shack and looked to Prodigal as two guards and two tribesmen pounded the wooden door. It was not long before one large guard used brute force to break the door down.

They found Ben, the swordsmith, laying dead on the floor. The swordsmith's face had paled. The sadness of his eyes touched Kairu in a way he did not expect. *This man killed Lord Alton Rowe…and would have killed me.* However, the dead man lying on the floor would provide no clues as to who had commanded him to kill. "What good is he dead?" said Kairu, frustrated.

"A dead man," said his friend, "has much to say, Kairu…sometimes." Prodigal leaned over the body and pointed to the dirty floor. "These footprints are not his, see…" He pointed to a set of footprints before lifting the swordsmith's right foot. The sandals worn had no pattern. However, the other set of footprints had left definite marks.

Kairu smiled at his friend, impressed. "Thank you, Prodigal, I would not have seen this."

His friend then tapped the hilt of the dagger, which had been thrust forcefully into the swordsmith's chest. "I do not think the killer meant to leave this behind, Kairu."

Kairu nodded. The hilt of the dagger was made of silver and decorated with elaborate engravings and inlayed gems. Kairu cringed, closing his eyes as Prodigal pulled the dagger from the swordsmith's chest. After placing the weapon aside along with the bows given to them by the maker of bows, the Nuba boy searched the swordsmith's shack for some time before producing the longbow; this, the swordsmith had carefully hidden within a large oaken chest. Nothing else of consequence was found within Ben's shack. Kairu sighed. His purpose that day had been to find Lord Alton Rowe's killer; however, it had not occurred to him that he would find him dead. "I must speak with the king at once."

## CHAPTER TWENTY
### *The Queen's Gift*

The girl sat before her, seeming lost. Queen Bernice shook her head, disappointed by what she saw before her. It seemed Genesis, her son's betrothed, had become weak, or it may simply be the case that she had not been strong at all. "Mind your posture, dear girl. You shall be my son's queen someday." Queen Bernice walked around the girl's chair, watching her weep. "Will you weep so as you utter your vows for all Qev to see? Shall they know how unhappy you are to marry a prince?"

"Your son loves me not." The girl's sobs were unbecoming—unfit for a queen.

The queen sighed. "I shall not blame you," she said. "It was not your fault…being baseborn, but you must be thankful I have given you a chance to rise above your station." She lifted Genesis's chin. "What is love? Tell me." The girl's pretty eyes seemed empty of thought. "A queen is a mere figure, for it is the king the people love, not us. But you must be strong nonetheless. Take comfort in the fact that you can be more than what they see, even if in secret."

Queen Bernice looked down at the girl who once shared her husband's bed. "You were a fool to ever think he loved you." She locked eyes with the girl. "My husband may have filled your little head with lies...but he never loved you. A king puts his realm above all. This, you must never forget." The queen walked to her dressing table and lifted a golden jewel from a padded box. "This belonged to my dear mother. It is precious to me. It is my gift to you."

The girl's eyes widened in awe at the size of the gem. "Your Grace!"

"Yes, child, a yellow diamond...authentic and rare." My son will give you many gifts—more gems and various jewels than you can dream of. But those are mere trinkets. Today, I offer another gift of far more value than that diamond. Advice." The girl seemed to struggle, as she could hardly decide whether to look at the jewelled ring or her queen. "A queen with heirs is untouchable. My son will be free to take anyone to his bed, but you, child, will not. For a queen to take another man would mean giving the king and the realm a bastard."

"But Your Grace, Prince Kevan—"

"Yes, child, my son already shares his bed with anyone who would oblige. This, I know. But your duty to him is to give heirs to the realm. You need not worry about the bastards Kevan has spawned, for they are all dead." She watched the girl's eyes bulge from shock. "A queen does what she must to protect what is dear to her." She wiped Genesis's tears away. "You mustn't weep so. Go now, child. Your wedding draws nigh and you must look beautiful for all of Qev to see."

After the girl left, Queen Bernice walked into her antechamber, where she had kept her brother waiting. She had kept Percival waiting long before the silly girl had come crying to her, begging for a way out of the marriage. She fixed her brother with a cold stare. "What now?"

><<<<o>>>><

Percival looked to his sister with loving, humble eyes, for he indeed did care for her. Save for her children, Bernice was the only family he had left. "Sister." They stared at each other for some time, his sister refusing to break the contact of their matching grey eyes. Percival waited, endured the torture as long as he could, but he was no match for the queen. Bernice had always been stronger than he. *Father knew it*, thought Percival. *No wonder he always wished she had been born a son…* "By the Gods, Bernice, must you force me to demean myself even when we are alone?" He bowed low.

"I am queen," she retorted. "Now, what is it you want. I have a wedding to see to." She swept by him and busied herself before the mirror, examining an already perfect hairdo and looking at her jewelled hands. Bernice had not changed at all. "Well, don't stand their gawking. Why have you come to disrupt my day?"

Percival cleared his throat. "I…ummm…come, Sister…" He paused for a bit longer in order to choose his words carefully. "Out of concern for your son…my nephew." Already, he could see anger blazing in those cold eyes. "Bernice, I was young once…I know what the boy is going through, but he has caused havoc among the camps. Several noblemen have come to me personally…out of respect, for Kevan will one day rule the realm."

"What of these noblemen?" Bernice turned abruptly from the mirror to face him.

"The boy has bedded four young daughters, virgins, Bernice. And their fathers have come to see me—not your husband. They expect me to fix this, for I am his uncle." Percival did all he could to at least appear as if he cared for the boy, for he knew his sister's son loved him not. The earls, lords and dukes have all threatened to go to the king. They say Kevan has spoiled their daughters, claiming no husband would touch them after the young prince had plucked their virginities."

"Nonsense." Bernice dismissed her brother's concern with a wave of her jewelled hand. "I do recall what you did with the young maids in the stables when we were young, Brother. Do not think I didn't spy on you." She actually smirked at him. "And from what I recall, you hadn't much to please those wenches. Thankfully, my son is duly remembered for what he can do behind closed doors…"

Percival shifted his gaze. The thought that his sister had spied on him shamed him. "Ummm…I came to discuss the failings of your son, Bernice, not mine. All I ask is that you speak with the boy—get him in line. It seems only you are able to get through to him." Percival gazed into his sister's eyes again, wondering what she would do were he to reveal what he knew of her secrets. He held his peace. They were older now. If only his sister could realize that.

"You needn't worry of my son's failings, Percival. Think on yours." Now, her grey eyes blazed with anger. "Think on the fact that you are not a father. Father found you a wife with a handsome dowry; how you squandered it all. Your wife died but a year after you were wed, leaving you childless and alone." She backed away from him with a look of scorn. "You would be nothing without me, Percival. I married a king, ugly as he is, and made you what you are today. So don't you dare stand before me and think you are fit to judge my son." Her grey eyes bulged. "My son! For you are not worthy enough!"

Percival feigned boldness, bowed before his sister, queen of Qev, and left the room without uttering another word. *The day shall come, queen, when you will grovel at my feet…and I shall respond in a brotherly way…*

## CHAPTER TWENTY-ONE
### *Ties That Bind*

She would be a princess by sunset. Her hand would be joined with the prince of Qev and her life changed forever. Genesis sat before her dressing table, surrounded by several ladies-in-waiting, her former peers. Now they waited upon her, the woman once favoured by a king. She wore the queen's gift upon her finger, her bridal gown hung just steps away from where she sat. The gown and the queen's ring were the most beautiful things she had ever owned; Genesis studied her reflection, admitting that she had never looked or felt so beautiful. How had Queen Bernice done it? The queen had made a life next to a king seem so simple, yet Genesis could hardly endure the thought of standing before the Gods and the citizens of Qev, ready to bind her hand in union with her betrothed. She scrutinized the face of each girl waiting on her and could not push unwanted thoughts from her mind. *Which of you will my new husband bed this night, the night of his wedding? Which of you has he taken to bed already?*

Genesis bowed her head in regret, fearful that Queen Bernice had doomed her to a life of misery. The queen had seen her as a threat, yet here she sat, betrothed to Prince Kevan. She had been a fool to embrace the queen's goodness. *She loves me not.* Genesis thought on what she had done to deserve the prince's hand. Nothing whatsoever. She had brought nothing but grief to Queen Bernice's life; why then would her kindness be pure and true? Her mother-in-law's affection was false and the love she feigned concocted. But to what end, Genesis could not tell.

Prince Orin pushed through his brother's servants and into his rooms, for they were nothing to him, not even the guards. The anteroom of Lucas's suites was unkept and dark. "Come out, little brother," said Orin. "We mustn't be late for our brother's wedding." He pushed open the doors to his brother's bedchamber and found him seated by the window. "Come, come, little one," Orin teased again. "Do not let the death of the smith trouble you so, for he was nothing but a murderer."

Lucas shot him a scathing glance. "He was not."

Orin shook his head. "Lucas! We've talked of this before. The smith was nothing more than a common servant; his life meant nothing." The second prince of Qev studied the way his young brother held a sword crafted by the smith's own hand. "You are most ungrateful, young brother. You came for my help when Father's black eunuch summoned you for questioning." Orin could hardly believe what he had just said. He had expected more of his father, king of Qev, for it was unnatural for one whose rightful place should be a slave, to interrogate princes. "'Tis bad enough," said Orin, "we have a weak father." He took the sword from his brother's hands. "…A weak king."

"We should have told the eunuch the truth." Lucas's eyes were tired. "He knows I've lied about knowing Ben."

"Brother, you are a prince. Father's black eunuch mustn't be feared." Orin tossed the sheathed sword to the floor. "Beautiful as he may be, the eunuch has no power; he only wields what powers our father gives."

"The eunuch is clever." Lucas said this with his eyes fixed upon the sea.

Orin conceded with a nod. "A valid point, young brother."

"What must we do? This black eunuch has become a thorn in our sides." Orin watched his brother rise and retrieve his sword.

"Your hunger for vengeance clouds your mind, Lucas." Orin scratched his chin in thought. "The eunuch spends much time among the scrolls and books of the library, yet I cannot tell what it is he seeks."

"And he must have found something," added his brother. "Why else would he leave the citadel?"

Orin concurred with another nod. "'Tis unusual, the eunuch leaving the citadel on the eve of the royal wedding."

"He's taken the other one with him."

"Two black eunuchs on a king's errand…and to what end?" The second prince bit his nails. "I predict this errand will bring us nothing but grief…"

><<<<o>>>><

"Could this not have waited, Kairu?" Prodigal moved uncomfortably in the saddle, for unlike what he had expected, he detested horses. The beasts never seemed to like him. Kairu, on the other hand, rode his palfrey with such grace. *Even beasts bow to him.* Prodigal pulled on the reins again and the stallion he rode whinnied, as if to scold him. Riding before them were three royal guards; two tribesmen, appearing just as frustrated with their mounts as he, followed behind them. Prodigal did not feel unsafe, for there was peace in Qev, and no one would dare provoke the king's wrath by harming them. He looked ahead toward King Earvin's royal standard. The red banner trimmed with gold bore the image of a wild boar; this was their protection outside the walls of the citadel. Neither King Earvin nor any of his kin were present, so by tradition, his powers were temporarily extended to Kairu, descendant of the El Molo…just a boy of the Maasai. How strange it was, thought Prodigal, to see his friend wield the power of a king.

Kairu remained as calm as ever beneath the hot sun. The dirt road was rough and dusty, and as Prodigal shifted in his saddle again his inner thighs ached. "Will you not answer me, Kairu." The Nuba boy looked behind; the citadel was no longer in sight. He did not expect to see the citadel, for they had left the castle just after sunset the previous evening.

The El Molo boy lifted his chin with pride and conviction as though he were king of Qev. However, before he replied he looked behind as if to ensure they were not being overheard. "We have so little time," replied Kairu. "It is the king's command." The boy of the Maasai said nothing more. In fact, as they rode onward, Prodigal could not push one thought from his mind. He could not help but think that Kairu did not trust him.

><<<<o>>>><

The piece of parchment bearing the face of a woman long dead was secure inside a leather satchel. After discovering the body of Ben, the swordsmith, a determined Kairu had walked the castle with the painted parchment, making certain every servant saw the dead woman's face. The black eunuch had nearly given up hope when a young scullion directed him to the only person within the castle who could identify the mystery messenger. "Ol' woman Gertie," said the young maid. "I reckon she'll know…"

Kairu had left the castle immediately after speaking with the old woman, Gertie, though they had to spend the night at an inn. What he learned from Gertie had brought the black eunuch closer to the dead woman, Petrona. He reached into the satchel and pulled out the image of Petrona's face. *What secret did you take to your grave?*

"The old woman said Petrona lived alone, Kairu." Prodigal's impatience since they left the citadel had become unbearable. "What good will come of riding this far today?" asked Prodigal. "We will not get back for the wedding, Kairu…so many have come for the feast."

"The ride back will not be long," said Kairu. "We will be back in time for the feast." He pointed ahead. "There!" The cruck house was by no means large, yet this place with a garden, now overgrown, was once the home of the dead woman, Petrona. The walls of the cruck house were of wattle and daub and the roof of thatched straw. Once inside, Kairu and Prodigal found nothing within but a table and several stools, and a bed of straw on the dirt floor.

They found no valuables within the cruck house other than the objects needed for daily living. Kairu left the dwelling disappointed. But as they mounted their beasts an old crone appeared from the thicket. "What business have you in my neighbour's house?" She used an old branch as a cane. She looked from the guards to the royal banner. "What business does the king have with Petrona?" The old woman had her eyes fixed upon Kairu. "The talks be true then," said the old crone, "…of the false king's dark men from across the sea."

"You are mistaken, old woman." Kairu locked eyes with the crone. She was short, ugly and obviously sound in mind. "There is but one king of Qev."

She smiled at him, bearing broken, rotted teeth. "These be Lord Theo's lands." Her right eye, which was larger than the left, widened. "'Tis the Theo house should have rule o' the land."

"What do you know of the woman Petrona?" Kairu would not allow the crone to speak ill of the king.

"Good woman, was she." She watched Kairu suspiciously. "Ain't set eyes on her a whiles…"

"She lays dead."

The crone nodded. "Expected such."

Kairu dismounted and approached the crone. He towered above her. "Dear woman, I beg for your help." He produced a golden coin. Her larger eye brightened.

She looked deep into Kairu's eyes as she reached for the coin. "There's much to tell, black master from across the sea." She reached to touch Kairu's skin with a grin. "Me thinks she died for what she 'ad to tell."

The black eunuch nodded. But before the crone could utter another word, Kairu motioned toward the cruck house. "In there." As he shut the door behind them Kairu saw displeasure in his friend's eyes.

## CHAPTER TWENTY-TWO
### *Royal Wedding*

The saviour of Qev. This name, the killer of so many had given himself, for only he could set things right. He alone would right the wrongs of many, now long dead. He had endured the wedding ceremony with distaste. It seemed all of Qev had come to witness the joining of Prince Kevan and his betrothed, the wench who once shared King Earvin's bed. Seated among the nobles, the one responsible for the death of King Earvin's friend carefully observed the newly crowned princess. The poor girl was lost, terrified it seemed, for she had damned herself to a life of sorrow and turmoil. Her prince, as handsome and royal as he looked, had no passion for her, yet the king, it seemed, could hardly shift his gaze from the girl. *The false king, they say…this is what they say you are…*

It was not that he had no love for King Earvin; overall, he was a good man…but a fool he was. The saviour turned his gaze from the king and examined the queen. She could not take her eyes off the boy. He knew what she had done; her betrayal was abominable—something that should never be spoken of. *It is you I protect, king.* The saviour had trouble sleeping as of late—a result of having too much blood on his hands. What he had done was for the good of the realm; he could not forget this. But why then, he thought, had he not told the truth? Why had he killed to keep truths from the king? *I can't stop now,* thought the saviour. *I mustn't, for all those I've killed will have been for naught…*

The king's black wench, the thing he had brought from across the sea, was a clever one. It was he who should have died. *But I have had my eyes on him. He gets closer…so much closer…* There was only one option left. The black eunuchs had to die. The saviour had made certain they would find nothing at Petrona's dwelling. Finally, the saviour smiled. Anyone watching his face would have guessed he smiled at the prince and his bride. By sunset the secret he had killed to protect would be entirely safe. Only he should know it…only he should use it…

Kairu of the Maasai…Qev's saviour had heard this name uttered a thousand times. However, as he observed everyone within the great hall he found the eunuch's absence refreshing. Ben had failed in ridding Qev of the beautiful beast, but he would not escape again—not this time. King Earvin had been a fool, thought the saviour. He had elevated the black eunuch above his station, for as beautiful as this Kairu was, he was not worthy enough to change the bedding of the lowest of the common folk within the realm. The thought that his king had made the black one his advisor angered the saviour. *You forced my hand, King. You made me side with your enemies…and now I fear I cannot stop what I've started.*

><<<<o>>>><

The dances at the feast had begun, and Lord Hayden Bourne made certain he was the first to save the king from obvious torture. As quickly as he could he glided across the floor and greeted the royal highnesses with the lowest of bows. "Cousin, I must protest," said Lord Hayden. "For you have kept your beautiful wife to yourself all evening." He bowed before Queen Bernice. "May I be presumptuous, my queen, to ask for the next dance?" He took her hand before she extended it, pulling her from the king's weak grasp.

Queen Bernice did not resist. In fact, she allowed her body to relax as they swayed away from the king toward the centre of the dance floor. "Thank the Gods you've rescued me from that horrid man." Her grey eyes became narrow slits.

"But you make such a splendid couple…Highness." He grinned with sarcasm.

"Don't be silly." The queen dug her nails into his shoulder. "He sits by my side, still longing for the little wench. I fear I have erred, the girl isn't worthy of my son."

The king's cousin rolled his eyes. "Do I see jealousy in the eyes of the queen?" Lord Hayden spun the queen ever so gracefully, knowing many eyes were upon them. "The girl carries a pretty face, she shall produce lovely heirs for the realm."

She dug her fingers deeper into him, eliciting a sudden, quiet gasp. "My son must have the throne; that is all I need."

"And what of your other children, loving mother?" Lord Hayden raised his brows. "I can assist with putting the boy on Qev's throne, but—"

"Make Kevan king!" The icy spheres widened and the queen's body tensed. "It is Kevan's line that matters, not theirs. I am content to see them live well, but none of my other children should ever inherit the throne."

"And of the two concubines?" questioned Lord Hayden. "The news comes directly from my cousin's black eunuch." He saw sudden interest in her grey eyes. "Yes, Majesty. The boy does make mistakes."

"Where are these concubines? Who are they?"

"Worry not, Highness, we shall find them."

She eyed him with suspicion. "How did you learn of this? The eunuch could not have told you."

The king's cousin grinned. He held the queen away from him, with such grace that others around them cheered, as they moved so well with the music. "No…that eunuch, my queen."

"Ahh…the strong one." Her gaze brightened. "Have you shared this with our friend?"

"Yes, Majesty." Lord Hayden Bourne glanced over his shoulder; his cousin, the king, had brought his beloved daughter, Cylene, to the dance floor. "It is arranged."

"Yet," said the queen with scorn, "you made a mess of things." She made certain no other could overhear her words. "I am furious! Lord Alton Rowe was not supposed to die—no one was supposed to die."

Lord Hayden Bourne now saw coldness in her eyes. "Pity the fool is dead." He spoke of the swordsmith. "He was but a messenger to me, nothing more." The regent whispered his words through gritted teeth.

"Then who else could have killed him if not you?"

"I know not." He paused briefly, allowing others to sway by them. "I'd have killed him myself, but the fool never reported back to me after I sent him off to deliver a message to our friends." He looked into the queen's eyes and saw the same reflection of worry, for he had assumed it was she who had the brute killed. Finally, Lord Hayden Bourne smiled. "Our lowly friend, it seems, had another master."

"Who?"

He pulled the king's wife close to him, just so his lips slightly grazed her ear. He could feel her body tense in his grasp, and for a brief moment he wondered who tended her needs, for every woman had certain needs… "Your guess is as good as mine, Majesty."

><<<<o>>>><

King Earvin danced with his beautiful daughter, yet as he swayed, joined hands and turned her time after time, he could not help but watch as though he were a vigilant watchman. Cylene moved gracefully with him; however, the king was not entirely with his daughter. Instead, his eyes watched his friends…and his enemies. It was evident many of his lords and captains were not with him, for he saw it in their eyes…the tension in their bodies when near him. *Even now they look at me strangely.* The king exchanged nods with countless nobles.

The queen still danced with his cousin; Kevan had left his bride alone to dance with an earl's daughter; and this new bond between his two younger sons, though strange, was refreshing. His children seemed content. Orin and Lucas had not left each other's side since the wedding celebrations began. The king's brows converged. "Where has the time gone, Daughter?" He gazed down at Cylene, amazed by her beauty. "Kevan marries his bride…" he cringed at the utterance of his words. "What shall I do for my other children? You too must be betrothed…and your brothers also need wives."

"Oh Father, why must you fuss about such things." Again, Cylene gazed off to the right of the great hall.

King Earvin followed her gaze and locked eyes with Lord Theo, commander of half the realm's army. The two exchanged nods. Next to Lord Theo stood his only son, Cedric. "Surely, Daughter," said the king, "you are not besotted by Theo's son."

Cylene laughed. "No Father, but they have not looked away since our approach to the dance floor." No sooner than Cylene had finished her words, Lord Theo himself rose and left his retinue with the young lord at his heels.

"And here they come," said the king. "I dare say the good captain shall ask that I give you to his son."

"I would die first."

Lord Theo and Cedric were upon them, leaving the king no other choice but to pause their dance. "Your Majesty." There was no sincerity in the way Lord Theo bowed. "It seems my son cannot keep his eyes off your lovely daughter." He bowed low. "Princess Cylene. The Gods have blessed you with beauty." Cylene responded with a modest bow of her head.

"Might I have the...pl...pleasure...Your Highness?" Cedric's hand trembled as he extended it toward Cylene.

"Not her, you fool," scolded his father. "You asked the king—the father's permission. Have I not taught you the protocols of courting a royal maiden?"

"Sorry, Father." The boy shifted his gaze and extended his hand toward the king. "Your Highness...I beg..." He wiped sweat from his brow.

In an effort to rescue the boy, King Earvin presented Cylene hand. "You may have one dance, Cedric." The boy seemed to be in awe that the king remembered his name. Cylene went reluctantly.

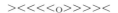

Things could not have been better. The royal wedding had been a great success; however, her dance with Hayden had vexed her spirit. Their conversation had left her worried, for the fact that Lord Alton Rowe's killer had been killed by someone unknown to them was troubling. The queen was seated at the royal table, doing her best to ignore the useless babbling of her two younger sons. The two had eaten their fill and had lowered their babbling to a whisper. It had taken several attempts to get through to Kevan. *Stay by your bride's side,* she had warned. Yet, he had insisted on dancing with every beautiful maid within the great hall.

Queen Bernice had kept her eyes on Earvin and Lord Theo as the two conversed out on the terrace. From afar, the two seemed inseparable—a king and his captain enjoying the evening breeze. But the queen knew what they presented to nobles and common folk alike was false. There should always be peace between a king and his captain, for this was good for the realm.

Cylene had danced with Lord Theo's brute several times before being rescued by the boy's attendant, a handsome, strong boy who seemed no older than the prince.

"Young brother," said Orin. "It seems our dear sister has found herself a suitor." His words were followed by his childish giggle.

"Nonsense." The queen studied the attendant, noticing the way in which he held her daughter. "A princess cannot marry below her station."

"And why should we care about one's place in life?" said Lucas. "I stand with Cylene; she should be free to choose whom she loves, whether it be a nobleman or a man of low birth."

"Do not torture me with such talk, Lucas." The queen lowered her head, shaking it in frustration. She returned her attention to her daughter and Lord Theo's attendant. The boy was handsome—a perfect match for her daughter, yet there was a hardness to him she could not stand. Their smiles were sincere; Cylene had never seemed happier. Queen Bernice closed her eyes and allowed herself to be swept back into the past, basking in nostalgic bliss. She was as happy as Cylene now looked—happier even. She too had wanted a man well beneath her station—a member of the king's guards. And he had served Earvin's father, King Bernard, true and faithful. Earvin was just a boy, but he was the only prince of Qev. Her only true love was long dead—murdered by Earvin's own hand. However, she took solace in the fact that her love had taken a part of Earvin with him to the grave. "He took your life…and you took his face," the queen whispered. "If only you had lived and he had died…" Queen Bernice got hold of herself and blinked the tears away before they surfaced.

## CHAPTER TWENTY-THREE
*Throne, Crown, Power*

The black eunuch and his best friend had ridden for their lives, for all their guards were dead. The first two of their protectors—the two strongest—were shot down by arrows, while the others fought hand-to-hand and gave their lives to protect the eunuchs. That had been their king's last command. Two nights had passed since the attack, leaving the two black eunuchs exhausted and famished. The last word from their protectors was to ride. Kairu could still hear the booming, deep voice as the guard fell with the blade of a bandit's sword in his chest. Kairu alone had killed several of the bandits, but there were too many of them.

"What shall we do, Kairu?" asked Prodigal. The Nuba boy had been wounded by a bandit's blade—stabbed in the abdomen. The two had ridden hard and did not stop until they found refuge at a quiet farm. They had tied the beasts in the thickets and travelled on foot to the quaint dwelling, which appeared to have sunken into the ground, for only the roof was visible atop the greenest bed of grass. There had to have been dozens of mounds, all covered with the greenest grass Kairu had ever seen. They had hidden themselves among the stalks of corn, just as the sun disappeared behind the clouds. And now, here they were, comfortably resting within the sunken dwelling with the towering tree above it.

"We must get to the king," replied Kairu. He looked at his friend's wound. "…I must get to the king."

"No, Kairu. You will not leave me here with them." Prodigal's eyes shifted to the two grinning children.

"They have been good to us, Prodigal." He looked toward the twin boys and smiled wide at them. They were frisky little ones. Kairu leaned close to his friend. "Besides," Kairu whispered, "their sister—"

"No, Kairu! I am content with the woman my master has given me."

Kairu had not revealed a word of what the crone had told him. What he knew was to be told only to the king. Kairu sat before his friend, frustrated with himself, for the answers he sought had been right before his eyes, there on the shelves within the castle's library.

"Kairu!" Prodigal raised himself ever so slightly and gripped his arm. "I will not stay here alone, Kairu. We leave together." There was a look in his large eyes that forced Kairu to respond with a conceding nod.

><<<<o>>>><

The two eunuchs rode through the gates of the citadel with haste. Something had changed. As Kairu dismounted he noticed the absence of the king's tribesmen. The familiar faces among the king's guards had been replaced with faces he did not know. He could feel the eyes of the guards digging into him from all angles. "Something has changed, Kairu."

Prodigal's eyes became filled with worry. His friend looked from the face of one guard to the next. "We shouldn't have come back, Kairu."

"I must see my king." The black eunuch looked toward the stone steps ahead, but felt his friend's sudden grip to his shoulder.

"Kairu, please." Prodigal had tears in his eyes. "I do not think your king is alive, Kairu…" He shook, his head. "I have killed him."

The El Molo boy looked to his friend, puzzled. "What have you done, Prodigal?"

"I wanted to tell you, Kairu…but…they say he is false. They say he stole the throne…" Prodigal fell to his knees, even as the guards formed a circle around them. "Forgive me, Kairu."

As they were dragged up the steps of the castle Kairu locked eyes with his friend, the one he had thought to be his brother. "Take me to the king at once!" A painful blow to the face from the back of a king's guard's hand quieted the black eunuch.

When the two were brought before the massive doors of the throne room, Kairu sighed with relief. "He asks to see the king," said the strong guard. "Open the doors."

The double doors swung open slowly. *My king will send them all away,* thought Kairu, *And then he will punish those who plot against him.* His eyes caught view of the white throne. There were many others standing before it. The guard loosened his hold on him and Kairu took one step forward before collapsing to his knees. His body had become weak, with hardly any strength left to cry out, but Kairu moaned sorrowfully. Through tear-filled eyes, Kairu, descendant of the El Molo, the black one of the Maasai, saw seated upon the white throne someone who had no right to it. The guard pushed him forward with a hard kick. "There's your king, black eunuch. Crawl to him and kiss his feet." Kairu heard laughter. Everyone laughed, even the queen.

*"You are Kairu…you are a descendant of the El Molo. Remember this, my son."* The black eunuch heard his father's voice resound inside his head, and found strength to rise. He would not crawl to this new king. As dirty as he was, Kairu walked the aisle toward the white throne, and there, seated with a grin of concocted poise, was Prince Kevan.

His finger bore King Earvin's ring. "And now you bow to me, eunuch…for I am king." His eyes were cold.

Kairu looked around the great hall. How could so much have happened in so short a time? The eunuch did his best to serve as Ade had instructed him; however, as he bowed, he felt no joy in it. "Gr…Great King." To utter such was worse than death, for this boy seated upon the throne was no king. Kairu cast his eyes to the floor, but not after engaging the grey stare of Queen Bernice. He did not see Princess Cylene or the other princes. "I wish to see King Earvin."

"In time, eunuch." The new king stared at him with what appeared to be a lustful gaze. "Dear mother, what shall I do?" He adjusted the crown upon his head before turning to Lord Theo, who stood to the right of the throne. "Regent, shall I permit this…thing to see my father?"

Lord Theo kept his eyes fixed upon Kairu. "Let him see his false king."

The wound to his abdomen throbbed, yet the pain of sorrow Prodigal felt was far worse. He wept silently as his friend, Kairu, was stripped of his beads and red shúkà. The naked black eunuch stood next to his naked king. King Kevan had commanded that everyone leave the great hall—all except his mother, his uncle, and Lord Theo and his retinue. They all watched Earvin, the false king in his nakedness.

It was the false king who broke the silence. "My own son," he said. "You've been a fool, boy. They have used you to get to me…who will they use to rid themselves of you?

Queen Bernice spoke for her son, for the boy appeared to still fear his father, though it was he who had crown, throne and power. She looked down at her husband, who had been forced to kneel before his son, and spat upon him. "It is you who are the fool, you ugly dog."

"Woman, you have damned this realm and your children." He looked to Lord Theo. "You put the future of Qev into the hands of a cruel line…their blood is cursed, I tell you."

"And you killed the man I loved. You took my Asquith from me." She slapped the scar on his face. "My father gave me to you, for I was his to give. And he knew how much I loved Lord Theo's brother."

"Bernice, the man was a dog! They were the ones who waged war against my father, and your hand was deep in their plot. I had to kill him."

"Careful how you speak of my blood, false king!" Lord Theo's hand went to the hilt of his sword. "I will skin you right here."

King Kevan clapped both hands together. "Enough." But somehow, no one within the hall seemed to heed his calls. "I am king!" Lord Theo's hand grabbed King Kevan's neck and squeezed, his eyes still upon the false king. King Kevan choked.

"You keep your mouth shut, boy." He stopped his own son's sudden burst of laughter with one quick glance before dragging King Kevan from the throne.

"Silas, how dare you? Kevan is king!" The queen rushed to her son.

"Shut it, woman." He snapped his fingers and suddenly two of his guards moved toward the false king. "At midnight, the bells shall toll to announce the death of Qev's beloved king. The boy shall be crowned, and I shall be named regent." A faint smile surfaced.

"You promised Kevan would rule over all Qev," cried the king's mother.

"That was the agreement, Lord Theo," said the queen's brother. "The boy is to sit on the throne and the rule of the realm fall to the council…and the regent…of course."

"Plans have changed." Again, Lord Theo snapped his fingers. He tapped the hilt of his sword as his attendant stepped forward. Prodigal knew him, for it was the same attendant who had rescued him long ago from the young lord of Theo Manor. Cedric Theo had not mistreated him from that day forth. But as he drew his master's sword from its scabbard Prodigal cringed. Ayden Thorne looked to the false king with hate-filled eyes.

The false king looked Ayden Thorne in the eyes, even as the young attendant raised the blade with skill and brought it down ever so swiftly. The cut to the false king's throat was clean and precise; as the false king gasped and his blood streamed down his chest toward the floor, Kairu's scream was shrill and his sobs uncontrollable. Queen Bernice buried her face against her son's heaving chest. Lord Percival turned his back upon the massacre, leaving only Lord Theo and those of his retinue looking down at the corpse of a fallen king. Prodigal shut his eyes.

## CHAPTER TWENTY-FOUR
### *Revelations*

The black eunuch sat with his body immersed in a tub of scalding water, yet he still felt dirty and defiled. It was late at night. Kairu had put out all the candles himself, and had even drawn his own bath, for he was no longer permitted the luxury of servants. Nearly all within Lord Theo's retinue had made use of him. Kairu had been from one noble to the next for nearly five suns—lord Theo's gift. The puppet king, Kevan, had not been seen since his coronation, for he was just a symbolic figure for the people of Qev. The true ruler of the realm was Lord Silas Theo; it was he who sat upon the white throne. The boy was intended to use the throne only when protocol dictated.

Prodigal's attempts to see him had been futile, for Kairu had little desire to speak with his betrayer. The Nuba boy had told his master of King Earvin's plan to sire new heirs. The two concubines now lay dead at the hand of the tyrant, Lord Theo. Even in passing, Kairu heard Prodigal's pleas of forgiveness, but the black eunuch had hardened his heart and closed his ears.

Kairu closed his eyes in sorrow, for he lacked whatever energy was required to weep. His king was dead, and a powerless king sat upon the white throne. But the one thing that hurt him most was the fact that Prodigal seemed to relish his new post, for it was he who commanded the servants within the castle, as Kairu once did. He quickly rose from the large tub, as it too had become a source of the sorrow which enveloped him. He had been much younger when the dark old man's blade made him a eunuch; however, Kairu remembered it vividly, though he had been sedated. He dried his body quickly, for his new master had commanded that he visit another's bed this night.

As always, Kairu arrived at a different room within the castle, unaware of who awaited his arrival. His duty was to serve. The rooms were dim and no servant attended. Kairu pushed the door shut behind him and shuddered at the thought of whom he would find in the darkened room. The last pale-skin was old and had drunk too much of the castle's wine. It had become common for the black eunuch to simply lie quiet while those he served took what they liked, for it had become his purpose. He would not forget what his papa had told him—that everything happened for a purpose…

Leaving the anteroom, Kairu entered the bedchamber silent as a cat. He approached the bed and saw no figure lying there. He breathed a sigh of relief and was about to turn and leave when a hand grasped his shoulder. Kairu yelped. "Do not fear me, black eunuch." He recognized the voice—Kairu would never forget it for as long as he lived. This was no man, nor was he a noble. It was the murderer—the killer of his king. The murderer caressed the side of Kairu's face; the black eunuch closed his eyes and turned his face away. "I do not wish to take you by force," said the man who slew the king.

"My king's blood stains your hands." Kairu stepped away from Ayden Thorne. "And your master now gives me to you as reward." The eunuch wept, even as Ayden Thorne grabbed his arm and pulled him close.

"You are not the same as the other," said Lord Theo's man. "You are…beautiful."

"And your heart is black, for you killed a king." The black eunuch pulled himself away with more force.

"A false king." The smell of wine was strong on his breath. "He deserved to die," said the attendant, his words laced with uncertainty. The slayer suddenly gripped Kairu's throat, and the eunuch winced as his beads dug into his skin. The murderer pulled Kairu's body against his. The two were the same height, so their stares were locked. There were tears in the murderer's eyes. "He was meant to die…false king…"

As the weeping killer fell to his knees he clung to Kairu's leg. The eunuch looked down in awe. What was he to do? He watched Ayden Thorne, unable to react, for he felt no pity for this man who had killed the King of Kings. Yet, Kairu, descendant of the El Molo, boy of the Maasai, stooped low and placed a hand upon the killer of his king. He realized that Lord Theo's attendant was just a boy who had never taken a life. "Why?" asked Kairu. "Why did he deserve to die?" And he saw the answer within the tear-filled eyes. Ayden Thorne had killed a man, not for his own beliefs, but for those of another—Lord Silas Theo.

Ayden Thorne appeared to be immediately enveloped by sudden realization. "I…I don't know. I wanted to prove myself worthy…" His body trembled as his sobs escaped.

Cylene walked into the library to find her mother, Lord Percival, her uncle, and her siblings, all waiting impatiently. She had not left her rooms since her father's body burned upon the bier near the sea. All of Qev had mourned the death of King Earvin, the last Godfrey to sit on the white throne. Her gown of embroidered black silk fit so closely she could hardly breathe. The library was silent, for those she found there did not utter a word, so the princess decided against breaking the solemnity within. However, she did wonder why she had been summoned by the black eunuch. Had her father left specific instruction with his servant?

Since her father's death, Cylene had felt nothing but contempt for the man with whom she had danced at the royal wedding. In fact, she had hardly seen this Ayden Thorne since he murdered her father. She glanced at her mother, who sat alone near the window. The queen's face was cold as ice. Kevan had come alone. King only in name, he seemed lost. His bride had not left her rooms since their union, for her new husband had refused to visit her bed the night of their wedding.

Her two other brothers, Orin and Lucas, sat together, also silent, for it appeared that they too grieved the father they once despised. It seemed grief had brought the brothers even closer, for they had become inseparable long before their father's slaughter. The silence within the library was suddenly broken with the arrival of Lord Hayden Bourne.

"Ahh, I'm not alone." As always, her father's cousin grinned cynically. "How foolish of me to assume that the black eunuch summoned me here for the sake of having me all to himself." He brought finger to his lips. "Shhh…I've heard talk that all in Lord Theo's retinue have had my dear cousin's leavings…"

"You are a dog." Cylene's eye cut into him like knives. "Our father, your own cousin, is dead, and this is how you speak of him."

"Forgive me, Highness," said her father's cousin after a mocking grin. Lord Hayden Bourne extended his arms and displayed the most exaggerated bow. He was well aware that Lord Theo had kept them alive simply because the people of the realm would rebel, were they to discover that he had wiped out the entire royal family.

"Enough!" Cylene's mother still stood near the window; she twisted a black lace handkerchief in her hands. "I can endure no more of this."

"You were part of the plot, Mother." Orin's gaze was unforgiving.

"It was not supposed to happen this way," their mother answered. "Kevan was to sit upon the throne."

"But he does, Mother." Orin seemed disappointed. "Our brother sits upon the white throne, tamed and powerless. Your plot failed…and we're all left here, lucky to have our lives."

"You betrayed us all for him." Lucas motioned toward Kevan, who simply sat there biting his nails. The once arrogant Prince of Qev, heir to the white throne, now seemed shaken. "How else did you expect this to end, Mother. None of us could ascend with Father still alive."

"Oh dear." Lord Hayden Bourne moved across the room with flamboyance. "I fear my presence has caused…a bit of…friction." He was about to say more when the black eunuch entered the library. All eyes turned to the doors.

Kairu's entrance was, as always, graceful. Cylene observed this *descendant of the El Molo*, as he had always been announced, still intrigued by his elegance. It was not that the eunuch was effeminate or ladylike; however, he carried himself with a sense of innate confidence that commanded all to forsake other thoughts and actions and look to him. The black eunuch's bow was slight; yet, there seemed to be something majestic in it…something royal. The library had fallen silent again, and it seemed no one would utter a word until this dark eunuch permitted it. Cylene sat with her eyes fixed upon this creature, amazed by his poise and his presence. She glanced at her brothers and saw that they desired him; her father's cousin too looked at the eunuch with longing, while her mother eyed the esteemed eunuch with scrutiny. Only her uncle appeared unscathed by Kairu's presence. "Greetings." His gaze told them all there was no need to respond. The eunuch walked toward the large desk with cause, and showed no sign of fear.

Cylene found that she could not ignore the beauty of the eunuch's full lips. She admired the smoothness of his dark skin, the length of his legs, as well as his long arms. Even the mark of his branding appealed to her. The black eunuch had only said one word—that was all it took to send tingles throughout her body. Visions of his lips against the nape of her neck sparked inside her head like lightning against a rainy sky. She saw his long legs wrapped around her and could almost feel the sensation of their tongues touching…

"Why have you summoned us, eunuch?" Lord Percival's lips curled with distaste as he looked the eunuch up and down.

The black eunuch was calm. He was not afraid. Again, Cylene watched Kairu with a sidelong glance, for surely the Gods had not created this creature simply for use as a mere servant. This Kairu of the El Molo was destined for greater things; of this, Cylene was certain. It was the way he looked at them—something in his eyes. Kairu's gaze seemed deliberate as he addressed Cylene's uncle. As always, his words were preceded by his slight bow. "I have come to tell you a story," said Kairu. His eyes shifted from Cylene's uncle toward her mother. "…A story of three births."

## CHAPTER TWENTY-FIVE
### *The Book of Births*

He saw flashes of worry within the eyes of the queen and her brother. Kairu paid little attention to the others within the library, for he was not yet ready to address them. The black eunuch was ready to tell all of what he had discovered; however, he needed something to help present his tale—*The Book of Births*. So he gracefully moved from behind the desk and retrieved his proof—a record of the births of all those who had claim to Qev's white throne. It did not matter how small that claim was, nor did it matter if this claim was of the past or in the future. The large book was carefully bound—made to last ages. The metal clasp had kept the book properly sealed; however, it had not prevented the pages from aging. As he unlocked the latch Kairu looked to the individuals he knew had knowledge of what this book of births could tell. Lord Percival and Queen Bernice exchanged swift glances; Lord Hayden Bourne's eyes were fixed upon the red book, embellished with illustrations of flowers. Finally, Orin examined the book with a finger pressed to his lips. The studious prince seemed puzzled; it was impossible to glean anything from his blank expression.

Lord Hayden Bourne moved forward. "Ahh...*The Book of Births*." He took quick glances about the library before looking upward to the dome-shaped ceiling. When his eyes met with Kairu's again he said, "I tend to forget our eunuch is able to read."

Kairu opened the great book and leafed through the pages of times and births; however, he had already marked the pages he needed. The eunuch took his time. Finally, he looked to the queen, Bernice. "Tell us of the day your first son was born."

"I do not have to answer to you, eunuch. For you are nothing." Her grey eyes were like steel. "Speak what you know and be gone..."

"Bernice..." Her brother rubbed his palms together as he moved closer to his sister. He leaned in close enough to her ear to ensure his whispered words were not heard. The queen nodded, suddenly calmed by the words of her sibling. "My sister is...not well." His grey gaze was identical to his sister's. "Why do you bring such questions...such disquiet, you insolent dog? You have brought nothing but trouble here. I advise you to leave the citadel, or by the Gods, I shall go directly to Lord Theo!"

Kairu bowed in acknowledgment, for he knew Lord Percival's intent was to instill fear. "Then be prepared to report to him," said Kairu, "how you had Lord Alton Rowe murdered." Lord Percival was not an old man; however, hearing Kairu's words, a sudden wave of vulnerability seemed to sweep over him. This, Kairu realized, was uncertainty, for it was evident the queen's brother was simply attempting to guess how much he knew.

"Nonsense!" His palms met once again, this time held upward as if in prayer to the Gods.

Kairu pointed to Kevan, who had no claim whatsoever to the white throne. "You are no son of King Earvin…you never were." The princess, Cylene, gasped; however, Kairu continued. "He is son to Lord Theo's brother, now long dead." He looked to the queen. "Isn't that right, Your Majesty? Prince Kevan is no prince at all, for he is neither the king's son…or yours."

The queen scoffed. "All Earvin needed…all he wanted of me… was a son. An heir for his kingdom. I gave him what he wanted, but I did so on my own terms." She wrenched her arm from her brother as he attempted to silence her. "I must speak, Percival. I can bear this burden no longer." The queen bowed her head after looking to her legitimate three children. "I loved your father." Her words were directed to Kevan, who simply stood by with his mouth ajar. The realization that he was not of noble birth, as well as the fact that the queen was not his mother at all, was evident in his eyes. The queen continued to free her conscience.

"I did the only thing I could to have my vengeance. After Earvin had Asquith killed I discovered he'd had a bastard—born just days before my own son. The midwife told me, you see. And there with a swollen belly before me; with pain to my back and sweat on my brow, I pushed with conviction. I wished the child dead, for the Gods had given me my vengeance. It had to be the Gods, for the mother of Asquith's new son had died in childbirth. She'd been poor—just an alewife, I was told. When Petrona laid Earvin's son upon my breast, I was suddenly displeased…the blue eyes…" The queen clamped her eyes shut. "I wouldn't look at him, for I'd already disowned the boy."

Kairu watched the faces of the queen's three children. They had drawn close together, shocked by what they had heard. Yet, the faces of Lord Hayden Bourne and Lord Percival showed no signs of surprise. Cylene, Orin, Lucas and even Kevan all looked to the queen, intrigued.

"At first," she continued, "I never thought the midwife would agree. But for enough silver, the low ones will do most anything…every dark deed has its price. It took no time to convince Petrona to do as I asked." The queen eventually paused and seated herself upon a plush cushion. Her eyes studied the lace handkerchief in her hands. She breathed deeply before resuming. "I commanded the woman to fetch the child and have it brought to the castle immediately. All it took to distract Earvin was a simple lie. The midwife told him there were complications—a long painful childbirth." A smile swept over her lips. "I'd not expected it to be so easy. By dawn the next day I had a new son…one I could truly love. And I did love him. Never think I haven't loved you, Kevan…for in my eyes you are my son." She did not find the courage to look to Kevan or her other children.

"And what of our brother?" asked Orin. He looked to Kevan with scorn. "The scrolls tell of the feud between the Godfrey and Theo houses, and you raised their own blood, their kin among your own children? Do not speak love, Mother…for you know nothing about love."

Queen Bernice began to weep. "If you only knew what he did to me. Your father was a monster."

"Your tears mean nothing." Orin's attempts to abate the sorrow which enveloped him failed. His voice quaked and his body convulsed. "You taught me to fear him…to hate him. What sort of woman are you?"

"He was a vile man."

Orin now mopped tears from his eyes. "I remember having nightmares, all for what you told me—that Father was a beast…a monster." Cylene rushed toward her brother and consoled him with an embrace.

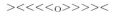

A mere servant sat presiding over them—nobles. What had Qev come to? Lord Percival paced the library as his sister spoke of the past, while Earvin's eunuch presided over them as if ready to deal death and judgement. He had advised against answering the eunuch's questions, for not even Lord Theo would discuss what occurred so long ago. He was no fool, not such a fool as Bernice. *I answer to the Gods alone, for only they can judge me.* Lord Percival had blatantly refused to answer the eunuch's questions, so it had been left to his sister to reveal the truth of what occurred so long ago.

"Percival knew what I did." He stopped pacing at the sound of his name and glanced at his sister. Bernice had managed to compose herself. She had tucked her lace handkerchief inside the sleeve of her black gown. "I had to tell my brother, for we shared everything. Percival knew what I'd been through…he knew what Earvin had done to me." She looked to her children with pleading eyes. "I did not love your father, and I couldn't—not after being in love with another man. But my father had made his choice. I begged him, pleaded with him, I did. My own father told me that love meant nothing. I was to wed Earvin Godfrey, prince of Qev, and it was final.

"I was a young girl in love when I was given to Earvin." She looked toward the window. "He took me that night knowing how much I loved Asquith. He even laughed at me…taunted me, for he could hardly stand me; this he told me, even as he entered me and spilled his seed. And I hated him for all those long months with the child growing in my womb. So, you see, I could never have loved the child. He was dead to me."

"But what became of our brother, Mother?" It seemed Lucas, like all the rest, was afraid to hear the answer.

Lord Percival had had enough. "There is no brother, boy." He said. "The child never survived the night." Percival watched the eunuch carefully. "When Bernice sent for me I went immediately, so pleased to be the first to see and hold my nephew. I was terribly vexed when Bernice spoke of what she had done, for she had commanded the midwife, Petrona, to toss the boy into the well or leave him in the woods." The queen's brother reflected upon his own unfortunate life, for the Gods had not seen it fit to bless him with a family. His wife had died not long after they were wed. "But when she revealed this abominable plan I begged her to reconsider…but your mother," he looked to the three siblings, "is not easily swayed. And she had a way of getting exactly what she wanted, especially when we were children." For a moment Lord Percival's mind drifted. He could do nothing else but smile.

When the doors opened and servants brought food, Lord Percival welcomed fruit, cheese and wine. The wine was strong and much needed. "It was the perfect plan. Word had come from the midwife that Asquith's paramour had had a bastard, one he knew nothing of. And what did it matter? Asquith was dead—killed in battle." He turned to Earvin's children. "Your father and Asquith despised each other. Earvin was prince; Asquith felt his rightful place was to be prince, for it was the Theo house which had held power in ages past. They were never friends, and while their feud had lasted all their young lives, many said the prince only begged his father, King Bernard, for Bernice's hand, not because he loved my dear sister, but because he knew Asquith did."

He was about to continue when the black eunuch interjected by lifting his arm. Lord Percival sniggered, shocked by the audacity of the lowborn scum…

The sudden shock, which had paralyzed Kevan's entire body, was beginning to ebb, yet, he could not evade the thoughts which seemed to attack from all corners of his mind. Again, he wiped sweat from his brow with the back of his hand. It had been awhile since the others within the library had looked his way…already he was invisible to them. If Kevan could have quietly left the library he would have, for with each detail, he realized he did not belong with the Godfreys. *I am of the Theo house, and now, they have the power.* He remained quiet, calm as still water. Kevan willed himself to come to terms with what had occurred. He had been stripped of his titles of king and prince of the realm; however, he was not without worth. He was of noble birth—son to Asquith Theo and nephew to Lord Theo, ruler of the realm. He would let the fools have their say, for that was all he could do…at the moment.

It made sense now, knowing that Earvin Godfrey was not his father. The distance between them had been justified, for they were never father and son. King Earvin must have known who he was. *He must have seen something of my father in me…* Suddenly, the desire to know who he really was overwhelmed him. Kevan needed to find out all he could about his father. He looked to the woman he had loved all his life as his dear mother. She had loved him all his life; however, Kevan could not decide whether that love was sincere or simply remnants of her affections, which were intended for a man long dead. The black eunuch would not stop leafing through the massive book. He stopped Lord Percival with a wave of his hand. The man Kevan had known to be his uncle all his life fixed his grey stare upon the black eunuch and clenched his fists.

"I have spoken with Petrona's friend," said the eunuch. "The old woman told me all she knew." The black eunuch smiled, as if he relished the power of some knowledge he possessed that the others with him did not. "The woman Petrona had come to report all she knew to Lord Alton Rowe…and you killed him." His eyes were fixed upon Lord Percival.

"No one was supposed to die…I simply wanted to keep things the way they were." Lord Percival shook his head as if to apologize. He looked to his sister. "The midwife had been well paid, but it seemed no amount of silver could quell a guilty conscience—"

"The woman was a fool," blurted the queen. "You had a right to have her killed."

Kevan saw this new woman with different eyes, for she was not his mother at all. She had made certain that all the young maids he had been with disappeared. Had she killed them too?

"Quiet, woman!" Lord Percival seemed shocked that he had spoken harshly to the queen. He bit his lips and rubbed his palms together.

"Petrona told all she wished to tell Lord Alton Rowe to the old woman." Kairu still leafed through this *Book of Births*, casually. Unlike Orin, Kevan had not shown interest in the books and scrolls of the library, so he watched the black eunuch, puzzled. What was it he needed them to see within the book? "Your Majesty." He looked from the book to the queen. "Your natural son was taken by Petrona to be killed or left for dead. Lord Asquith Theo was dead, but after his paramour had given birth she died. But there was another birth. Another woman had a child. Three births are involved in this plot, not two. Three mothers, all connected to a single purpose, devious as it was. Three sons had been born. But one was dead."

Lord Percival, the queen and Lord Hayden Bourne watched the eunuch with interest. As for the three he thought to be his siblings all his life, Kevan saw that they were as eager and shocked as he. But no one uttered a single word.

The eunuch rose from behind the desk and lifted the massive red book. "*The Book of Births* tell us all," said the eunuch. "My king had blue eyes…but all of his line had different eyes." The black eunuch paused and slowly looked from one person to the other before continuing. "Except one." He raised his dark brows slowly.

"You speak in riddles, boy." It seemed Lord Percival had lost all patience, for he lifted his trembling hands and dragged them down his face.

"The woman, Dorcas, had given birth to a stillborn son." The black eunuch placed the red book upon a cushioned chair and beckoned everyone close. Kevan looked with interest at King Earvin's name on the parchment. A detailed description of the king and those of his line followed. Kevan even saw his own name there. "Nothing of this child was recorded within this book," the eunuch pointed out, "for he was of low birth." He turned the pages of the book as he looked to Kevan. "Lord Asquith Theo was of noble birth." As the black eunuch's finger moved down the page and stopped at the small illumination, Kevan staggered back, for this confirmed the tales of Lord Percival and the woman he had known to be his mother. Kevan wanted to speak and could not.

"By the Gods!" Orin leaned over the book and touched the drawing, which had been left upon the parchment long ago. The birthmark, which had been recorded at the time of Lord Asquith Theo's birth, looked identical to the mark Kevan knew he had on his shoulder. Orin looked to Kevan. "You have the same mark, Brother." He grinned at Kevan with satisfaction.

"This is true," confirmed the eunuch. "Prince Kevan is the natural son of Lord Asquith Theo."

"And what of this other child?" asked Lord Hayden Bourne. "I'm afraid you've left us confused, eunuch."

"The old woman spoke of a woman named Dorcas. She could tell me no more of her, for Petrona, the midwife, had said nothing of her—only that the true prince had been given to this woman as replacement for her stillborn son." The queen gasped; however, the black eunuch continued, even as she cupped her face with both hands. "The true prince of Qev lives. The midwife's last words did not make sense." He fixed his gaze upon the queen's brother. "You commanded the swordsmith to quiet the midwife, Lord Percival…after she had come to you with word that she could keep your secret no longer."

"She said nothing of this other child…that Bernice's son lived," said Lord Percival.

"Petrona would have told all to Lord Alton Rowe. But you had him killed. Before he died, Lord Alton Rowe begged me not to utter a word of what the woman said to my king. And I obeyed. I was wrong."

"But what has become of our brother, eunuch?" Lucas asked. "We must—"

"Forgive me, Your Majesty…I do not know." The eunuch bowed with reverence. "The midwife told the old crone nothing more of this woman, Dorcas. She raised your brother as her own son…but this was somewhere near or within Lord Theo's lands. I did not have time to find this woman and the prince. All Petrona told the old woman was that Dorcas could not have endured the shame of not having a child. She feared her husband would have put her aside for another. And since the midwife did not have the heart to kill the innocent baby or leave it in the woods to be eaten by savage beasts, she gave the child to Dorcas to ease her sorrows and bring happiness. She did not want the blood of a child on her hands…"

Tried as he could, Lucas could not imagine what his eldest brother could possibly look like. However, he took comfort in the fact that the true heir to the throne of Qev lived. They were all still gathered around *The Book of Births*. Lucas looked down at the page of the book, still shocked at what the eunuch had shown them. He had seen Kevan's birthmark ever since he was young; he had been afraid of the dark mark at first, but seeing it painted on the parchment brought happiness. The brother he had loathed all his life was never really connected to him, for he had been a false prince.

He turned to look at the false brother and quickly gripped Orin's shoulder. "The brute has run off!" All eyes looked to the spot where Kevan stood. He was not within the library.

"Oh dear." Lord Hayden Bourne lamented by lifting a hand to cover his brow. "We are all dead. Dead!"

Lord Percival bowed his head and allowed his body to fall to the cushioned couch beneath him. "There's only one place that boy could have gone." He looked to the black eunuch, as if to seek advice. "What now? You have sealed our fates, eunuch."

"Mother, you must go to him," Cylene urged. Her cheeks had reddened and her eyes widened. Lucas knew she would do no such thing. All her life, the brute had been her weakness.

"We must flee the castle as soon as we can." Never had he seen Lord Hayden Bourne so nervous. "I implore you," said their cousin. "Lord Theo is a ruthless man…he will—"

Suddenly, Orin moved toward their cousin and looked up into his face. "I know what you did, Cousin." His eyes burned with sudden rage. "You were never loyal to my father." Orin was swift. He pulled their cousin's dagger from its scabbard, which dangled at his side. "I should have known all along that you were the source of the rumours." Lord Hayden Bourne, their cousin, cringed as the blade was pressed against his chest. "This dagger…" Orin's eyes shifted to the hilt. "Ben's work. The smith made this, for he made a similar one for Lucas." He pushed the dagger inward. "What was your business with the swordsmith, dog?"

Their cousin closed his eyes. "He will kill us all, boy. Turn me loose and let us all flee from this place at once."

The black eunuch gently touched Orin's shoulder. "We must not be found here, Your Majesty."

"We leave when he tells me the truth. Did you have grandpapa killed?" Orin lifted the dagger and pressed it against their cousin's slender neck. "The rumours said Father murdered Grandpapa to ascend to the throne. What do you know of this?"

"It…it was no plan of mine, I tell you." Lord Hayden Bourne sniffed. "The smith delivered my messages to Silas's messenger; I merely wrote the letters."

"Ben couldn't read," added Lucas.

"Why…yes…but…it was Silas Theo's plan to move King Bernard out of the way. Earvin had nothing to do with it."

Lord Percival's groan echoed. "What a fool I've been. The smith took our coin…"

The eunuch nodded. "He killed at your command, Lord Percival…and would have killed the king himself if he could." He shifted his gaze to Lord Hayden Bourne. "Lord Theo gave a command to kill the king. Lord Alton Rowe once told me King Bernard may have been poisoned." The eunuch raised a brow.

Lord Hayden Bourne opened his mouth to reply when a loud noise resounded. The library doors burst open and a flood of guards were upon them. They were quickly surrounded. Moments later, Lucas watched as the false prince entered with the eunuch Prodigal behind. The two eunuchs exchanged glances in the silence before Prodigal spoke: "Take them to the king."

King? Had this dog, Lord Theo, proclaimed himself ruler of Qev?

## CHAPTER TWENTY-SIX
### *Escape*

Lord Silas Theo sat upon the white throne as though he had had the access and the right to it for all his life. It did not appear as though he simply aspired to be king, or even wanted to be ruler of the realm. He believed it, for it glowed from within him through his eyes. At first, Kairu refused to engage the usurper's gaze. However, he soon had a change of heart. *Let him kill me where I stand…for I do not fear him.* This, he wanted the false king to know; he wanted this man to see and know that Kairu, descendant of the El Molo…the black eunuch of the Maasai, was not afraid to die. Silence reigned over the great hall as the two lost themselves in a challenging gaze. Kairu had his arms clasped behind him; he had long decided he would not bow before this king.

He could see Prodigal standing to his right; however, Kairu had also decided he would not speak with the betrayer. He could hear Lord Percival's deep breaths behind him. Kairu would not look away from the false king; he did not blink. Finally, the false king smiled. He shook his head in denial, though he had lost. "I am king. I can have you skinned alive where you stand if I wish it, black eunuch. But I have other uses for you." The usurper snapped his plump fingers. "I am king. Kneel!" His rumbling voice echoed within the massive hall.

The sharp sting of a leather whip to his legs forced Kairu to fall to his knees in agony. Yet, he did not look away from those wretched eyes. The false king's son, Cedric, stood to the right of the white throne; Kevan had found his place to the left. His retinue was scattered about the great hall, while the guards lined the walls. King Earvin's killer stood behind the false king with one hand on the hilt of his sword. It seemed he had forgotten how much he had wept after killing a true king.

"I would have been merciful, but it seems you've decided to side with this." The false king motioned toward the black eunuch. "I've been to their lands…I know what these people are. Worthless."

"I was once told," replied Kairu, "that I was worth more than gold." *What would Ade say if he were to see me now…defying a pale-skin?* His teacher had once said that his very life belonged to his master. Lord Theo was no master of his, thought Kairu. The false king's eyes gave the command and another lash of the whip stung, this time to the eunuch's back.

"We would be grateful…for your mercy, King." Lord Hayden Bourne stepped ahead of Kairu and fell to his knees. "Great king, show us your mercy."

"The traitor." The new ruler of Qev regarded King Earvin's cousin with a sniggering gaze. His eyes moved again with commanding might; there was also a nod. As Lord Hayden Bourne rose two royal guards moved swiftly to King Earvin's kin, once regent of the realm. "I'd be a fool to think you could ever be loyal to me; after all, you could hardly be loyal to your own blood." Another nod. When one of the royal guards unsheathed his sword and slit Lord Hayden Bourne's throat, two shrill screams resonated. Kairu turned to see the queen and the princess clinging to each other. Lord Hayden Bourne brought both hands to the wound; his eyes widened in shock. He soon fell sideways, his body twitching.

Kevan smiled. He now stood boldly beside his uncle, for he seemed to have forgotten the fear that had crippled him within the library at the revelation of who he really was. "It is as I've said, Uncle…Your Majesty. He knows all." Kevan pointed an accusing finger at Kairu. "Queen Bernice's natural born son lives…as alive as we are now." The queen gave a sudden start, seeming hurt that the boy she once loved and cherished as a son all his life had addressed her as *Queen Bernice*—not *Mother*.

The false king glared at them all with bulging, angry eyes. "Where is this prince the midwife was too weak to rid us of?" His fist pounded the arm of the throne. "Tell me, eunuch! I shall find him and kill him myself."

"I do not know." Kairu would not address him as king. He bowed.

"The child was given to a woman…she was of low birth and had a husband." Kevan pinched his chin as he considered carefully. Suddenly, the false prince snapped his fingers. "It was the woman, Dorcas! That was her name…a woman named Dorcas who had been barren. She got the child!"

When the false king and his son both glanced at the king killer simultaneously, Kairu gasped. How could he not have seen it before? Ayden Thorne was swift. He unsheathed his sword instantly and backed away. "My guards, to me now!" shouted the false king. The sound of steel within the hall was deafening. Ayden Thorne looked around with fear, suddenly feeling like a trapped animal cornered on a hunt. He had been completely surrounded.

Kairu looked from the false king and his son to Ayden Thorne, and he knew instantly that they would kill King Earvin's eldest son, the rightful heir to the white throne.

Princess Cylene and the queen still clung to each other; however, could not shift their gazes from Ayden Thorne.

"Give up, boy," said the false king. "There is no place to run. I do not blame you for what you are…but you see…" The usurper smiled slyly. "I have to kill you. You have served me well."

Ayden Thorne's blue eyes danced. His hands trembled as he gripped the sword's hilt with both hands. But when the first two guards approached him with swords held high, the prince moved with stealth and skill. They moved against him, with force, yet Ayden Thorne parried while the sound of metal against metal echoed within the great hall. Eventually, the first guard fell dead, but not before his sword cut into the young prince's abdomen. At that moment, Kairu witnessed the bravest effort a young boy could ever have made. The Gods must have been with young Prince Lucas, for he pushed his way toward the dead guard and swiftly picked up the blade. "Brother!" He said this as the blade skewered Ayden Thorne's second opponent. Kairu and the others could do nothing, as they were soon encircled by a flock of royal guards with blades pointing toward them.

Surely, Kairu thought, the princes would die. Yet, again, the Gods must have been with them. Young Prince Lucas grabbed his brother's arm and dragged him beyond the white throne, and with a quick push of the wall a secret door was opened. The way was dark—Kairu saw it; however, in a flash, the newly reconciled brothers were gone. After the secret door was pushed shut, the false king bellowed. "After them, you fools!" But their efforts to open the doors was to no avail. Kairu smiled. He had known of the secret passages; however, he had not explored them.

"It's of no use," said Kevan, the false prince. "You shall never find them. The passage doors can be locked once you get in. No one will get that door opened now."

The false king eyed Kairu and the others with contempt. "Throw them to the dungeons," he commanded. "Surround the castle. No one leaves the citadel until Ayden Thorne is found—dead or alive."

><<<<o>>>><

The secret passages of the castle were pitch black at first. Lucas led the way without uttering a word, and though he could have moved much faster within the dark, confined space, the young prince was restrained, as he was leading the wounded. Lucas thought of what he had done within the great hall. Where had the courage come from? And why had he saved this brother of strange? They had had to stop several times before, as Ayden Thorne had become weak. The wound bled profusely. Lucas had cut away a portion of his own cotehardie and bound his brother's wound. It seemed like ages since he, Orin and Cylene had played together in the passages; however, Lucas's memories of the place were vivid. *I can almost find my way with my eyes closed…*

When the two exited the bowels of the castle, the scent of sewage stung his nostrils. "We mustn't delay," Lucas urged. The sun still shone bright; it was a large risk to go where he intended to go by daylight; however, it was their only chance of survival.

Ayden Thorne paused, taking deep, laboured breaths. "Go."

"I will not leave you here to die." said Lucas, more determined.

"I…I killed your father."

"Yes, you killed our father. Maybe I will kill you," Lucas replied. He was suddenly enveloped by sorrow, as he had come to realize what a fool he had been. With his father now dead, Lucas was plagued by regret and guilt. Why had he not spared at least one moment to show his father how much he longed to be like him. Their mother had done all she could to make them fear the king; however, Lucas had always loved and adored his father. Now he was gone, dead.

The sun hung against the backdrop of the blue sky like a golden disc. Lucas looked into his brother's blue eyes as they leaned against a massive black boulder, and saw his father's eyes. He had not paid much attention to the stranger before, as he had been just another of Lord Theo's dogs. Ayden Thorne had murdered his father, yet Lucas had not looked into his eyes.

"You'd best kill me now…end my misery and be done with it," Ayden Thorne replied. "For I've killed a man I was taught to hate…my own kin, my blood. My father." He hung his head sadly and wept. "All my life I thought I was nothing. And here I am with you, a brother I never knew I had."

"Come." Lucas knew they could not linger. "Or we both die this day."

He knew precisely where Lucas was taking him, for he had been there before—many a time. Ayden Thorne limped behind his brother, though he wished the Gods would take him. He was not worthy to have lived. *I have killed a king—my own sire.* Lucas relayed the convoluted details of their lives, all that the black eunuch had told. To suddenly learn that the woman he had adored all his life—the mother he loved—was no kin to him, but that his natural mother was queen of the realm was impossible to accept. It was impossible to point blame to his mother, Dorcas, for all she had ever done was love him with all her heart. A sudden surge of pain forced him to fall to his knees once more; it was the pain alone which reminded him that he had not been in a long, treacherous dream. When his brother rushed to his side and offered his shoulder, Ayden Thorne hung his head shamefully. "I cannot repay you for what you have done." He could not look into Lucas's eyes. "My life shall not be the same," said Ayden Thorne. "I shall have no peace for as long as I live."

"Then you must live," said Lucas. "Your life shall be your penance." His brother pointed ahead. "We've made it."

Again, Ayden Thorne hung his head low. He knew the cave well, for he had met the smith there many a time. The cave seemed a different place entirely by day. Ayden Thorne could not have explained why he had kept his knowledge of the secret entrance to the citadel from his master. His smile was faint. "We must get to my mother at once."

"We've got no horses."

Ayden Thorne nodded. "I shall remedy that."

## CHAPTER TWENTY-SEVEN
### *I am Kairu*

The dungeons were cold and dark. Kairu sat upon a bed of straw and could feel insects and other vermin crawling over his feet. The stench of urine and feces was near impossible to endure. From the small hatch high above, Kairu could see that it was night. Already, three suns had passed since the false king imprisoned them. The black eunuch bowed his head low in defeat. This could not have been the life Ade had intended for him. "I should have left all alone," said Kairu. Lord Alton Rowe had been a good man and was now dead. King Earvin too had died…and a few others. Had Ade seen what was to come? Had he even foreseen what Prodigal would do? Kairu shook his head and whispered again, "Papa…all things happen for a purpose…"

Prince Orin was held in the cell next to him. Lord Percival had been placed at the far end, while the princess and Queen Bernice were locked together across the cold, narrow passage. And what had become of Ayden

Thorne and the young prince…brave Prince Lucas? Kairu had not expected the prince to have grasped a dead man's sword and fought…and killed.

When the door to his cell creaked open, Kairu looked up to see Prodigal standing in the dark. The Nuba boy stood and gazed at Kairu as though he had not seen him before. Finally, courage came. "You must forgive me, Kairu. I did not—"

"You betrayed me, Prodigal. Because my king is dead…and so are his concubines and his heirs."

Prodigal fell to his knees. "You must believe me…it was Nadira I told."

"The woman he gave you?" The black eunuch saw his friend nod.

"It was Nadira I told, Kairu. She must have told him." The Nuba boy pushed his hands against the sides of his head. "I am a fool. I will help you, Kairu. Let me set you free from this place before he…" There was a look of sadness in his eyes. "I haven't much time, Kairu. I free you and the others from this place."

Kairu took his arm. "Only if you come with us, Prodigal.

><<<<o>>>><

King Silas Theo. This was his new name. Yet, the people of Qev knew him not, for they still believed that it was Kevan, son of their beloved King Earvin, who now ruled the realm. "The actions of that woman may one day ruin all I've worked for." He looked to his only son, Cedric, his mouth bitter with disappointment, for it was obvious he had no clue of what was really at stake. The Cedric Theo he knew would welcome Earvin's son, still thinking him closer than a brother, and all the while this boy, with the blood of the Godfreys running in his veins, would plot to slit his throat and regain what the Theo's had reclaimed. Silas looked to Asquith's son—all along he knew what the boy was. *Why shouldn't he still serve a purpose greater than himself?* Silas knew Cedric was incapable of ruling the realm. The boy was an idiot. *And I was a fool to think of Ayden Thorne as the son I never had…the son I so longed for…*

Ayden Thorne would have done anything for him once—once when he believed he was just the son of a poor widow and the best friend of a young lord. But now, for obvious reasons, the boy had to be blotted out like a dark error on the richest piece of parchment. Silas looked again to Cedric. The boy looked everything like him—the reflection of a true king. But what good was physical likeness, Silas pondered, if heart and valour were lacking? For these a true king could not live without.

It was his nephew who offered a solution to their problem, while his son stood there and looked toward the window as though he longed for the boy, Ayden Thorne, who would have killed him. "Uncle…they will seek to put him in your place." Kevan moved closer to the white throne. "You must kill the black eunuch; he knows all. Ayden Thorne must be hunted down," said his nephew. "Kill the sons of Earvin Godfrey. Spare the women." The boy grinned. "They need not know who I really am, the people of Qev. Let me tell the people what you wish them to know, Uncle."

Finally, Cedric found the courage to speak. "Will you give my father grandsons?" Cedric shot his cousin a scathing stare. "You've had your chance. Let me have mine as prince."

Silas smiled. Was it shock that suddenly swept over him or was it pride?

When the new chief of his guards burst through the doors of the great hall Silas leaned forward upon the white throne of Qev. "What is all this?"

Klyos was young and strong but fear clouded his eyes. "My Lord." He shook his head in failure, eyes fixed upon the floor. There on one knee, with a hand upon the hilt of his sword, Klyos spoke it loud and clear: "The prisoners have escaped us, great King."

*Great King.* Silas was somewhat distracted by the title. "Speak sense, dog. There are many prisoners in my dungeons."

"I speak of the queen…Your…Majesty." Klyos wiped sweat from his brow. "She and her kin are nowhere to be found. The black eunuch is with them, my king."

He could not contain his fury. Silas's voice filled the hall. "I commanded that eunuch to keep watch!"

"It was he who freed them…My Lord. Six of your guards are dead. Poisoned."

"And Prodigal?"

Klyos cleared his throat nervously. "Gone with them, My Lord."

Silas fell backward upon the white throne and shouted aloud, for only that was enough to stop him from weeping.

Klyos removed a length of parchment and extended it toward the throne. "The black eunuch, Kairu, left this with the dead…Great King." With a nod to his nephew, Silas commanded that the message from the eunuch be read aloud.

Kevan glanced at Cedric as he snatched the parchment from Klyos's hand. "It comes from the black eunuch, Uncle."

"Read it."

Kevan read. "*Your time upon the throne, false king, is near an end. This I promise you. I am Kairu.*"

## CHAPTER TWENTY-EIGHT
### *No Crown For A King*

They had acquired strong steeds to take them to safety. Ayden Thorne's wounds had been properly bound and now he sat upon his steed with Lucas, his brother by his side, eyes fixed upon the place he once called home.

"Do you think it safe?" questioned Lucas. "We have watched the house all night long. No one has come or gone."

"And yet," said Ayden, "I have not seen my mother." It was unlike his mother to allow the sun to go down without tending her garden. Something was amiss. "We've wasted days," said Ayden, "…lingered far too long."

"You were injured and would have died if we had not stopped to rest."

"He has taken Mother captive—this I know." Ayden gripped his sword's hilt. "Let them kill me, but I will not let Silas Theo harm my mother."

"They will outnumber us," replied Lucas. He looked carefully from the cover of the trees. "But there are no horses."

"I grew up around this man, Lucas. I know him."

"Then what must we do?"

"We face him—die if we must."

"You are my brother now," replied Lucas. "But you speak folly. I did not risk all to save you for the sake of sacrificing ourselves to your false king."

Ayden smiled. "False king…that is what I called our father all my life…" He unsheathed his sword with determination. "I am grateful for what you have done, Lucas. If I die this day, may the Gods be with you. You are not bound to follow me, Brother."

Lucas's eyes were filled with tears. "And where shall I go, if not by your side. You lie. For I am bound to you. You are my brother…my leader…my king." Lucas dismounted, sword in hand. "I will follow you."

><<<<o>>>><

Lucas and his brother ran side by side as they charged the quaint cruck house. Lucas had meant every word of what he had said to his brother Ayden; if his moment had come to die, then it would be so. The young prince was terrified, for though he would soon be a man he had yet to live. He had not yet known a woman. Simply put, Lucas had not yet lived. These things flooded his mind as the youngest of King Earvin Godfrey's sons charged forward with a sword in his grasp.

Lucas was just several paces behind when Ayden crashed through the door with force. The two shouted as though they charged with the company of a thousand men. They found themselves inside the cruck house brandishing their swords before seven others. The woman, Dorcas, called out to her son. Lucas and Ayden stood with their backs together. They paused in shock as their swords were lowered. "How can this be?" said Lucas.

The black eunuch spoke for all. "The Gods favoured us, Highness." Kairu's white teeth sparkled as he smiled with a bow of reverence.

Cylene was upon him moments later. "Oh Lucas, my brother, I thought you dead."

He held his sister at arm's length, still in shock. Lucas looked from one face to the next. His uncle, Lord Percival, stood close to his mother; Prodigal lingered near the window; and the one face he did not know had to have been that of the woman Dorcas. Orin, his brother, greeted him with a beaming smile before joining with their sister in a loving embrace.

"We must not linger here too long, Your Majesties." The black eunuch's voice interrupted their brief reunion. "We waited as long as we could."

"The eunuch knew he would come for his mother." Orin fixed his gaze upon their brother for just a brief moment; his eyes contained neither respect nor contempt; he simply regarded the brother who had made them fatherless with a blank, meaningless stare.

Ayden Thorne pivoted nervously before looking to the woman, Dorcas. "Mama…I…" He said no more, for the woman rushed into his arms. Ayden fell to his knees and wrapped his arms around her waist, his fingers clutching the fabric of her cotehardie. Ayden Thorne wept.

"Forgive me, my son…" Her sobs filled the room.

"No, Mama. I cannot blame you for what you did. You are…my mother."

"Oh, Ayden…my boy." She looked down at him with pure adoration. The woman, Dorcas, smiled amidst her tears. She wiped Ayden's tears away with the palms of her hands before kneeling to kiss his face. Lucas, the brother who had lived a luxurious life within the royal castle, watched in awe. The love he saw before him was mutual, sincere, real. He would give all he had for what he saw before him. Lucas, Prince of Qev, had never before felt such envy. He could not look at his own mother.

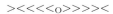

It was deemed unwise to remain upon Lord Theo's lands, so all agreed to Ayden Thorne's suggestion to retreat to the town Lunaris, known for its beauty beneath the night's moon. They left before sunset, all in the guise of poor, common travellers. Kairu still wore his beads beneath his cloak. The group of nine had left the house of Dorcas with nothing but the rags they wore, several loaves of maslin bread, some cheese and, only for when it was needed, a satchel of gold coins. Their valuables had been left in Kairu's care; all had agreed to this, except Lord Percival. Even Queen Bernice's ring bearing the royal seal had been given to him. The three women were carried by the steeds, while the men walked.

Now with the blazing sun behind them, Kairu walked in silence, pondering. How would they manage to carry out this plan they had concocted? And what would become of them were they captured by the false king? Surely, they would not live. Had he been made a eunuch simply to die in this world that was so different from his own? Kairu walked along, confused, for his king was dead. He had lost his purpose. Forced to think of his father again, the black eunuch wished he could at least ask these questions of the man who had sold him. "Papa," he whispered. What had become of his family?

Prodigal's appearance at his side pulled him away from his thoughts. "You are troubled, Kairu." His friend caressed his arm. "I have failed you, Kairu...this I know. But I beg you...forgive me."

Kairu nodded. "You are always my friend, Prodigal, my brother. We were created together, you and I." He looked to Ayden Thorne—King Earvin's son walked beside his mother's steed. "Must we forever run for our lives?" asked Kairu. "What will become of us? We go to this place, Lunaris. Ayden Thorne tells me it is a poor, abandoned town—the last place the false king would think to look."

"What other choice do we have, Kairu?" Prodigal pushed his hood away from his face.

"Our faces must not be seen, Prodigal." The Nuba boy nodded. "We will retreat to this place and wait...but for how long, I do not know."

They reached Lunaris at sunset. Kairu saw nothing but old dilapidated dwellings all inhabited by poor, malnourished folk. Many heads looked out from windows and from behind ruined walls to see the strangers passing through their village.

The group found refuge and rest inside an old cruck house, and there they set up camp. By nightfall they were all comfortable around a fire and gladly ate maslin loaves, whatever wine Ayden Thorne had found from an alewife, and cheese.

Lord Percival finished his second cup of wine before posing the same question as before. "I come from a noble house. Look at me now. Look at us! How long must we live as vagrants? Shall my dear sister, queen of this realm, live as a beggar for the rest of her days?"

"My Lord"—Kairu swallowed his last piece of cheese—"the people of Qev will follow the true king—"

"A king they do not know, boy." He shook his hand at the eunuch before biting into his maslin loaf.

"Patience, Uncle." Orin sipped his wine. "Our eunuch speaks sense. Ayden Thorne must seize the white throne, for he is father's rightful heir." He still could hardly look at his brother and king.

"I shall soon die if I am to live like this," said Queen Bernice. She had yet to speak with her son, the king. Only Cylene and Lucas seemed to have welcomed and forgiven their brother. Kairu wondered whether he could forgive any man who had killed his father. Many a time, he had seen the queen watch her son. The queen he once thought a cold, vile woman, now seemed vulnerable and sorrowful. The woman before him was cumbered by pain and regret. She needed to hold her son, for she could not bear to see the woman, Dorcas, comfort the king.

Kairu rose and moved from his place around the fire, for there was but one thing he needed to do. They did not have much, yet he found what he needed to complete his task. The black eunuch filled his cup with wine. He approached Ayden Thorne and knelt before him. "Highness." The discomfort in Ayden Thorne's eyes was evident in the way his eyelids fluttered. Taking his hand and leading him closer to the others, Kairu asked King Earvin's eldest son to kneel. "Your Highness. I pledge to you my service and my allegiance, for you are king of Qev. Only through you can the rule of the realm be restored to the Godfrey house."

"I am not worthy."

Kairu looked to the others. They gathered around as he poured the wine from the cup upon his sovereign's head. "Great King. Son of Earvin Godfrey and ruler of the realm. We pledge to follow you." The black eunuch allowed the king to rise. "You are a king without a crown, My Lord. But I serve you still. He was first to kneel at his king's feet before the others followed. "How may we serve you, King of Kings?"

King Ayden pulled Kairu to his feet. "Rise, eunuch."

"King of Kings, I am Kairu. I am a descendant of the El Molo. I am of the Maasai."

King Ayden nodded. "Kairu."

They all knelt before King Ayden, as it was required of them; however, it was obvious that Queen Bernice, Lord Percival and Prince Orin bowed before him for duty alone and allegiance to the realm, not because they loved him. Later, while most slept, Kairu spoke with Queen Bernice. "Majesty, I see the way you look at your son. You grieve for him."

"What do you know of my life, but for my wrongs?" She looked to the spot where the woman Dorcas lay. "I cannot undo what I've done…"

"But you have your life, Your Majesty." Suddenly, all seemed to make sense to Kairu. "All things have a purpose." He looked out the window at the fullness of the moon. Something about the glow of the silvery-blue disc made the night more beautiful. "What you did to your son was meant to be, for if you had not sentenced him to his fate he may well have died. We know not what his life with this woman was like, but I look at them both and I see promise. He shall be a great king—even greater than his father before him. My Queen, I believe it was meant for Dorcas to raise him, this was her purpose." The black eunuch smiled as he took the queen's hand. She was cold to touch. However, her tears seemed warm enough as they streamed down her cheeks. "You are here now with him, Your Highness…still to fulfill your purpose, for even I have deeds to fulfill." Kairu looked to the woman Dorcas. "She sleeps. And your son is awake. Go to him."

Kairu settled himself upon his bed of straw and watched as Queen Bernice walked out the door into the moonlit night to speak with her son.

## CHAPTER TWENTY-NINE
### *For Qev*

His king had summoned him. What was he to do but obey? Orin had agreed to accept his brother as king, but he could not accept the fact that Ayden Thorne had killed their father. "I cannot even give him our father's name." He walked to the third of three cruck houses that were used as dwelling places for the royal family. Orin found it strange that a king lived so poorly—a poor king living like common folk. His brother Lucas, however, had little trouble adjusting to their new life, for it was he who convinced the common folk of Ayden's claim to the white throne. Many of the common folk had never seen their true king. Orin had listened to many of the tales of his father and what he had looked like before he was vanquished. Little children shared stories they had heard—news carried from afar. In their minds, King Earvin had been a giant, a deformed man with a cruel face and a monster of ruthless mind. Among these people of

Lunaris, Lucas had found peace. Again, winter was drawing nigh; the long summer had ended.

It seemed so long since he had left the citadel, and even longer since his father's death. Orin went on his way toward his brother, the king without a crown. The folk of Lunaris had grown to love their king. The tale of King Ayden and his black eunuchs had been sent to all the forgotten areas of the realm—towns and villages that meant nothing to the man who had falsely proclaimed himself ruler of the realm.

He found his brother alone within the cruck house, which had been made with all the comforts fit for a king. These comforts, however, were nothing compared to what any noble was accustomed to. He greeted his brother with the slightest of bows. "You sent for me...king." His brother's humility had always angered Orin. *Where was this humility when you slit our father's throat?*

Orin's eyes or tone must have betrayed him, for his brother stiffened. "You are my brother. I cannot change that." King Ayden looked no different than his father did, now that he had Kairu by his side, ever advising him. "And I cannot change what I've done. I can only hope to amend my wrongs—make things right."

Orin still could not look into his eyes. "Our mother taught us how to hate—not to love," said Orin. "The first victim of my hatred was our father. But now he lays dead and I realize I may not have hated him at all."

"I wish I knew him...Brother." His brother, king of the realm, took a knee before him. "If you could tell me...help me to know him..."

"I cannot." Orin wept.

"I beg of you."

Orin turned away and walked toward the door. He was about to leave when something stopped him... "You have his eyes."

"I know...I looked into them as I..."

When he turned to face his brother, Orin first noticed the black eunuch's eyes. Kairu nodded with encouragement. "Something left me the day you killed my father—something I never knew I had. Father gave me hope…that day I lost all hope, for he was gone. And I am ashamed, for the day he died was the day I realized how much I loved him…needed him." Orin did not resist when his brother embraced him.

His sister had become a changed woman. Night had fallen; Lord Percival sat alone and watched as the mothers of the king sat and laughed together. The princess was with them. The cruck house they all shared was warmed by a welcoming fire. But most of all, the hearts of the folk in this place, Lunaris, were filled with love. Winter had come and the night wind brought a chill, and the folk of Lunaris were happy nonetheless. Children danced around fires, and their stomachs were not full but their faces bore happy smiles. Lord Percival had not known this to be possible. One's wealth and possessions now seemed hardly enough to make one happy. Lord Percival bowed his head in shame, for he had always had wealth and could remember the times when his need to attain power had been his only drive. Now, after Kairu had spoken to him of his purpose, Lord Percival searched deep within himself to see whether he could find it. The eunuch had said to him once that all things happened for a purpose. What then had been his purpose for killing. What other reason did he kill but for greed?

Now his new king was preparing for war, for only thus could he attain the white throne and the crown. The plans had been made. The eunuch Prodigal had been sent with newly trained warriors to bring others to the king's cause. Lucas too had travelled for the same purpose. And Orin, had been asked to remain by his brother's side, for he had knowledge of the protocols and laws of the realm. As for their king, Ayden Godfrey had taught every able man how to wield a sword, even Kairu, his black eunuch. War was coming, and still, Lord Percival, brother to a queen, had no purpose…

They had already endured half the winter. Life within the town of Lunaris had not been easy. Cloaked within layers of wool, a hooded Kairu walked alone through knee-high snow and had become short of breath from the effort. He had gone to visit the king's mothers as commanded by his new master, and the women of the royal family could not have been happier to see him. News of King Ayden's existence had spread across the entire realm; many had pledged their allegiance to him, both nobles and common folk alike. Those of the nobles who had come to greet the king were of the oldest houses; they knew the history of Qev too well, and had expressed their fears of having the rule of the realm in the hands of the Theos. Of the common folk, they too had not forgotten the ages of war between the two most prominent houses of the realm. A treaty of marriage had ended a long war after most of the Theo house had been vanquished. Desperate for their survival, the head of the Theo house had capitulated. A Godfrey took a Theo as his queen, thus becoming king. However, when the young queen was radiant with child she mysteriously took to illness and died quickly. The Theo queen and their heir to the white throne were dead. The Godfrey king then took a new wife, a distant cousin who was said to be already with child, and thus the feud between the two houses continued.

    This history had been recorded within Qev's *Scrolls of Times*. Kairu had read them himself. He suddenly thought back to the life he remembered as a child. He was a man now. The black eunuch smiled; he considered himself a man in a world where he was just a eunuch—ọmọkùnrin wa ni omobirin. *Boy turned girl.* As the cold winds bit into his skin Kairu pulled his hood over his face and quickened his pace.

He found King Ayden by the fire. "King." Kairu approached slowly and bowed before the new king. "Your mothers, Dorcas and the queen, are well. Princess Cylene longs to see you, King of Kings." Kairu finally looked into his eyes. "Majesty, why do you hide yourself from them?"

"They accept me," he answered, "while I struggle to accept myself." King Ayden covered his ears as he took a long, deep breath. "I cannot close my eyes without seeing his face. I dream of him whenever I lay my head to rest, for I am not at peace." The king's eyes were tear filled. "It is as if the Gods have told him who I am…for he haunts me…"

Kairu caressed his king's face. "You are king."

"I did not ask to be king, Kairu!" He clenched his fists and pounded the sides of his head. "I cannot think. I cannot make decisions, for my clouded mind. And now these great lords come to me from all corners of the realm—all pledging their loyalty. And some bring gifts…only wanting to be rewarded in return with lands and titles when I sit upon the white throne. I know them, these noblemen…they are fickle." He looked to the black eunuch with pleading blue eyes. "Kairu, what am I to do? Already three earls have offered their daughters to me. A king is nothing without a queen, they say. Nothing without an heir."

The eunuch bowed. "You must take a wife, Majesty. But take no gifts until you have decided which maid you will take to be your wife. The castles and lands they offer shall be her dowry."

"I have not seen these maidens, how am I to choose?"

Kairu allowed his cloak to fall to the floor, for the fire had warmed him. "You must send word to all the noblemen. Plan for a feast. Invite the fathers and a bride shall come."

"And what then?"

The black eunuch took several moments to gather his thoughts. "The family of your bride must have strong connections to the realm's army. Lord Theo controls half of Qev's forces, my king, this you know." They stood by the fire in silence for some time before Kairu stooped to remove the large shoes from his feet. King Ayden towered over the black eunuch, simply watching him. As the eunuch rose slowly the king took his arm. "Come, Kairu. Sit with me." He bid the eunuch sit and knelt before him cradling the eunuch's feet into the palms of his hands. "Your Majesty…" As the king's fingers massaged his cold feet Kairu's head tilted backward as he released a satisfying moan. He was instantly reminded of the times his mother rubbed fish oil into his skin as a boy. The king's hands moved up his calves, still gently massaging them. His fingers were long and their touch sensual. Kairu closed his eyes as the fingers travelled beyond his knees; he released an involuntary gasp.

"Kairu, why must I take a bride when there is you?" His words were a mere whisper. "I have always…needed—"

The door to the king's cruck house opened, letting in a sudden rush of chilly air. Prodigal entered. "Forgive me, Your Majesty." The Nuba boy hesitated. "Kairu." His eyes fell to the floor instantly. "Please…," said the Nuba boy. "I will leave you now."

"Prodigal." King Ayden did not speak with a commanding tone. His tone was not demanding. "Please sit." Kairu and Prodigal locked gazes. The black eunuch remained silent as his friend sat next to him. He could still feel the warmth of King Ayden's hands upon his thighs.

The king's eyes pleaded with them; the eunuchs disrobed in unison. And even as the king pushed their faces together so that the fullness of their lips touched, Kairu did not resist, for what he felt for Prodigal was real. Slowly, the eunuchs undressed their king and the three lay naked together upon the padded couch. With the blazing fire before them and the fullness of the night's moon visible from the window, Kairu clung to Prodigal while his king clung closely to him. No other night in the town of Lunaris had been better…

## CHAPTER THIRTY
### *Garring Fort*

Garring Fort was built upon a cliff, making it possible to view all lands around it. Beneath the cliff was a river, which got its supply of spring water from a massive waterfall. It was beautiful. There was another identical cliff on the other side of the river, but while the castle stood upon one, the other stood bare. The servants of the castle had spoken of Lord Garring's ancestors' plans to build a twin for the beautiful stone castle, for a bridge extended from one cliff to the next, making it the perfect fort. The bridge was the only way of entry to the Garring Fort.

It was nearly summer again, and Orin sat within Garring Fort's small library feeling homesick. King Ayden had moved his retinue and his family to this place, nearly a full day's journey from the citadel. Lord Garring's castle was by no means inadequate; Orin simply longed for home. He missed seeing the turrets pointing toward the blue sky; he longed for the large library with countless books and scrolls. The prince had waited long enough; it was time to have his old life back.

His brother, the king, had been given the option of choosing one bride for his queen. Seven potential brides were presented to his brother; for days he pondered, for they were all beautiful. But the king could not decide, for he worried he might err. Seven great lords watched with keen eyes the night their king was to pick a maiden, and each wanted his daughter to be queen of the realm.

That night, when Kairu, the black eunuch, leaned and whispered in the king's ear, Orin knew Kairu's solution would be the wisest. A thin smile surfaced over his brother's lips; Orin would not forget it. Ayden, King of Qev—the king without crown and throne, had made his choice. Boldly, he stood, with the eyes of seven fathers fixed upon him as he prepared to make his announcement. "I shall wed them all," his brother said. At first the nobles recoiled, shocked; however, it took just several words from the black eunuch to convince them. Thus, the seven lords gave their daughters to one king. Seven queens would sit with the king of Qev. Qev would have its harem. The first queen, Clarissa, had won the king's heart. The others would be second wives. Orin had underestimated this black eunuch, for with just words, the beautiful Kairu had managed to bond powerful lords of great influence to their king.

Now, all within the realm knew of two kings. War was inevitable. Orin had spoken with Kairu and his brother of the secret way through the caves, for he was certain the false king knew nothing of it. This would be their way to victory.

Garring Fort had become a busy place. Kairu sat upon a great black stallion, still shocked that he, a black eunuch from across the sea, had acquired yet another name. From the moment he saw the light of the world, he had been Kairu, descendant of the El Molo, from the Maasai. He was also known as *black one*—the meaning of his name, Kairu. And when his purpose changed, Kairu knew himself as eunuch, ọmọkùnrin wa ni omobirin. *Boy turned girl.* King Earvin gave him other names: amanuensis, advisor and *Chief of the Girls*. But now he had another name—warrior.

His new king insisted that he and Prodigal be trained as warriors. "Even eunuchs must know how to wield a blade in times of war," King Ayden had said. From that point on the two eunuchs were trained by generals of King Ayden's new army. Even the king himself had helped train them.

"You seem to be in a trance, Kairu." Prodigal reined his beast alongside him. As Kairu took a deep breath Prodigal smiled. "Do not be afraid, Kairu."

He was not aware his fear could be seen. Kairu adjusted himself in his saddle. "Do not mock me, Prodigal. It is bad enough my shoulders ache from this heavy armour." Lord Garring's plan was keenly strategic; he had convinced the king to strike first and take Eldford Castle, for this well-guarded fort was a gateway to the lands surrounding the citadel. "We may very well be riding to our deaths," said Kairu. "The false king would be a fool to not have this castle heavily defended."

"It would be a great victory, Kairu." Prodigal touched his arm. "Your desire to live is all you will need, my friend. Do as the generals taught us. Let go of your fear."

Kairu shrugged. "It is easy for you to say this, for you have already killed." Suddenly the events of that night swarmed his mind. Prodigal had killed that warrior, who would have ravaged him and left him for dead…

"I could not help it, Kairu."

"Lord Garring wants the glory, that is all." Kairu had begged King Ayden to remain within the safety of Garring Fort…but his king would have it no other way. He would fight. "No harm must come to our king, Prodigal." His friend nodded. They looked long into each other's eyes. "And you…you must stay alive, Prodigal, for I cannot be in this place without you." Prodigal's eyes calmed him, just like they had the day they first met beneath the brightness of the golden sun. "I am bound to you…"

"I am bound to you, Kairu."

The war horn sounded. Hundreds of warriors pulled the reins of their mounts, and before long, the sound of pounding hooves against the ground resonated. Horsemen rode bearing the king's banner; Kairu could hear beats of drums among the throng. The king rode between Kairu and Prodigal as they set off to battle.

## CHAPTER THIRTY-ONE
*Eldford Castle*

The walls of Eldford Castle were well guarded. It was dusk, and all seemed calm within the stronghold. Kairu sat upon his mount beside the king. The rapid slam of his heart against his rib cage echoed inside his head; however, the eunuch took comfort in the fact that the false king's men appeared ignorant of the imminent attack. The black eunuch rubbed his palms together. He had never taken a life. As he looked to the castle with tall walls extending from one large mountain to the other, Kairu wondered how his king's army would penetrate the wall of stone. The fortress seemed impregnable. "King of Kings," said Kairu, "the night comes quickly. How will one see his enemy in the dark?"

King Ayden laughed. "We shall storm the castle as soon as our scouts send the signal." The young king spoke with confidence. "Eldford shall be ours by the morning."

"What signal, my king?"

"Look, Kairu." Prodigal pointed toward the fort. Kairu saw a faint flicker of light near the edge of the mountain. "Our prince has done it, Your Majesty." The Nuba boy had seen Kairu's confusion and smiled. "It is Prince Lucas, Kairu. He took the task of opening the gates."

Before Kairu could question his king the battle horn sounded. He could hear sudden commotion beyond the walls of the fort. As they charged toward the walls of Eldford Castle many horsemen rode out to meet them, all clad in armour. Kairu could not tell how the young prince and his companions had managed to open the gate, nor did he know what had become of Prince Lucas. As the enemy charged toward them Kairu unsheathed his sword, and as the two sides met with a sudden crash, all thoughts immediately left his mind, for instantly, a horseman was upon him. His blade clanged against one of his enemy, sending vibrations down the length of his arm and into his shoulder. The black eunuch tried to recall all he had been taught, and just as Prodigal had said, his desire to live was paramount. Kairu's one aim was to ensure he remained seated upon his mount; at that moment, his one task was to get to the next enemy after cutting down the first. He could feel sweat rushing down his forehead from beneath his helmet. The mail shirt he wore, combined with sudden fear, felt heavier now, and as he parried with a stranger, Kairu, descendant of the El Molo, glanced into the enemy's eyes. Somehow, the hairy warrior became distracted, giving the black eunuch his only chance to strike. Kairu took his chance, for he realized this man was much older, stronger. The enemy had lifted his sword arm upward and had started to bring it down with all his might when Kairu jabbed, swiftly, like a snake. The enemy let out a faint cry as he tilted sideways upon his mount.

The black eunuch's body tensed as a rush of adrenaline swept over him. He veered and again faced his enemy, who still sat leaning upon his mount, chagrined, for he still looked to the eunuch with eyes of admiration and shock. Kairu charged forward, refusing to engage the enemy's gaze. With one downward chop, he finished his task. Kairu, black eunuch of the El Molo, had killed his first man…

With the small battle won and Eldford Castle taken, the king and those who followed him dined within the great hall. The wine from the castle's cellar was of the best quality and the cooks had prepared a feast fit for King Ayden and his warriors. Prodigal sat a distance from the king and Kairu, for they usually dined side by side. *Kairu of the El Molo*. He noticed the way the king looked at his friend…his Kairu. But what did it matter that he felt bound to the beautiful one? Prodigal did not envy his friend, for Kairu's beauty was a curse—even Ade, their teacher, had seen this. But he said nothing. The battle outside the gates of Eldford Castle had been short-lived, for they far outnumbered the enemy. No sooner had the gate been taken and the first few were struck down than the others dropped their swords and surrendered. Many knelt before King Ayden and pledged to serve him, for they knew him when he once served the false king.

"Friends!" The king's eyes still beamed with victory. "Great lords and generals. I thank you this night. For I could not have done this without you…it is you who brought the victory!" The crowd of warriors roared as they hailed the king. "Tonight we drink to victory…but the road to a greater victory is long. Soon, all of Qev shall rise victorious, and shall serve the false king no more." He sipped wine. "I return to Garring Fort at dawn. My brother, Prince Orin, has been given charge of this castle; it is his to govern and protect. Obey and serve him as you would your king." Prince Orin, though small in stature, rose boldly, still clad in his bloodstained armour.

It was dark when Prodigal joined Kairu and their king in the royal chambers. And it appeared he had arrived too late, for the king's only desire that night was to talk and issue commands. "You will remain here by my brother's side." The king's eyes were fixed upon Prodigal.

"But Majesty—"

Prodigal ceased to speak as his king raised a hand to silence him. "I have decided."

Prodigal looked to Kairu and saw in his eyes that he and the king had already decided his fate. *It was I who watched over you in battle, Kairu. I, Prodigal—not your king.* He kept the thoughts to himself, ever gazing into Kairu's eyes…

## CHAPTER THIRTY-TWO
### *Cylene*

"This is not what our father would have done!" Cylene faced her brother-king with fierceness. She hated him, even if just for that moment. "I cannot wed that old fool," she resisted. "I will not." She refused to face her mother, for this pairing had been her devious idea. The princess made every effort to ensure that the king's commands were carried out to their fullest, but to wed an old man was completely out of the question.

"Daughter, you are a princess…the only princess given to the realm." Her mother moved like a snake around her son's chair before her hand rested upon his shoulder. She then laid her eyes upon the woman, Dorcas, and the two exchanged mutual smiles. Cylene felt her own defeat, for it seemed her mother had long forgotten her past deeds and the sorrows they had brought. It was these deeds that had left her father dead and the realm at the brink of war. Cylene pitied Dorcas, for it was obvious the woman had quickly succumbed to her mother's plotting ways.

"I would speak with my brother alone." Cylene's gaze was fixed upon the black eunuch, for only he could convince the king. The eunuch's plea was wordless—it took just one look to soften her brother's heart. As her mother left with Dorcas, her eyes lingered upon her daughter.

"My sister, your marriage would bind another of my enemies to me. We must make the offer while Lord Theo is weak. Already he sends an offer of truce." He lifted a parchment bearing the enemy's seal."

"What truce?" She was shocked to hear such news. "What is the false king's offer?"

Her brother smiled. "He gives me half the realm to rule—a dual rule."

"Yet, Highness," said the eunuch, "there is dishonesty in this truce." He caressed his beads as he stepped from behind the king's chair. "Lord Theo would be high king, while our king rules the lesser lands."

"My old master is hoping that my inexperience will work to his advantage."

"Yes, Your Highness," said the black eunuch. "The false king has even offered payment—gold and lands in exchange for a kingdom."

Cylene thought a moment. "This truce the false kings extends, what part does our dear mother play in it?" She stared at her brother. "Know that our mother's ways shall never change." That was all she needed to say. Her brother looked at her as if puzzled. "She is the reason we stand here this day. Do not forget this. I will wed the false king's general. But I tell you this, Brother…Father would have fought. He would have loosed his rage upon the enemy and claim the realm, which had long been his." She bowed to her brother-king before she left him…

"I tell you, Sister, nothing good can come of this." Lord Percival wanted nothing to do with his sister's plan; however, her will was stronger than his. "The boy has the Gods on his side. Do you not see how quickly they follow him?" Lord Percival clutched his sister's shoulders and pleaded in vain. "Why must you always meddle?"

"Is it really him they follow?" Her grey eyes cut through his defences. "They follow an idea left by a king long gone from this world. They harken to the voice of a mere servant; it is he who decides what must be done; he who dictates times of war; and it is upon his will alone my son relies."

Percival could not help but smile. "So now he is yours…" He turned his back to his queen. "Sister, the boy is destined for greatness, even you must see how the Gods favour him."

"What are Gods? We are but puppets to them…it is they who need us." A thin smile crossed her lips.

Percival's eyes widened in shock. "Do not mock the Gods."

"We determine our destinies—not the Gods." She moved toward the door and smiled as she opened it. When the woman, Dorcas, entered, Percival clutched his chest. "What have you done, woman?" He challenged his sister with a fearful gaze.

# CHAPTER THIRTY-THREE
## *The Visit*

The doors to the great hall opened to the king's two visitors. King Theo had commanded that all leave him, save for those closest to him. But he especially asked one of his retinue to remain, and this person he kept close to his side. He watched the two cloaked figures approach; both still concealed their faces with cowls. But the king knew who paid this visit. He knew them well.

"Greetings, King." He knew the voice well.

"He refuses my offer," said the king. "A messenger arrived several days past. Earvin's son has chosen war, death."

Cedric moved closer to the white throne, ever determined to outshine his cousin. "Do not trust them, Father." This he said after the visitors pushed back the cowls from their faces.

"Shut your mouth, boy." His sidelong glance was stern. "Learn from your cousin how to hold your forward tongue."

"Your Majesty." The first visitor addressed him with an empty bow. "I…we…have come with terms."

"Then speak." The king turned to gaze upon his nephew, Kevan. "Do you not agree, Nephew?"

Kevan nodded. "Yes, Uncle." The boy moved from where he stood and addressed the visitors. "What are your terms?" Like the son he had always wanted, Kevan made King Theo smile with pride.

He was the prince of Qev and would be ruler of an entire realm someday. This, Cedric had always hoped for. The throne room was now empty. His father's business was done. Now, the prince sat alone, as was custom, for none within his father's retinue favoured him. Seated upon the white throne, Cedric thought of days long past, days when he would bask out in the sun with his one true friend. Now, it was Ayden Thorne who called himself king, for all along he carried the Godfrey blood within his veins. All his life, his father had spoken of regaining the throne and the crown, for in truth, the Godfreys had usurped his birthright. And now…now when this had finally come to him, his cousin, the dog raised by Godfrey himself—he who was once prince, comes to take his place. Cedric blazed with rage, for his father had sent him away again, while he kept his dead brother's son by his side…this Kevan, the boy who carried the Godfrey stain. "He carries their curse with him," said Cedric. He heard his own voice echo within the great hall. The sudden sound of footsteps echoed behind his voice.

"Who goes there?" No answer. Suddenly, from behind one of the large pillars, he saw a lone figure. It was the very person who was at the centre of his thoughts. It was the snake.

"Cousin." Kevan stepped out from the shadows and slowly approached the throne.

"What is it you want of me." Cedric noticed how his dear cousin refrained from greeting him with the reverence due a prince.

"I merely come to see how you are doing, Cousin." There was no trust in his eyes. Kevan smiled at him. "I remember sitting there once…when I was prince. It seemed so long ago. I've even had my chance at being king."

Cedric spat on the floor. "Dog!" He did not raise his voice. "I see you as nothing. You may carry my dead uncle's blood…but you are no kin of mine. You are spoiled."

The dog smiled again. "Will you say the same, Cousin, when you meet your friend in battle? Will you hesitate to cut him down with your blade without remorse?" Cedric nervously shifted his gaze. "Uncle knows what you will do, good cousin." The dog's grin grew more cynical. "He knows you would betray him for the love of your friend—a Godfrey."

Cedric could contain his rage no longer. He shot his cousin a baleful glance as he sprang from the white throne and fell upon him. His roar of anger echoed aloud. But, while his cousin had been taken off guard, he was by no means weak. The two wrestled upon the coldness of the stone floor and exchanged blows until Cedric tasted his own blood. When the guards came and finally wrenched them apart, the cousins shouted curses at each other, even in the presence of the king.

King Theo towered over them and looked down in disgust. "You will not shed Theo blood before my throne." As Cedric rose his father struck him to the face with the back of his hand. "You disappoint me, boy." He then moved to Kevan, seizing him by the throat. "Do you think I need you?" He cast a swift glance to his son. "I will gut you right here to prove it. We are of the Theo house. We are family."

Left alone with his father, Cedric wept. He would not beg his father's forgiveness. "All my life…my whole life, I've longed for your acceptance," said the prince. "Longed for your love…one pleasant word, or even a word of encouragement. But forever you show me that I am not enough—never good enough. Father, what have I ever done to make you hate me so?" His father offered no reply. He simply sat upon the white throne and looked toward the floor with a frown.

They called him a prince, but he was a prince without the respect of his subjects? Cedric had rushed to his rooms after his father's silence told him all he needed to know. He had met his cousin in the hallways of the castle, and all Kevan did was smile at him, a boastful, mocking smile. Cedric Theo felt alone again—just as he had when his mother had died when he was young. His father had been busy with battles, basking in the glory of them. And his father had not taken another wife; he had not even thought to find his son a mother.

When Ayden Thorne had come into his life, the loneliness had departed. Cedric Theo had made a friend. The friend was now lost—all forfeited because of a crown. The rage within him had not subsided. Cedric sprang from his bed determined not to fear his father. He arrived outside his father's chambers and was denied entry. "He's not here," said the guard. After attempting to get back to the throne room with no success, Cedric thought of the only other way he could get close to his father. He returned to his room and searched until he found the doorway to the secret passages. It was dark within the hidden corridors; however, Cedric endeavoured to make his bulky frame as small as he could, pressing his ear against the walls as he moved along, while viewing the image of the castle within his head.

Finally, he heard his father's voice. He was not alone. The prince unlocked the door and pushed it slightly.

"What they promise is impossible, Uncle." It was his cousin. "She raised me all my life…I believe she even loved me. But to trust the queen now would be foolish."

"Mind your tongue, Nephew."

His cousin laughed. "You and I are alike, Uncle. Am I anything like him—my father?"

Cedric listened keenly for his father's reply, almost holding his breath. "Asquith was everything I wanted to be. All the women wanted him, and every warrior wished him to be their captain." His father sighed. "And me, I had to live in my brother's shadow. Always second best." Cedric held his breath once more as the throne room fell silent. "I loved my brother." Another sigh. "But part of me rejoiced when Earvin killed him. I became the eldest. I was seen by those who had not even known I'd existed. And I became king…"

"And I can't blame you, Uncle. I did not know your brother."

"The queen…she comes to me with that liar, Dorcas. I think these women have a plan of their own. Queen Bernice wants a crown and the servant woman would not suffer her false son to die. Dorcas would have things as they once were." The king laughed again. "Fools they are."

Cedric pressed the side of his face against the door, fighting to compose himself. He had been present when Queen Bernice and Ayden Thorne's mother spoke their terms. The queen had offered herself to Cedric's father. This, she felt, would be gladly accepted by the people—a bond of peace between the two houses. She had offered the princess,

Cylene, not to the new king's son, but to his first general of war. And of the woman Dorcas, she needed a son, not a king. The woman had pleaded for Ayden Thorne's life by throwing herself at King Theo's feet.

The new king spoke again. "When Cedric was a boy I saw promise in him. Something about his eyes reminded me so much of Asquith…but the boy got older and grew to look more like me every day. What a curse. I look at my own son and his very face reminds me of what I wasn't."

Cedric clutched his head and allowed his body to slide toward the floor.

## CHAPTER THIRTY-FOUR
*"False King"*

Princess Cylene had sent an urgent message that he come to her at once. Kairu delayed as long as he could, for he could not leave the king's business simply because his sister had summoned him. Nevertheless, the black eunuch managed to leave the king in the capable hands of his squire, Rosario, a young man who seemed too eager to prove his valour to the king. Kairu left the two to continue their talk of battles and hastened to see the princess. Garring Fort was a gloomy place. Kairu had become familiar with it; however, the dim corridors and dark stone walls usually left him feeling lonely; they were nothing compared to the beauty of the grand halls at the citadel.

The princess was attended by female servants. As Kairu was admitted and asked to wait within the anteroom he wondered what it was the princess could have wanted, for it was long after sunset. Princess Cylene's servants eyed him as he waited, all the while giggling after sharing whispers. The black eunuch simply lifted his chin and paid little attention. Finally, the princess was ready to see him. As was his custom, the eunuch rose and bowed gracefully. "My Princess." Kairu was astonished to see that the princess had received him adorned in a long silky robe of white. Her raven hair cascaded well beyond her waist and her lips had been painted red. It was as though he had not noticed the princess's beauty before that moment, nor had he realized how much she resembled her father, the dead king. Princess Cylene's eyes glistened like two dark gems. For the first time in his life, Kairu stuttered. "P-princess." The giggles of the servants reminded him they were not alone. Kairu stood boldly; he composed himself so as not to insult the princess, for it was he who served. "I…fear I have come too early, Princess Cylene." He was wearing his beads and his red shúkà, skilfully draped at his waist.

When the warmth of her hands touched his chest, Kairu's body quaked. The passion he felt from a woman's touch was new and different. Kairu's eyes closed involuntarily; a chill swept over his body as the tips of the princess's fingers moved slowly over his nipples. "I am to be wed to the false king's general," said the princess. "I am to be joined with this man against my will. But he shall have me on my terms…he shall not be first."

"You must not do this, Princess Cylene. We cannot." He attempted to step away from the princess but found his back pressed against the wall. Again, the giggles filled his ears. Princess Cylene reached for his lips; her lids veiled the blackness of her eyes, bringing relief to the eunuch, for he found he could no longer look into her eyes. "Your betrothed expects you to be pure, Princess Cylene. It is dishonourable to—"

Kairu gasped as her hand moved down his torso. "You are capable of this task, are you not…Kairu?" Her fingers crept beneath his shúkà and tugged at his loincloth.

The black eunuch could not lie, for as Princess Cylene's fingers caressed his manhood it began to swell instantly. "I use herbs…Your…Majest—"

Her touch induced the urge to moan or scream with pleasure. Kairu felt passion in a way he had not experienced it before, for this was the first he had ever been touched by a woman. She was his sovereign—a royal princess, yet the black eunuch could neither repel her advances, nor withstand the effects of her caresses. With the servants present, Kairu, descendant of the El Molo, the eunuch of the Maasai, unleashed the beast which had hidden itself somewhere inside him. She had torn away his shúkà and loincloth. Kairu groaned as he grasped tresses of the princess's black hair and tilted her face upward before leaning in and tasting her lips. He saw submission within the pupils. But he also saw passion, hunger. As he licked her red lips and pulled her tongue inside his mouth, he pulled her tightly against him. Kairu tore away the silks and exposed the paleness of her skin. His eyes beheld rounded breasts; instinct compelled him to cover her pink nipples with his lips. The eunuch marvelled at what he had done, yet he felt no need whatsoever to entertain regret. The princess moaned as her body trembled. Kairu stood with his legs apart as his sovereign knelt before him, a eunuch created to serve. The warmth of her lips upon him encouraged Kairu to grasp more tresses of her raven hair within his fist. The unleashed beast could endure the tortures of pleasure no longer…blissful torture…

The black eunuch forced her body down to the floor; she did not resist him. He cupped her breasts with both hands; he could feel her legs twine themselves around him; her eyes widened at his first unrestrained thrust. She exhaled. "Kairu…"

><<<<o>>>><

He had deemed his new king even more terrible than the first. Prodigal stood upon the stone walls of Eldford Castle and gazed out into the distance as far as his eyes could see. Ever since Kairu left with the king he had not seen his friend. The days were long and the nights treacherous, for he could not endure being without his El Molo boy. King Ayden's decision was deliberate, Prodigal knew this. "If only you would open your eyes, Kairu." As his words drifted away with the wind, Prodigal wiped tears from his eyes and his mind drifted to thoughts of home. Standing atop the castle's wall was nothing compared to perching upon a branch of the great Marula tree. Prodigal would have given anything to feel the embrace of the tree's massive branches. He needed to feel the evening breeze upon his cheek, the ray of the sun blinding his eyes. It had not occurred to him so long ago that he would pine over Ade's temple of eunuchs.

The princess was to wed the false king's general, Lord Sewell. The Nuba boy had not been given leave to attend, though Prince Orin had already left for Garring Fort. He was to remain at Eldford Castle; this was the command of his king.

Although many had come from all over the realm, the false king did not attend the wedding. This puzzled the eunuch, for the marriage of the princess and Lord Sewell had been intended to be a union for peace. King Ayden was furious when he was given a message bearing the false king's royal seal. He had commanded Kairu to leave him but the black eunuch had not. "Your Majesty." He adjusted his king's crown a second time before kneeling before him. "You are ready, My Lord."

"He does not respect me as king," said King Ayden. "I am nothing to him…he will forever see me as the poor boy he took in—the son of a widow." King Ayden pounded the palm of his hand with a clenched fist. I should not have listened to her…my mother."

"Lord Sewell waits, Your Majesty. All your guests—"

"Cylene warned me of this." He suddenly seemed troubled. "Kairu, I have been a fool. Lord Theo thinks me a boy. He offers peace, but to what end? I have known him most of my life; this false king demands absolute control. He would never give up half the realm. There is a plot, Kairu." The king looked to Kairu with intense eyes. "And whatever the plot, it will happen this day."

"But Majesty, surely we cannot send our guests away." Kairu took his king's ringed hand and kissed it. "What must we do?"

"The false king's absence is no coincidence." King Ayden pulled the golden crown from his head. "What say you of this, Kairu?"

"You speak sense, Majesty." His thoughts of Cylene sent tremors of pleasure through his body. He had visited her rooms each night since their first. "The princess spoke with wisdom, Your Highness." He averted his eyes as he mentioned the king's sister. "Lord Theo would cut down every link to the white throne, save for those of his own blood."

"What must I do, Kairu."

He stood motionless for several moments. "If there is a plot, Your Highness," said Kairu, "I fear the false king has fixed his gaze elsewhere."

King Ayden grimaced. "By the Gods! Eldford Castle. He means to seize it." The king placed the crown atop his head. "Send for my mother," he commanded. "And my mother, the queen." Kairu was about to leave the room when the king called to him. "Wait."

# CHAPTER THIRTY-FIVE
## *The Plot*

Queen Bernice entered her son's presence and knew immediately that something had gone wrong. She entered the Garring Fort's great hall continuing to hold her head high. The boy had summoned several of King Theo's own men. Her brother Percival stood near Cylene, both seeming puzzled that they had been called before the king just moments before an important wedding celebration. Even Dorcas had been called, as insignificant as she was. She looked to her son and saw a frown upon his face. Her other sons, Orin and Lucas, flanked the king's makeshift throne, a high chair embellished with gold plating. There was a slight buzz within the hall, mostly from those of Lord Sewell's retinue. And as always, the elegant black eunuch moved around the hall gracefully, but ever watchful. It was impossible not to notice the black beauty, yet one seemed to dismiss his presence; it was almost as though the eunuch could make himself not seen in some magical way. Lord Sewell entered the hall and the whispers ceased. At that same moment her son nodded. His brothers and the eunuch must have understood whatever unspoken command he had given.

Her son cleared his throat and the hall fell silent. Queen Bernice shifted her body and all she could hear was the ruffle of her mauve silk gown. Her eyes connected with those of her son's and her body tensed. *He knows.* The queen could see it in his eyes. She nervously adjusted her necklace before glancing at the woman Dorcas. *I will say nothing. Let the boy do with me as he wishes.* She turned her gaze to him again and was instantly angered, for his was no different from those of his father's. *He haunts me still, even from the grave...*

"My friends,"—her son smiled, though he still wore a frown—"I must welcome you all to Garring Fort, and I thank you for attending what would have been my sister's wedding." His brows arched at the sound of grumblings within the great hall...

><<<<o>>>><

Prince Orin studied every face within the great hall. Many displayed puzzled looks, for they had been called away from what was set to be the wedding of peace, but the prince saw many other faces which bore looks of worry; their eyes betrayed them. His brother's suspicions had been correct, for indeed there was a plot against him. Orin again exchanged glances with the eunuch; Kairu nodded. Their king's plan was in place.

Lord Sewell bowed before he addressed the king. "Your…Majesty." His distaste for the king was obvious, for it could be heard in his voice, seen in his deceitful eyes. Why had Orin not noticed this before? "Your words confuse me, king. Your dear sister and I are to wed this day."

"I was a fool to think a man such as yourself was capable of honour, Lord Sewell. Do not take me for a fool." Orin watched his brother with pride, for in him he saw traces of their father. "I was just a boy when the false king took me in; I was no fool then…and I am not a fool now." When his brother gave the command with a single look, Orin nodded back.

The true prince of Qev opened his mouth and shouted his command: "Guards!" The king's protectors rushed in from all ends of the great hall. Several stood by their king, while others surrounded Lord Sewell and his men.

"What is the meaning of this?" Lord Sewell stood with hands at his hips; he had no sword. "Is this how a king treats his guest of honour?" His beady eyes widened.

"You will tell my brother all you know of the false king's plot!" Lucas drew his sword as he approached the man who would have been his brother-in-law. "Speak!" Orin had never seen Lucas so enraged. As he struck Lord Sewell's face the great lord's retinue reached for their swords; however, they were quickly deterred when the guards surrounded them. They were outnumbered.

Cylene made the effort to approach her brother; however, as Kairu placed his hand upon her bare shoulder, the two exchanged glances. His sister was instantly calmed and obeyed when the eunuch shook his head. The princess of Qev was subdued by the servant. Orin searched the faces of others around, wondering whether anyone else had noticed this strange interaction between the eunuch and the royal princess. The prince quickly returned his focus to Lord Sewell.

"You won't get a word out of me, boy." His eyes were fixed upon the king. "Torture me—kill me if you must. But you won't have any help from me…or my men." A thin smile swept over his lips. "I will never betray my king—the true king of Qev." Lord Sewell crossed his arms over his chest and his men did the same. Orin looked on, shocked, and he saw this also in the eyes of his brothers, and even the eunuch. They had not anticipated such a reaction from the deceiver. But it was Kairu who again brought things to light.

The black eunuch approached Lord Sewell while bidding the guards to stay their swords. "The laws of Qev dictate that a captive is bound to serve his captor, for it is honourable not only to man but to the Gods."

"Do not speak to me about our laws, black man. In ages past, my ancestors helped write them. You are nothing here." He spat upon the floor. "Go back to your wooden hut across the sea, black eunuch. You have no power here." He glanced toward the king as he spoke. "…Only in your master's bed…"

The black eunuch grasped a guard's sword and held it to Lord Sewell's throat. "I am Kairu!" Orin had never seen rage within those calm eyes. The black eunuch looked deep into Lord Sewell's eyes, as if to speak to his soul. "I am a descendant of the El Molo. I am of the Maasai!" His rage was sincere, yet the black eunuch pressed the sharp blade against Lord Sewell's skin with such control—just enough to draw blood, not to kill. "You are not bound to answer to me," said the eunuch, "but you shall answer to my king." Lord Sewell could feel the sting of the blade as well as the warmth of his own blood. He swallowed slowly. "Speak, or I shall slit your throat."

"My king comes." Lord Sewell lowered his eyes in defeat. But at the last moment the strangest thing happened.

"Stop this now!" All eyes turned to the woman Dorcas. "I cannot endure this…this war…the killing." The woman once known to be mother to Ayden Thorne turned to the king. "My son. You are my son…but you must forgive me…I did what I did only because I love you. I could not give you up."

Orin's brother-king frowned. "Mother…woman, what have you done?" Ayden leaned forward in his seat. "You could not have betrayed me—not you."

"Foolish woman!" Orin looked to his own mother, the queen, and suddenly understood. She looked to Dorcas with scorn. "You are weak."

Dorcas approached Queen Bernice and struck her with such force that she fell backward to the floor, looking up shocked and embarrassed. "I am not weak"—Dorcas curtsied—"Your Majesty. You are ungrateful—unworthy of the Gods' gift of life, for how can a woman despise her own issue? You are no mother!" Neither Orin nor any of his siblings went to their mother's defence, nor did a single guard move forward to assist her. Orin's uncle, Percival, nodded with satisfaction.

Kairu turned to Dorcas. "You will tell the king all you know."

Dorcas turned to the king. "My son, forgive me." She wept profusely and pointed to Orin's mother. "The queen summoned me and begged that I mention nothing of what she was about to do." Dorcas covered her face in shame. "Lord Percival was there when I—"

"I warned her against it, Your Majesty. My sister has never listened to my counsel."

"Yet," said Ayden, "you failed to come to me, Uncle."

"Forgive me, Your Highness." Lord Percival withdrew, ashamed.

"The queen told me I would be helping you, my son…saving you from a life of turmoil and pain." Dorcas threw herself at the king's feet. "I only wanted things the way they were, you needn't be king…I would love you just the same—even more. King Theo promised you would not be harmed—not if he and the queen were to be wed. She agreed to wed him. You were to be exiled…and I would have followed you, my son."

"You have doomed us all, foolish servant. I should never have included you." The queen finally rose to her feet, ever determined to restore her dignity. "I am Queen." Her grey eyes pierced into her eldest son. "I look at you and I see him—ever haunting me. The Gods curse you, for I cannot sleep at night. Your father, the monster, lives within you and I cannot see you without seeing him, and hate him so…"

Orin saw his brother with new eyes, for he managed to cage the rage within him. He turned his gaze from their mother and never looked at her again. Orin never expected he would ever acknowledge her presence. King Ayden sat silent. No one else uttered a word. Finally, the king spoke. "And what of the false king?"

Dorcas spat out the details she knew. "King Theo planned to take Eldford Castle; he may be there even now…but he is to arrive here…after…"

The queen eyed Dorcas with contempt. "Keep your mouth shut, woman."

Dorcas ignored the queen. "She planned to put the entire castle to sleep," said Dorcas. "The sleep potion is in the wine. And while you slept, the false king would come. All would be held captive. But I was to leave with you, my son…the king promised this himself."

"The king?" Orin brought his hand to his lips. "Speak sense, woman."

"We went to see King Theo ourselves…at the citadel." Dorcas shook her head in shame. "The queen and I were taken to him…someone let us pass through the gate at Eldford Castle."

Kairu turned to the king. "If we lose the castle, Your Majesty, I fear we shall have no hope."

King Ayden nodded. "Orin, Lucas. Assemble the rest of my army. We go to battle this night." As Lord Sewell and his retinue were restrained the king issued final orders. "Return Lord Sewell and the queen to their false king. His retinue remains in custody."

"Brother"—Lucas raised his shoulders in dismay—"you plan on releasing him?"

"Lord Sewell, give your false king my blessing." He did not respond to Lucas's question. "But he must wed his betrothed quickly, for by nightfall tomorrow she shall again be a widow."

As she was ushered from the king's presence with Lord Sewell, the queen gazed at all her children before turning to her eldest son. "After all I've done for you…you side with him. I curse you all. Ungrateful children!"

## CHAPTER THIRTY-SIX
### *The White Throne*

King Theo was camped behind one of Qev's largest mountains, not far from Garring Fort. It was nearly sunset and he smiled with satisfaction, for surely Lord Sewell would have wed the princess by now. He turned to his nephew, who sat closest to him inside the massive tent. "The boy is weak as his mother said. Earvin would never have agreed to such a union."

"That is true, Uncle. Mother…I mean…the queen proposed a wise plan." His nephew glowed with pride.

"Our marriage will simply strengthen my claim," said the king. He looked to Cedric, who had said nothing since he had been summoned. "Isn't that right, Cedric?" The boy nodded. He accepted the slight acknowledgement and turned back to his nephew. "I suppose my union with your mother will bring us even closer, Nephew. You are like the son I never had." He took note of Cedric's grimacing face and felt satisfied. The veins in the boy's neck had nearly doubled in size and there was sweat on his brow. He was about to throw salt in the wound when the flap to his tent opened and a guard brought in two guests.

"Lord Sewell and Queen Bernice, Your Highness."

The king's heart raced. He clenched his fists as he leaned forward. "What trickery is this? You are supposed to be at a wedding feast."

"My Lord." Lord Sewell knelt before him. "I have failed you, my king."

"What news do you bring for my uncle?" Kevan's eyes fell upon the queen and his eyes softened.

Lord Sewell would not engage the king's gaze. "The plot was discovered, My Lord. King…the boy has banished us and has kept my men captive at Garring Fort."

"You are hopeless, Lord Sewell. Maybe I should reconsider my decision to place you at my right hand."

"He speaks true." The queen appeared lost. Empty. "They knew something was amiss…and then the foolish woman told all."

The ruler of the realm did all he could to remain calm, yet he found it impossible to contain his rage. The woman before him would be worth nothing without a victory; he saw in her grey eyes that she too had come to that realization. "What would you have me do, woman?"

"I shall never see my children again," said Queen Bernice. The king glared back at her with disappointment. "They would sooner see me stuck here with you than say a kind word to their only mother."

"You don't need them…Mother." Kevan finally rushed to her and embraced her. "You have me, your only son."

The king turned his face away, for he had little patience for the weak. As he rolled his eyes in disgust they met with those of his son. Cedric's sad eyes were haunting. *Shall I always have such gloom around me? Surely, the Gods are against me.* He stared back at his son disdainfully and wondered what he had done for the boy to hate him so. After all, he had given him a home—a good life. Cedric was destined to inherit all his possessions; he would be lord of Theo Manor. "We cannot waste the day away in loving embraces while the enemy plots to supplant me." He would have to choose his words carefully now; he needed the queen now more than ever. "To plot against a king is treason—punishable by death. But most kings seldom sentenced their mother's to death. Ayden Thorne is such a king; he will not harm you, for he was soft, weak."

Queen Bernice released herself from Kevan's embrace. "I've come with nothing but this gown. What shall become of me—a queen on a battlefield?"

"Battlefield?" said King Theo. "Speak sense, woman. The boy had no idea I am camped here."

"You forget these are Lord Garring's lands. You fought next to Earvin in many battles; surely you are aware they will leave no stone unturned until they find you." She pressed her hand against her bosom. Her face bore an empty, sad look. "Besides, only the Gods know what Dorcas told them, for I can hardly remember it." Again she sighed. "Even my own brother betrayed me…Percival had always stood by my side…"

"My men shall escort you back to the citadel. They will use the old roads." He turned to his son. "You will go with them, Cedric." The boy gave no answer but immediately started to prepare. "And you must go too, Nephew. If I should fall in battle, you must take my banner and my men back to Theo Manor." He noticed the sudden tension of Cedric's body before the boy glared at him. "What? I am merely giving your cousin instructions."

"You give him my birthright!" Cedric pointed an accusing finger at his cousin. "And you take it gladly…as you have always done. You are a thief."

"Enough!" The king's eyes bulged. "You will do as I command. Both of you."

"And what of me, Sire." Lord Sewell had yet to look into his eyes.

"You do what a king's general should. Prove yourself worthy. Win the war!"

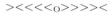

The journey by way of the old roads was long and tedious. Queen Bernice sat alone during the bumpy ride looking out the window. She had never taken the time to admire the beautiful days of summer, for all her time had been spent preparing Kevan for his rule over the realm. "Where did I go wrong?" She had pondered this since they left King Theo's camp. Her only love, Asquith, had died at the hand of her husband, and she hated him for it. She had vowed to make the beast pay. "I should have killed him myself," she whispered. "Would I now be bound to wed another beast had the boy not lived?" Kevan's mount trotted alongside the carriage. If only he had not learned who he really was…

"You seem troubled…Mother." She heard the hesitation in his voice—even saw it in his eyes. "You loved me all my life…I know now that I was truly yours." He offered a faint smile. "What was he like…my father?"

The queen felt a sudden surge of energy. "Oh, how I wished I could've spoken of him. I see him in you. Such courage…"

"Was he like uncle?"

"He was everything Silas never was." She felt her smile spread over her face. "There wasn't a woman who didn't want him as her own. But they were not good enough for him—none of them were." She continued even as Cedric rode up on the opposite side of the carriage. King Theo's son kept the pace in silence. "I have no regret for what I did. My conscience is clear."

"What will become of us," asked Kevan, "should uncle lose the battle?"

"If the battle is forfeit," she replied, "I fear we are doomed, for it will mean the Gods are against us."

"And why would the Gods wait so long, Mother? Why would they sit idle while your true son lives a life of poverty and want?"

Suddenly, it occurred to the queen why two kings were about to meet in battle. "It was him—the black eunuch from across the sea. His presence here changed all things."

"You speak true, Mother," agreed Kevan.

It seemed Cedric had heard enough, for after shaking his head, the king's son galloped ahead. "The poor boy." She looked to Kevan with a smile. "He has spent a lifetime trying to please a father he adores. I pity him." She saw a grin of satisfaction appear briefly over Kevan's face. "My son…you are not my issue, but you are all I have ever lived for. All I have left. The eunuch…this Kairu, he will forever stain the ways of our realm. Qev needs him not. He has Ayden's ear—he manipulates the son as he did the father, and this shall lead to the ruin of all…"

## CHAPTER THIRTY-SEVEN
### *Battle Horns*

Kairu stood by the window of his rooms and watched the darkness of night vanish like a cloud of mist. Sunrise came much too quickly, for with the rising of the sun came the horns of war. Kairu rose from bed that morning knowing many would die that day. He had taken lives at Eldford Castle and would do so again this day. He sat before a breakfast tray and could hardly eat. He had already seen the king and the princes, for they dined together, with talk of a victory spewing from their mouths. Not one of them seemed to fear death. He left the king and his lords within the great hall, for he could no longer endure the battle songs. Lord Garring had a gleam of pleasure in his eyes while the royal family broke their fast. The young queen sat speechless next to her king, beaming with innocence. Kairu sincerely believed she loved him—yet he had not forgotten that the king had taken Lord Garring's daughter for his queen simply to strengthen his claim to the white throne. And there were six other wives, all daughters to wealthy men of great influence and power. These other wives had been left in Kairu's care, for he was to be *Chief of the Girls*. King Ayden would have his harem. The black eunuch thought it ironic that the very purpose for which King Earvin brought him across the sea was now to be fulfilled.

News had come the previous night that the false king and a vast army had gathered near the walls of Eldford Castle; they had made no attempt to take the fort. Eldford Castle was known by many as *the gate*. It was said to be the only path to the citadel; however, there were other paths to and from Qev's capital—by the old roads around the twin mountains. Kairu turned from the wind and faced his armour. It was lightweight, made specially to allow him to move with agility. He had cleaned it himself, making it shine so bright. He retrieved his beaded necklace, for he would wear it this day. "If I am to die…" He could not say the words. The black eunuch donned his colourful beads with thoughts of his mother. Again, he saw her smile and heard her voice. "Mama…"

After he was clad in armour and a sword by his side Kairu sighed. He would kill again this day…or be killed.

Eldford Castle was built between the twin mountains, and its walls, which seem to emerge from both sides of the towering hills, were of grey stone. King Theo rubbed his hands together and looked across the vast space before him, for on the other side of the field, just beneath the left mountain, stood those who opposed him. Behind him stood thousands. Many of his warriors waited afoot while others were seated high upon their mounts. He heard the clang of metal, the jingle of chain mail and the whinnies of stallions, all unsettled by the smell of war, for much blood would be shed this day. Earvin's lost son had come; the drums boomed from the other side of the dry field. "Lord Sewell, if I die here today the fool will spare my house. I know the Godfreys well." The king turned to his first general. "All will not be lost."

Then came the deafening sounds of swords against shields. The time for battle had come. It was custom for two kings to meet upon the battlefield, and so the king rode forward to meet the boy who once served him as squire. Moments later he was just an arm's length from Ayden Thorne—this he shall always be. Their mounts stood side by side, each king facing the other's army. "A king who takes seven wives to buy himself an army is no king at all, boy." King Theo laughed with scorn.

"My father was king." The boy's eyes betrayed him, for they showed the pain he felt.

"A father you killed with those hands," said King Theo. "By my command." He looked beyond the boy and saw his eunuch, clad in armour." The king laughed aloud. "The boy brings his eunuch to war." The king saw the eunuch and remembered how he had been taken from him. "That eunuch belonged to me when Earvin took him—all because he was king. But I will stand over your body this day and reclaim my property." One last look at the eunuch enraged him. "Don't be a fool, boy…I refuse to have your leavings…and your father's. I will kill the black eunuch before your eyes as you draw your last breath, and I shall take your seven wives for my own—even wed your virgin sister."

"I will only take the white throne," said the boy, "and my crown." He turned his stallion and galloped back to his army.

When he saw Prodigal emerge through the gates Kairu closed his eyes and thanked the Gods. The battle horns sounded from both sides of the castle walls. Kairu sat upon his mount next to his king, while the princes, Orin and Lucas galloped along the vast army of men shouting commands. The army responded with echoing roars and battle cries. They were ready to fight. Prodigal's horse had galloped half the distance from the gates when the false king's army charged. Then came the cry from Prince Orin.

"Archers Ready!" The prince lifted his sword and gave the command. "Release!"

Kairu recoiled as the blue sky became blackened by a cloud of arrows. Many of the false king's horsemen fell while others galloped back to safety. When Prodigal arrived before his king he did not look into the blue eyes, which gleamed from behind his shiny metal helm. "King of Kings," said the Nuba boy.

King Ayden greeted Prodigal with a nod. He spoke aloud for all to hear. "Stay clear of the false king," he commanded. "His life is mine to take."

"Brother, think of what you say." Orin did not shift his gaze from the enemy across the field. "I am certain Lord Theo has promised to endow whosoever strikes you down. You must not honour him."

"Orin is right, Ayden." Lucas pointed his sword toward the enemy's army. "This is a battlefield, not the council hall."

The king adjusted his helm and unsheathed his sword. "I have given a command."

The princes looked to Kairu and he spoke immediately, patting his stallion's thick neck. "Majesty, it would be unwise to do this. Remain here on guard; watch the battle, for you must live."

"I will have my vengeance"—King Ayden had tears in his eyes—"and my crown. What good is a crown if it is merely handed to me—what value shall I place on this white throne if I do not seize it from the usurper with sword in my hand?"

"My Lord, ride with me awhile." The black eunuch trotted off and his king followed. He would make their conversation quick, for the generals had already begun moving the army forward. "You shall have your vengeance, King of Kings. But should this vengeance come by shedding Lord Theo's blood?" His king remained silent. "I implore you, Majesty. Do not engage him, for this is what he expects of you. I know you mourn him…he was your father. King Earvin was a good king. He was not governed by his passions…or his grief. The king, your father, is dead—struck down by your own hand. Do not sacrifice your own life, for it cannot bring him back from the dead." Kairu smiled as he thought of his own father and the last words he said to him…

"My King, my own father betrayed me—he sold me for two sacks of gold. I do not know why he did it, though he loved me. I know he loved me—that I can never doubt. Your father died by your hand…for a purpose. Before he left with his sacks of gold, my father said this to me: *You are Kairu. You are a descendant of the El Molo…remember that, my son of the Maasai.* Do not let his death be in vain, Your Majesty." Kairu looked into King Ayden's eyes, just as he had done his father. "Do this for me, King of Kings."

"I have no peace at night." This, Kairu knew. The king quickly wiped his tears, for he would not let his army see him weep. "Stay with me, Kairu…of the Maasai." He adjusted his helm. The king rode back to his generals and issued his command aloud. "I shall owe a great debt to the man who slays the false king. Bring him to me alive if you must." The army roared. "But I shall ride out with you; today you fight for me and I shall fight with you."

Kairu observed the king and his brothers. They were all young, just as he. He gripped Prodigal's arm. "Was this why he made us? Ade feared there would be war and now we are here—eunuchs with swords."

"I do not know, Kairu." Prodigal's grip was strong. "Know this, Kairu…you have done all that Ade said you would. You have charmed the hearts of kings. But remember this, my friend: it was I, Prodigal, who loved you."

Kairu saw tears in his friend's eyes. He could not utter a word of what he felt within himself. Prodigal had been his friend—his protector since they were boys. And he could see the need in Prodigal's eyes—yet Kairu could not say he loved him. But he did; he had known it—felt it all along. He had served two kings and had done so with perfection—yet he could hardly tell his eunuch brother how much he cared for him. Why had he come to this realization at that moment…at the brink of battle? "Prodigal…"

King Ayden's eyes were fixed upon the eunuchs as he gave the command to charge ahead. Prodigal eyed the King of Kings with disgust. "You are blind, Kairu—"

"We cannot speak of this now, Prodigal." He charged his stallion ahead to ride next to the king. "We talk after."

><<<<o>>>><

They had fought their way through hundreds of warriors. His armour stained with blood, King Ayden lifted his head and looked to the skies. The Gods were with him. But the battle was far from won. The false king was still strong. He had surrounded himself just near the foot of the mountain to the right of Eldford Castle. The coward seemed content to remain behind the safety of his warriors while many died in his name. King Ayden took a deep breath, for he would be permitted a moment's respite. His right shoulder ached from swinging his sword; however, the king moved forward. He fought with the eunuchs by his side—Kairu to his right and Prodigal to his left. His brothers, Lucas and Orin, also fought close to him with their own squires and captains moving with them through the battlefield. Ayden had given a command for any man to slay the false king or capture him alive; however, his eyes were fixed upon the man he once admired and served. He had also searched the battlefield for Cedric and was pleased that his friend was nowhere to be seen.

His father-in-law was first to move against the false king. Lord Garring must have planned this with his retinue, for the small group of warriors moved with stealth and purpose, not through the host of men coming toward them, but around them. His father-in-law's group had several archers; no single swordsman would confront them. Before long, Lord Garring and the false king stood apart with no more than a few feet between them. King Ayden moved as quickly as he could through his foes, still flanked by his two eunuchs. What he witnessed next to him was magnificent, for the eunuchs fought well in unison—it was the most spectacular thing he had ever seen. Kairu and Prodigal moved together—as one—and while their first priority was to remain alive, protecting their king was paramount. He saw Prodigal cut down one enemy with swift accuracy before glancing at Kairu. Still moving toward another foe, Kairu nodded, as if to encourage his friend or to thank him. The eunuchs shared something special; the king saw this in the way they exchanged glances. And for a brief moment, his gaze was fixed upon the black eunuch, Kairu. Only when he felt a sudden sting to his left arm did he realize he had taken his eyes off one of the enemy. King Ayden cried out in agony.

"My King!" Kairu left Prodigal's side for just an instant and smote the enemy with his longsword. "Are you all right, Your Majesty?"

"I shall live," replied the king. He looked to his father-in-law. "We must get to him before he is slain." As he moved through men clad in heavy armour the king swung his sword; he parried with one large foe before he was overwhelmed. It took Prodigal's strength and Kairu's will to fell the warrior who had the appearance of a giant. When Lord Garring fell to his knees before the false king, King Ayden moved with haste. And even as the false king lifted his longsword and swung it downward, King Ayden fought on. More of the false king's men had surrounded them. "To me, my brothers!" Orin and Lucas rushed to his side. "My father-in-law has fallen," said the king.

Kairu joined with several others and formed an unbreakable circle around their king, for Prince Orin had been correct in warning that King Theo had commanded all his men to slay his king. Prodigal, who had no intention of losing sight of Kairu, placed himself to the black eunuch's right. Their king stood with his sword on guard directly to Kairu's left. Kairu's gauntlet was stained red; however, he held fast to his sword. Several of King Ayden's own warriors had made it through the false king's wall of men and metal only to be cut down before their comrades. King Theo had been wise to surround himself with his best warriors, for when a foe cut through his defences, it took him little time to slay the tired, injured warrior.

"You, Prodigal!" King Theo looked beyond Kairu to the Nuba boy; he had not long ago impaled a foe with his longsword, and now he pointed it toward Prodigal. With great commanding might, the King of Kings shifted his blue gaze toward the false king. Blood dropped from his pale skin, and it seemed his strength was almost gone. His entire body seemed laden by the weight of the blood-stained armour—yet, as he issued the command, something in his eyes betrayed him. "You will slay the false king," commanded the king. "Smite our old master!" Kairu gasped. Surely the king knew he was sending Prodigal to a certain death.

Suddenly, the battlefield became a blur; the echoes of steel against steel and cries of agonizing pain and death overwhelmed the boy of the Maasai. Kairu ceased his movements, still grasping his longsword. From the corner of his eye he saw that Prodigal paused, but then, as his figure moved ahead toward the wall of men and metal, it occurred to Kairu that his friend had quickly accepted his fate. Prodigal knew he was likely to die before he made it halfway to the false king. It was Prodigal's quick glance that gave Kairu the courage to move. Without a word, Kairu, descendant of the El Molo, eunuch of the Maasai, broke the impregnable wall around his king and stood beside his friend.

"Kairu, you stay with me." There was something threatening within King Ayden's blue eyes. "Hold the line!" He must have known Kairu would not comply. "I command you! Hold the line around me, eunuch!"

The boy of the Maasai gripped his longsword tighter. "I am Kairu...King of Kings." The black eunuch charged forward, for if his day had come to die he was certain it would be with his friend. Prodigal was already in the midst of four foes; Kairu slew the first with two swift swipes of his longsword. He had no time to look behind him, for the force charging toward them was overwhelming. His king had many to protect him; Prodigal had Kairu. His presence seemed to replenish the Nuba boy's strength as well as his will; Kairu felt it too—that sudden rush of invincibility. "I will not suffer you to die alone, for you are all I have."

Prodigal laughed aloud, though they were deep in battle and surrounded by many men. "Finally, Kairu," said his friend. "No longer are you blind, my brother! For only I am your true friend."

Kairu nodded. The two moved together as one with innate instinct. With backs pressed together they met every foe with untamed fury; for just one moment, the black eunuch felt confident that victory was near; the Gods were with them. But the Gods are fickle. For it seemed the false king had devised a plan that would guarantee his victory. Kairu heard shouts from their comrades, and what he heard enveloped him with fear.

"We are surrounded!" said one warrior as he pointed back the way they had come. "His warriors come from behind us!"

Kairu took a quick glance, his shoulder safely pressed against his friend's. King Ayden's reserve fighters had become engaged in another battle near the base of the left mountain—King Ayden's camp had been breached. "Look, Prodigal." They could not become distracted from the foes before them.

"We are doomed, Kairu."

"Then our deaths must not be in vain." Kairu blocked an attack with his longsword before pointing it toward the false king. "They will not follow a fallen king." The two eunuchs nodded in unison, knowing what they had to do. If King Ayden fell first, only a few of his warriors would pledge allegiance to the false king; however, if Lord Theo, the false king, fell, most, if not all who follow him, would serve the rightful king of Qev. The black eunuch had deemed Lord Theo's claim to the white throne weak, for his son, Cedric, had shown little desire or ability to command an entire realm.

The two eunuchs fought their way through the enemy; their king was close behind. They were close to the false king—so close that Kairu could hear the echoes of the usurper's grunts as he fought with great skill. He had underestimated this man who had seemed feeble and insignificant next to King Earvin. The false king's body was a bulk of muscle, not fat, and he maneuvered himself with great skill; this man knew his sword well and was able to anticipate attacks from any foe. They advanced closer and closer until, finally, Kairu found himself facing Lord Sewell, the general once betrothed to Princess Cylene. Prodigal was closer; however, it was he who faced the false king with sword held high.

"It is time to die, eunuch." Lord Sewell smiled.

"I am here to fight," said Kairu with a slight bow. "We need not talk." The eunuch thought on what he had been taught to do. He thought of the key principles, for he would need them more than ever if he wanted to conquer this foe. Timing and distance were paramount, but so was adversarial perception. Kairu knew he would die if he failed to cling to these principles. The tips of their longswords touched as they moved in a circle. Kairu could hear the loud clang of Prodigal's blows against the false king's longsword, but he dared not look. Lord Sewell charged with all his might, and as their blades met Kairu's entire body shuddered. He gripped his longsword with both hands and blocked each pounding strike. Lord Sewell was a large, tall man; he was as strong as a beast and his steely gaze was as sharp as the longsword he bore. Kairu could not withstand the swift, strong blows, for as much as he tried to block them, he found that his wrists ached so much that he felt the need to simply kneel and rest. But he did not kneel. Lord Sewell's next blow was so powerful that Kairu's grip loosened. His foe's blade slid downward against his own and struck his gauntlet, forcing Kairu to shout in agony. As he fell backward to the grass, still holding his longsword, Kairu blocked the blade with all his might. Kairu focused on Lord Sewell's thick, armoured legs, and as he rolled away from the next downward strike, the eunuch used his size to his advantage; he rolled to the right, though he could feel the armour dig deep into his flesh. The black eunuch slashed at the giant's thigh.

"Are you all right, Kairu!" Prodigal looked away from the false king for just one moment, and the false king saw his only chance. With a swift slash he struck Prodigal's shoulder with enough force that the Nuba boy too fell upon his back.

There was no time for Kairu to answer his friend, for he had discovered a way to save his life as well as those of many others. But he could not delay. Time was of the essence. Kairu saw blood oozing from Lord Sewell's thigh. The mighty general was wounded; however, he would not relent. Again he chopped downward, and again Kairu cut him with his longsword. The eunuch had managed to get to his knees and prepared for the right moment. He had studied the enemy well and had timed his strikes. Kairu blocked three forceful blows and waited as Lord Sewell lifted his longsword. It was then he took to one knee and aimed. He pointed his longsword, resting the hilt upon one shoulder; he waited for the point of the blade to make contact before he rose and plunged forward with all the strength left within him. He was of the El Molo, a boy of the Maasai, and his time had not come to die—not yet. As he pushed upward into Lord Sewell's chest Kairu felt the blade pierce through armour and flesh and bone. The grey eyes behind the helm widened, but the strong foe still had the power to strike. He lowered his longsword against Kairu's shoulder; the pain was excruciating. But the false king's general fell to his knees. He fell sideways and lay dead after the eunuch pulled his longsword from his body.

The false king was strong. Prodigal had done all he could but had not managed to strike one blow. King Theo, his first lord, was ruthless and strong; it was he who had paid a price for the Nuba boy. Prodigal had been offered to Lord Theo only after he failed to acquire the eunuch he really wanted, Kairu. The Nuba boy had not forgotten this. The wound to his shoulder bled profusely, but the eunuch could hardly feel it. If he failed to rise the false king would surely slay him. Prodigal saw his own death; he could hear it all around him. He had not seen war before in all his life, for he was but a boy when his father sold him to a life of service. But he had heard tales of wars such as this one—the smell of blood, the fear, the horrors of battle; war was a horrible thing. And here he was, fallen beneath a mighty king, though false. Prodigal looked up into the eyes of King Theo, ready to succumb to his longsword. His enemy's weapon came down fast. But before it struck Prodigal's blade another longsword blocked the deadly blow.

It was Kairu. Suddenly, Prodigal found the strength he so needed to face the false king, for again, his friend was with him. The false king looked from one eunuch to the other. "I shall skin you both alive…right here before your master. Today, you shall all die."

Prodigal did not reply. However, he understood Kairu's instructions in the Yoruba tongue. "Kolu kekere, Prodigal!" *Attack low.* This, his friend shouted to him above the sound of metal against metal. The Nuba boy understood. His strength renewed, Prodigal parried with the false king, his blows aimed at his legs. Kairu managed to wound their enemy to the chest; however, his armour took the brunt of the blow. The false king still stood strong. Prodigal glanced at Kairu, impressed by the way he moved around the enemy. The boy of the El Molo jumped high with longsword in hand, like a true warrior of the Maasai. This distracted the false king, for he quickly became confused, having to keep his eyes upon Kairu while still staving off Prodigal's attacks. The boy of the Maasai moved swiftly, lowering his longsword against his foe. Kairu released a shrill sound, which seemed to come from deep inside him. The first blow forced the false king backward, and he looked to Kairu, shocked.

Again, the El Molo boy parried; Prodigal was amazed at how well his friend was moving. Kairu did not deliver a blow each time he engaged his foes; he was not predictable. Now distracted, Prodigal jabbed at the false king with his longsword and saw the first sign of weakness behind his helm. Lord Theo's valour seemed to have abandoned him. When Kairu's last blow struck him, the false king fell to one knee. All seemed to stand still. King Theo drove his longsword into the earth with all his might—a clear sign of surrender.

"King Theo has fallen!" This came from one of his own men. "The king has surrendered!"

Prodigal fell to his knees as well, relieved, for he could already see many of Lord Theo's warriors preparing to surrender as he had. Prodigal looked to Kairu and smiled as he too leaned against his longsword. The El Molo boy stood just several paces away from him. "Victory, Kairu." But he had spoken too soon. Prodigal had forgotten the way of his vengeful master. Lord Theo released an echoing cry as he pushed his longsword sideways with all his might. The blade broke. As quickly has he could, the false king plunged the remaining half of the longsword into Prodigal's abdomen. The sting of the broken blade caused the Nuba boy to widen his eyes in shock and agony. And all the while, the false king grinned at him—even as Kairu's blade struck him over and over. Prodigal managed to keep his eyes open long enough to see the false king fall to his death…

## CHAPTER THIRTY-EIGHT
### *A Eunuch's Purpose*

Kairu stood upon the bridge that joined the two cliffs of Garring Fort and gazed over the edge at the waterfall. The stream below was beautiful enough to make Kairu dream. He wished there had not been a war—that so many lives had not been lost. He could not tell how many men he had killed, and standing upon the bridge, his entire body numb with pain, the black eunuch wondered why he now stood alive when so many others had perished on the fields before the gates of Eldford Castle. His king had gotten what he wanted—a golden crown and a white chair. Was that the value this world so far from his homeland placed upon lives?

The servants had tended his wounds shortly after the battle, and the treatments brought some ease. Though his wounds would heal, nothing could heal the pain he felt inside. What would Ade, his teacher, think of him now? The eunuch's had found wounds on his body he could not explain—cuts and bruises in places he did not feel while on the battlefield. The wound to his shoulder was severe; he would bear the scar for the rest of his life. King Ayden survived the battle; however, Kairu had not seen his master since the battle was won. It all still seemed a dream. After he slew the false king, Kairu had fallen upon his knees before his friend. He did not care that Lord Theo's warriors had thrown down arms and immediately pledged allegiance to King Ayden. Kairu shut his eyes, trying to force the memories from his mind. He could still see the broken longsword in the false king's hand…the intent to kill burning in his eyes…

He did not hear the approaching footsteps. "My brother summons you, Kairu. Will you not go to him?" He turned to see Princess Cylene. "I have spoken with Orin and Lucas, Kairu. They told me what he did."

"Then you know why I can never serve him." Kairu turned away from the princess…away from those pleading eyes.

"Ayden is king of all Qev," said the princess. "To defy him openly as you have may lead to your death." She grabbed his arm, causing him to wince in pain. "He has not been the same since you admonished him…shamed him."

"It was all I could have done, Majesty." Kairu watched the waterfall. He recalled what he said to the king, his master, after the battle had been won. The false king lay dead; his longsword was stuck in Prodigal's stomach; cursing his king was the only thing Kairu could have done. "No one knows what I felt, seeing Prodigal there on the ground." He could hear Princess Cylene's sobs. "I could have killed my king…my sovereign. I can no longer serve him, Your Majesty. His command was a death sentence."

"Think of why he did this, Kairu," said the princess. "It was for you…"

Kairu turned to face the princess. "Your Majesty, you are a princess of Qev. I am a servant. And although the pleasures between us are unforgettable, I know I could never have you. Would I then kill every man with a desire to wed you? Your brother was our king; Prodigal and I were bound to serve him in every way, but the king I fought for—the king I bled for—decided to put the one thing I have in this world to death by sending him alone to fight against many."

"He begs your forgiveness, Kairu. Ayden sent me to plead with you…if you would just visit him." She tugged at his arm. "He has refused to return to the citadel until you come to him. Three nights have passed since the victory. Now my brother lays abed weeping, for you, his compass. He has not forgotten your words, Kairu, for you deemed him a cruel king…no better than the one you slew in his name."

"Wish your king well," said Kairu. "I only ask that he permit me to leave with all I have. This is all I ask."

"He will not heed my words, Kairu, nor will he take my advice." Cylene's eyes quickly flooded with tears. "Go before him and he will grant whatever you ask of him."

><<<<o>>>><

The black eunuch went to the king early in the morning. The king's chambers were brightened with sunlight and he sat behind an oaken desk, surrounded by many scrolls. His squire stood behind him with tablet and quill in hand. King Ayden seemed in a daze; however, Kairu did not delay. "Majesty." He looked into the king's eyes as he bowed, though he could barely endure to gaze within the pools of blue. "I have come as you asked, Your Majesty."

"I called for you immediately after the battle was won, eunuch. Yet you did not come." At first Kairu thought he saw rage within the king's eyes, but he soon realized it was shame.

"Forgive me, Highness." Kairu lowered his eyes as he bowed again.

"You think me a tyrant? That is what you called me before my subjects." He looked to Kairu as if puzzled. "Why should I permit such insolence…such disrespect?" He did not permit the eunuch to respond. "I am terribly vexed by your words. You forget your station, eunuch."

"I am Kairu, Majesty, nothing more. Whatever else I am called, these were given to me and can be taken away if you wish it. But I am always Kairu…descendant of the El Molo…of the Maasai. My name cannot be taken from me, King of Kings."

The new king hissed, eyes now filled with anger. "My father owned you before me…and—"

Kairu bowed with a smile. "Your father was a good king, Highness." Kairu remained calm as the king clenched his fists. "You must remember who you are…where you are from. Do not be subject to a crown and a throne, for not long ago, any lord of Qev would have told you what you tell me now…that you had forgotten your station."

King Ayden's eyes softened. "Leave us." He looked to the squire and said no more until he and Kairu were alone. "I don't know what to do. They come to me with scrolls and decrees—things I know nothing of. Kairu, what must I do?"

"You are a young king," said Kairu. "But you are still king. Lean upon those who love you."

"But you…you, Kairu…you hate me now." The king's smile was grim. "I see it in your eyes. I should not have allowed my—"

"It is done, Majesty. We cannot change the past, for even an evil deed may yet lead to good." King Ayden nodded. "I beg your leave, Majesty." He did not wait for the king's permission to leave.

His walk back to his chambers was swift, for the black eunuch had much to do. As he entered he could see that the curtains had been drawn away from the windows and sunbeams brightened the rooms. Kairu quickened his pace, for he had left the windows shut. Upon entering the bedchamber, he saw a lone figure standing by the window. "I told you to stay abed…your wound!"

"I cannot stay in bed forever, Kairu." Prodigal turned from the window and winced in pain. "I will be fine."

With arms crossed, Kairu fixed the Nuba boy with a stern gaze. The bandages around Prodigal's abdomen were stained bright red. "You still bleed, Prodigal. The physician says you must rest." He rushed forward to assist his friend as his body began to collapse. "You must do as I say, Prodigal…for you and Mama's beads are all I have left." A new sense of determination enveloped the black eunuch. He would protect what was dear to him…

Prodigal was assisted back to bed without further protest, and as Kairu wiped sweat from his brow he feigned a smile, for he really felt the urge to weep. "You saw your king," whispered Prodigal. "What says he?"

"We will speak of this later, Prodigal." His attempt to rise from the edge of the bed was stopped by Prodigal's weak grip.

Prodigal's eyes were filled with hatred. "What says the cruel king, Kairu?" Prodigal shut his eyes in pain as he sat up in bed. "The Gods have spared me for one purpose, Kairu…I know this. This king will be the worst Qev has ever had. I can feel it, Kairu." The El Molo boy shook his head from side to side, but it was to no avail. Prodigal would not stop. It was not that he really disagreed with what his friend said…Kairu was terrified that what Prodigal said would truly come to pass. He could not say a word—all Kairu could do was sit and listen.

"You say all things, Kairu, happen for a purpose. You live by those words because of where they came from—what they mean to you. But what do we really know of these purposes, Kairu? How are we to know whether they are right or wrong…or good or bad? Why does what Queen Bernice did ages ago have to be bad, Kairu? Maybe her actions did have a purpose—to save the realm from the worst thing that could ever have come to it. What if you have reversed something that had happened for a purpose…what if Ayden Thorne was never meant to sit upon the white throne?"

The black eunuch shuddered and the pounding of his heart increased. He could only take Prodigal's hand and squeeze it in agreement, for he could not find the words.

><<<<o>>>><

No news of the battle's outcome had arrived at the citadel. She saw the procession from the window of the highest turret of the citadel, but Queen Bernice could not tell from afar which banner flapped in the wind. A surging throng had gathered by the gates of the citadel and flanked both sides of the path leading into the city, and although the queen was completely consumed by curiosity she would not go down to greet the victor. She had dressed in one of her best gowns, knowing she would be summoned by a son she detested or a betrothed she despised. However, deep inside she prayed to the Gods to grant her supplication. She prayed she would be wed and crowned queen again by sunset, for Silas Theo would need this union to strengthen his claim to the white throne.

Finally, the gates were opened. The loud cheers were carried to her ears from the mouths of what seemed to be tiny insects way down from where she stood. She looked out toward the blue sky and saw that the day was good; the sun shone bright—a perfect day for any king to claim a throne…and a queen.

But the Gods had betrayed her. The banner that came through the gates was not blue. It was not the blue banner bearing the black eagle of the Theo house. The banner she saw was that of her dead husband's—one of crimson and gold bearing the strong boar. Again, the Godfreys had prevailed. There would be no royal wedding. No crown for her. Her children had forsaken her, and all she was left with was a useless pretender. Queen Bernice smiled. She thought of her only love, Asquith Theo. The stone sill of the window was easy enough to climb. Queen Bernice did not give it a second thought, for even as she fell toward the ground below she did not utter a sound; she had no regrets. It happened quickly. Queen Bernice kept her eyes opened wide until that sudden feeling of fear swept over her and the sound of her heart slamming against her ribcage was impossible to bear. But then it all stopped…suddenly there was darkness, peace.

# CHAPTER THIRTY-NINE
## *King of Kings*

The long summer had ended and frigid winter had enveloped the entire realm. Kairu sat near the fire, warmly wrapped in fur. His day, like all others since the completion of King Ayden's harem, had been long. The black eunuch had not foreseen any of this, for nothing turned out to be as he had wished or expected. As Prodigal placed a tray of food before him Kairu shrugged. "You must eat something, Kairu," said his friend. "It is cold. Many say Qev has never seen such a horrible winter." Prodigal's eyes were animated, for he detested the cold as much as Kairu did. "These pale-skins have lived long lives in this world, Kairu…but we will not—we are meant to run beneath the sun." Again, Kairu shrugged. When Prodigal touched his shoulder the black eunuch startled as though he thought himself alone and someone had suddenly come upon him. "What troubles you, Kairu?"

The black eunuch sighed. "I was all wrong, Prodigal." He gazed into the orange flames. "This terrible winter…it is a bad omen. The Gods make it long because of what I have done. I put a murderous king upon the white throne. You were right, Prodigal, King Ayden was never meant to be king…the Gods knew this. What Queen Bernice did to her own child had been for a purpose…"

Prodigal nodded. "But you cannot blame yourself, Kairu. It is impossible to explain what was meant to be and what was not."

"I never listen. You warned me…you said I was blind…and I did not listen."

The flames from the fire were reflected within the Nuba boy's brown eyes. His smile was sincere and it quickly calmed the black eunuch. "You are *Chief of the Girls*, Kairu." Prodigal grinned. "You have charge over the king's seven wives and all his concubines. Be proud that he still favours you. He will not suffer to see me, Kairu, and I don't want him to."

"But he has put you to work in the stables, Prodigal. What has happened to you is my doing."

"I am glad he has not put me to death as he has others. Remember, Kairu, King Ayden commanded that his own uncle pay for his deeds with his life—Lord Percival was executed for all of Qev to see. And so was Prince Kevan." Prodigal's hand moved over the large scar on his stomach and he closed his eyes briefly. "We have only seen this king's mercy twice, Kairu—he did not move against me after you defied him on the battlefield. And he gave Cedric Theo his life, even after condemning him for being Lord Theo's heir. He took all his old friend had left, Kairu…all his lands, his father's legacy…but he was merciful enough to permit Cedric Theo to remain at Theo Manor—a prisoner in his own home."

Kairu nodded. "I do not fear him. But the princess does. She confides in me…tells me her worries." He saw a smile sweep over Prodigal's lips and quickly slapped his shoulder.

"What? You are the princess's lover…her eunuch." He smiled wide. "But you must be careful, Kairu…if the king should find out…"

There was silence between them before Kairu spoke again. "The princess tells me of her brothers. She says Prince Orin detests King Ayden's choices. But Prince Lucas adores the king—this is obvious, for there is a sudden rift between the two younger princes."

"What will you do now, Kairu…now that Qev lives in fear of this tyrant? Even his wives have grown to fear him."

Kairu looked to the door before he uttered another word. "The princess…she has asked for my help." He paused, knowing Prodigal had seen the look in his eyes.

"I do not trust them, Kairu. If King Ayden learns of a plot of any kind against him—"

"I will do what I can to correct this." He grasped Prodigal's arm. "I cannot let these people suffer and live in fear because of what I have done. This king has doomed our own brothers—he has made slaves of our tribesmen…of you. He surrounds himself with the same guards Lord Theo used, while the tribesmen—warriors of our land—have been put to work the fields, and some have been sold to citizens of Qev, men who are not nobles. He will bring more of our brothers across the sea, not to stand equal with guards in his service, but as slaves. I will not serve this king, Prodigal."

As Prodigal opened his mouth to speak there was a loud pounding at the door. "Open up in the name of the King!"

When Kairu opened the door he faced six of the king's guards, all armed. He bowed in his usual way. The captain of the king's guards had come himself.

"The king commands you come immediately, eunuch." The captain's eyes spotted Prodigal and pointed the hilt of his longsword toward the Nuba boy. "And you! The king would see you now."

The great hall was silent as the eunuchs were ushered in, but it was not empty. Kairu saw the faces of many nobles. Prince Orin and Princess Cylene stood together. Prince Lucas was to the king's right. It had become the custom that all who were brought before the king should kneel; this Kairu did, even as he bowed to King Ayden. Prodigal followed. "I come at your command, Majesty." Kairu lifted his eyes just as he would with King Earvin, though its effects had long lost all potency. King Ayden's face was stern and his gaze unbreakable. Kairu's eyes fell.

"I have seen my physicians and they tell me I have yet to produce an heir." His blue eyes blazed with what seemed to be rage mingled with shame—even fear. What good was a king if he could not produce heirs for a kingdom? Kairu looked to Princess Cylene and saw the faint smile upon her lips. Prince Orin's eyes sparkled with what seemed to be satisfaction.

"I am no physician, Your Majesty." The black eunuch rose slowly. "You gave me charge of your harem; I complete my task to the best of my ability." Kairu looked to the princess again. He had not had time to tell Prodigal of what he had done…that he had done all he could to ensure the king produced no heirs. The black eunuch had used the skills Ade had taught him of herbs; and as he was responsible for preparing the queens' and concubines' meals, Kairu had been able to make certain none would conceive. "What would you have me do, Majesty?"

The king pointed a ringed finger toward Prodigal. "You! You now have charge of my concubines." He looked back to Kairu. "You have charge of my wives."

The two eunuchs bowed in unison. But it was Kairu who spoke: "As you say, Majesty."

"Leave me!"

The black eunuch bowed low. "As you say, King of Kings." He turned with reverence and grace and walked toward the doors of the great hall.

"What have you done, Kairu?" Prodigal whispered. "He will put us both to death."

"Shhh…" Kairu caressed the colourful beads about his neck. "I have much to tell you, Prodigal. We have much to do."

"I don't understand you, Kairu."

"I know this, my friend…for I am Kairu, descendant of the El Molo, I am of the Maasai." He placed a hand on Prodigal's shoulder and smiled. "Everything I do from this moment on will be for one purpose…"

# I Am Kairu

## ABOUT THE AUTHOR

Gregory McEwan is a prolific writer with exceptional literary skills. He has developed a writing style that is both entertaining and thought provoking.
Born in the sunny Caribbean Gregory moved to the urban continental climate of Toronto Canada. This unique perspective enables him to create a truly inspiring fusion of writing that taps into the imagination and transcends the norms in both cultures.

Made in the USA
Charleston, SC
13 August 2015